W9-CEB-152

THE ARRANGEMENT

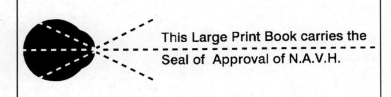

This Large Print Book carries the
Seal of Approval of N.A.V.H.

THE ARRANGEMENT

ASHLEY WARLICK

WHEELER PUBLISHING
A part of Gale, Cengage Learning

GALE
CENGAGE Learning·

Farmington Hills, Mich • San Francisco • New York • Waterville, Maine
Meriden, Conn • Mason, Ohio • Chicago

GALE
CENGAGE Learning·

LIBRARY OF CONGRESS CATALOGING-IN-PUBLICATION DATA

Names: Warlick, Ashley, author.
Title: The arrangement / Ashley Warlick.
Description: Large print edition. | Waterville, Maine : Wheeler Publishing Large Print, 2016. | © 2016 | Series: Wheeler Publishing large print hardcover
Identifiers: LCCN 2015051046| ISBN 9781410488510 (hardback) | ISBN 1410488519 (hardcover)
Subjects: LCSH: Fisher, M. F. K. (Mary Frances Kennedy), 1908-1992—Fiction. | Triangles (Interpersonal relations)—Fiction. | Adultery—Fiction. | Large type books. | BISAC: FICTION / Historical. | GSAFD: Biographical fiction. | Historical fiction. | Love stories.
Classification: LCC PS3573.A7617 A89 2016b | DDC 813/.54—dc23
LC record available at http://lccn.loc.gov/2015051046

Published in 2016 by arrangement with Viking, an imprint of Penguin Publishing Group, a division of Penguin Random House LLC

Printed in Mexico
1 2 3 4 5 6 7 20 19 18 17 16

For Marly Rusoff, who loved this book
when it needed it most

Tell me about the dream where we pull
the bodies out of the lake
and dress them in warm clothes again.
How it was late, and no one could
sleep, the horses running
until they forget that they are horses.
It's not like a tree where the roots have
to end somewhere,
it's more like a song on a
policeman's radio,
how we rolled up the carpet so we
could dance, and the days
were bright red, and every time we
kissed there was another apple
to slice into pieces.
Look at the light through the
windowpane. That means it's noon,
that means we're inconsolable.
Tell me how all this, and love too, will
ruin us.
These, our bodies, possessed by light.
Tell me we'll never get used to it.

— Richard Siken, "Scheherazade"

THE NEW YORK TIMES
M. F. K. FISHER, WRITER
ON THE ART OF FOOD AND
THE TASTE OF LIVING,
IS DEAD AT 83

BY MOLLY O'NEILL
PUBLISHED: JUNE 24, 1992

M. F. K. Fisher, the writer whose artful personal essays about food created a genre, died on Monday at her home on the Bouverie Ranch in Glen Ellen, Calif. She was 83 years old.

She died after a long battle with Parkinson's disease, her daughter Kennedy Wright said.

In a career spanning more than 60 years, Mrs. Fisher wrote hundreds of stories for *The New Yorker,* as well as 15 books of essays and reminiscences. She produced the enduring English translation of Brillat-Savarin's book *The Physiology of Taste,* as well as a novel, a screenplay, a book for children and dozens of travelogues. While other food writers limited their writing to the particulars of individual dishes or expositions of the details of

9

cuisine, Mrs. Fisher used food as a cultural metaphor.

Her subject matter, she said in an interview in 1990, "caused serious writers and critics to dismiss me for many, many years. It was woman's stuff, a trifle." But she was not deterred. In 1943 she wrote in her book *The Gastronomical Me:* "People ask me: Why do you write about food, and eating and drinking? Why don't you write about the struggle for power and security, and about love, the way others do. They ask it accusingly, as if I were somehow gross, unfaithful to the honor of my craft.

"The easiest answer is to say that, like most humans, I am hungry. But there is more than that. It seems to me that our three basic needs, for food and security and love are so mixed and mingled and entwined that we cannot straightly think of one without the others. So it happens that when I write of hunger, I am really writing about love and the hunger for it, and warmth and the love of it and the hunger for it."

In 1963, W. H. Auden called her "America's greatest writer." In a review of *As They Were* (Alfred A. Knopf, 1982) for the *New York Times Book Review,* Raymond

Sokolov wrote, "In a properly run culture, Mary Frances Kennedy Fisher would be recognized as one of the great writers this country has produced in this century."

Hollywood, California

1934

She'd made it sound as though her husband would be joining them for dinner. She'd made it sound that way on purpose, and then she arrived alone, lifting her shoulders in a vague wifely gesture of disappointment, and maybe she gave the impression of upset. She'd thought about this moment since she learned Gigi would be out of town. She wanted Tim's attentions to herself for the evening, and she'd planned accordingly.

"I reminded Al a week ago," she said, "and then again this morning. I don't know what he's thinking half the time."

Tim leaned to kiss her cheek, wrapped in his smoke, his trim dark suit, his sense of ease. His hair had always been white. "Well," he said. "Perhaps he'll join us later?"

"He had some kind of meeting. But perhaps."

She smoothed her hands against her skirt, rippled with electricity, and placed her clutch on the table to slip her sweater from her shoulders. Inside the clutch, she had a folded typescript, brought from strength of habit. She could be the schoolgirl, the devoted; it was, she understood, the way he met his wife.

But tonight Gigi was somewhere in the middle of the country, on tour with the other starlets at her studio, *starlet* the word for Gigi, bright and barely formed. She and Tim had married when she was only sixteen, and by then he'd loved her for years already, since she'd been a child. Mary Frances envied them their privacies and devotions, what she imagined to be their secret, richer life together.

She wanted a secret, richer life. She and Al had their late nights and closed doors, but there was something itchy and lonesome to her days since they returned to California, and she worried it was beginning to show. At a tea for the faculty wives, a woman with a blue winged sleeve draped into her saucer suggested mildly that she and Al had reached the time to start a family, said it as if she were reading from a textbook, and all Mary Frances could think was how there would be forty years of teas like that to come. She felt her face go hot again just thinking of it.

14

"Dear god," Tim said, peering over the top of the menu. "You're blushing. Are you nervous?"

"I never blush."

"I wouldn't have pointed it out if it wasn't so surprising."

"I'm showing off my French enlightenment," she said. "My continental permissiveness."

"Well. It's very pretty."

"Don't encourage me. Next thing you know, I'll be telling stories of the whores with their pastries and marc on the Place d'Armes."

"The scandal being the pastries or the whores?"

"Their beautiful long lunches. The wide-eyed boys lined up, waiting for them to finish dessert."

She could not believe she was blushing.

"Do you miss France?" he asked.

"Oh, yes."

"It is not a country where people do other things while eating."

He said this quietly, returning to the menu, and yet it had been the thing she'd been thinking for days, how busy it all was back here in California, how full to the brim with no room left over. Tim knew a little bit about everything, everyone. The electric

15

feeling returned, humming, and her hands pressed the linen in her lap to keep still.

The waiter stood by, and Tim gave him their order.

Gibsons came from the bar in their delicate open bowls. The gin was cold, shot through with slivers of ice. Trembling knolls of aspic arrived, flounced with cucumber, yielding to their spoons, and the thick gin again, and all around them the scent of roasting meats and the chime of silver on the plate, the far-off rumblings of the kitchen more necessary and coarse, like the plumbing of a body.

She took a deep breath and delivered her announcement: she'd published the essay about Laguna.

"The sun and the sand, how it's basically an artists' colony. I might have stretched that, but still, an essay and three drawings, with my name beneath them."

Tim raised his glass. "To Mary Frances Fisher. Her first publication."

"MFK Fisher. It's MFK Fisher."

"Really."

"It's how my mother signs her checks. I didn't really think about it, just sent the piece off with my initials. Later, a Mr. Hanna wrote from the editor's office to arrange a meeting with Mr. Fisher. I thought at first they were talking about Al."

"I don't believe you."

"They asked for Mr. Fisher."

"Even on paper, I don't believe you'd be mistaken for a man."

She laughed. She was a beautiful woman by any standard, with her heavy-lidded eyes and red doll's mouth, a pinpoint-sharp kind of beauty that was never so lovely as when she laughed and spoiled it, which she did often.

She said, "It's good to finish something, or to feel like it's finished. To get paid. Al had such trouble finding the job at Occidental, finding any kind of job in this day and age, and his poem —"

"Ah, the poem," Tim said, exhaling.

"Yes. That."

"The poem is always being written."

She laughed again and leaned toward him, and he liked how she didn't care to be quiet about it. She simply liked to laugh; she liked to eat and drink. He'd often thought she must like to do lots of things. Al was his closest friend, but the pleasure of Mary Frances's company was entire.

"And what does Al think of MFK Fisher?" he said.

"Oh, I haven't told Al. Yet. I haven't told

him. I wanted to thank you first, for all your help."

And as though she'd reached across the table and laid her hands upon his face, he understood she had not told her husband about their dinner here tonight.

Tim looked steadily into his plate, the last mouthful beside his spoon. His thoughts drifted one upon the next; how could a woman who talked so much still seem so guarded? She must have gone to such trouble to meet him here alone. He studied her face and her gaze seemed to shudder for a moment between frames. There was so much she was still deciding about herself, so much he couldn't know.

"You're talented," he said. "You've heard that before."

She lifted her chin, giving him the long white architecture of her throat. "Oh, I could stand to hear it once again."

And he didn't stop to wonder why him and not her husband, because years ago his cousin had encouraged him to paint and write, not his father, not his teacher; there was no charting who sparked what in whom. To Al, Mary Frances's writing would always be a hobby, like her drawing, her cooking and carving and knitting, because he did not want a wife for a rival, and really, who could blame him.

Tim told her again that she was talented, that she had discipline and a grasp of language, of reality, and they were alike in that way. Al was an academic, with his muses and inspirations, Gigi was a movie actress, but the two of them — he touched her hand — they were something else. She was writing a book that wasn't like anything else anyone had written. He knew how it must sound, but he meant it; he'd thought as much a thousand times, watching her lean forward over her notebook when they would talk about a story, or the way she leaned into her pages as she read them aloud. If it was admiration she'd come for this evening, that was easy to provide.

But too, he felt how her hand was kinetic beneath his — if he pressed, she would press back — and in this new light he wondered new things about her, if she'd been an athlete, played an instrument, if she'd bitten her nails, sucked her thumb, if she touched herself, if she ever wore perfume, his attention traveling her body, his mouth still making praise, but now he was thinking of her shoulder blade and how it fit into her back beneath the leafy sleeve of her dress. He felt her legs shift beneath the table, the conduction of her skirt across her lap; he saw her from all sides, all parts, because that was where his talent lay. Then it was his turn to take her by surprise.

"I wouldn't say this if Al were here. Not that it isn't true, or that Al doesn't know it himself. But I wouldn't say all this in front of him."

"And if Gigi were here?" she said.

"Oh," he said, letting go, leaning back. "I tell Gigi everything."

The waiter brought her trout under glass. He prized the flesh away from the spine in efficient sheets, pink and curling, though Mary Frances well knew how to use a knife; it was what a waiter did for a woman, what a woman allowed in a restaurant like this. Tim's face, cocked against his fingers; this had become fun or funny, she wasn't sure which, his eyes sweetly blue and blank as a baby's. After the fish, there was quail *en papillote,* the parchment broken and billowing the scent of dry grass, and her mouth became slick with fat and the second glass of wine. She forgot about Al and Gigi and what would be said about this evening later, and she ate.

If she understood art, if she could write, if she was beautiful and smart and a tangle of other things still taking shape, what she was truly good at was this. She ate slowly, she sat back from her plate, she allowed her pleasure to show on her face. And she was willing, always, to try the next thing.

Watercress with lemon, a slice of cake, bitter coffee, the last of the wine: it was late when they stood to leave, the restaurant still full of people radiant as flashbulbs on their own invented time. Mary Frances felt lightheaded; there had been so many endings to this evening already, so many possible moments to postpone or back out. Now it was almost over, and she'd made her announcement, thanked Tim, and nothing had really happened next. What was she waiting for?

Tim held her sweater, smoothing the shoulders after she'd slipped into it, his fingers slow to leave her nape and the dark knot of her hair. The valet had her Chrysler pulled around and lingered at their elbows, keys ready. Tim's hand covered hers where she'd tucked into his arm.

She thought again of the afternoon tea, the elegant parlor, the white gloves of the hostess. Someone's wife played cello, another recounted her year in China, another her love of bridge and how they must get together and have a club. No one asked her what she liked to do, and if they had, she would have lied.

Tim leaned to kiss her cheek. "I could drive you home," he said.

Mary Frances let her shoulder into his. "But then what about you? Who would drive you home?"

"If we only lived close enough to walk."

"Then what?"

His face, still warm from where her mouth had been.

"Mary Frances," he said. "I am honored Al worked late tonight."

"He might have, yes."

"As far as Al's concerned, we all worked late, my dear."

He opened the Chrysler's door and held her hand as she dipped behind the wheel, the green drape of her skirt brushing against his pant leg. He reached down for the edge of fabric that hung below the doorframe, testing it between his fingers.

"Tim?" she said.

He said good night then, or thought he did. There had been so much wine, so much talk. Her face still tipped up at him in the car window, now smeared and dappled in the lights from the restaurant's awning, as though she were swimming under shallow water. All that deep green dress, afloat.

Tim did not hear the valet until he

touched his elbow.

"Sir," the valet said. "Shall I bring your car?"

He was a boy, really, not even old enough to shave, an oil stain on the cuff of his jacket.

Tim clapped him on the back, flushed with energy now. He loved women; he loved his wife, Mary Frances in her deep green dress and polished mouth, the clever things she said. He loved his wife, and he was glad to be going home to an empty house. He felt like running for it.

"I'll get it myself."

He took off up Wilshire to the lot where the restaurant parked its cars, seeming to keep pace, for a moment, alongside the creamy fender of the Chrysler, in the wake.

Night in Hollywood kept falling, caught in the lights from the Paramount lot and thrown back across the sky, and Tim drove fast up the ridge of Mulholland, the city's swell and tow like some great sparkling sea, dipping at last into Laurel Canyon and the bungalows knit together against the hillside in the darkness. This house belonged to a producer's mistress, next door a dancer in the corps, the real traffic signaled by a porch light left on or out, a phone ringing once and not again, the real traffic after dark

23

between men and their lovers, because it was never night enough in Hollywood for anything but big ideas and getting caught.

If not for Gigi, there's no way he'd still be living here.

But he'd promised her California, that she could be a movie star, and for god's sake if she wasn't about to play Barrymore's secretary in his next picture. And if her star continued to rise, she would get better roles, where she would play another man's wife, girlfriend, mother someone else's children. He walked up the driveway of their house, squat and white, and he felt as if he were walking onto a set, that behind and beneath this place that looked so solid, people were working hard to make it seem real.

He left his keys on the table in the foyer next to the bowl of florist tulips, now ragged and sad in the time since Gigi left. He left his jacket on the table too, his tie and pants, skinned his white shirt over his head. He'd pick up in the morning, or the maid would on Friday; it didn't make much difference as long as he was here alone.

He woke to the double beat at his bedroom door, a woman's shoes falling from her hand into the parquet, one and then the other.

"You would not hear a person breaking

24

into your own house," she said.

He turned on the light. "Mary Frances? Are you all right?"

"The door was unlocked. I walked right in."

His body sank against the pillows, all ribs and sockets, lean and not relaxed. She remembered he had fought in wars, that he was trained to be prepared for anything, and still he was surprised to see her. She had surprised herself.

She placed her clutch on the bureau, thought ridiculously of the folded typescript she still carried. There was nothing left to pretend that might make sense: her house in the hills was the other direction, her husband the other direction, and yet the evening seemed finally sharpened to its point. If she was going to be here, it could be for only one thing.

She unfastened her watch from her wrist and set that on the bureau too.

Tim stared at her. "You're right," he said. "You never blush."

"I told you."

"Dear, what time is it? You're like the little girl, stayed up too late."

It seemed like a dare.

"Mary," he whispered. "Don't."

But she turned from him, her fingers at

the catch of her dress, the untoothing of a zipper. She was hoping that this wasn't as foolish as it felt, but it seemed the thing she had to do. If he didn't want her, she needed to know it, and if this was bound to happen, it needed to be now, and if she was about to ruin everything, then goddamnit, so it was.

Behind her, she felt the bed shift beneath Tim's weight, and then there came the barest tip of his touch between her legs.

She could not get her mouth around fast enough to take him in.

They will never, really, tell anyone about this. In the morning, at the beginning of next week, Tim will meet Gigi's train at Union Station, and he'll bring her a corsage. He'll load his arms with her cases, cutting the flock of other girls, their bottled hair waved, each of them like orchids, petals thick and flashy, with their men, and their arms full too. He'll take Gigi home. She'll sit at the piano, her ankles crossed and tucked aside, and she'll ask him what he's been playing since she's been gone.

He'll see the moment before him: he has missed her, he has always loved her, and people do the most surprising things by accident. He'll tell her a funny thing happened while she was away, and think of her washed in lights on that picture with Eddie Cantor, the heavy blond wig that concealed her body for the camera, a slave girl, a harem girl, her face lifted for her single moment in the shot, so like a racehorse, his Gigi, since she was thirteen. He'll tell her a funny thing happened while she was away, that their friend Mary Frances appeared in his bed in the middle of the night, and when he says it, he'll feel something new break over them, hot and bright and from above.

She'll place her small white hand atop his and say it doesn't matter. He'll notice then how she hasn't even removed her hat, that her small white hand is cool and ringless, the corsage heavy with lilies and their scent of powder, and he will not know what else to say.

In some small way, it is Mary Frances now who ate his words. She ate everything tonight, lush and drunk and wet, now she has her mouth at his ear, and she's saying things to him about what she wants and how, and she is strong against him, he can feel her strength in her legs and her grip and in her mouth still at his ear, but he can't make out words anymore, just something straining at its seams. Her slip drifts against him, and then she takes that, too, away, and they are naked.

There is nothing Mary Frances understands so much as nakedness, and looking
down between them, she can't bear to look
into his face, so she looks where things
make sense on him, the way each part fits
into the next, how compact and practical,
and she thinks of the waiter with his knife
over the fish, what a marvel it is to see the
works inside. She wants to keep seeing that
in Tim. She is afraid of what she'll think of
if she stops.

Her fear must show for just a moment,
because he says *what,* and stumbles on the
rest of it, unable to finish the question *what's
wrong, what is it,* because all of it is wrong,
but he asks anyway and stumbles, and nothing comes to her, nothing even to fill the
space, which is growing now, pushing up
between them. *Oh, goddamnit,* she thinks.
Goddamn. Before she realizes it, she's talking, and she nearly tells him she loves him
before his mouth comes down again to
cover hers, thank god, because it wasn't love
that made her want Tim, that turned her
car around on the dark highway and brought
her back to this moment, it wasn't love, but
rather an appetite's demand: direct, impera-
tive, true as love perhaps, but far more
dangerous.

All she's thinking now is *don't stop, don't stop. Don't stop.*

She left while he was still asleep, the folded typescript from her purse next to his jacket in the hall. She rolled the car downhill before she started it, flicked the headlights before she hit the main road, headed fast along the canyon to her family's summerhouse in Laguna, where she'd told Al she'd be all night. Funny, the things that just came naturally. When she unlocked the door and threw open the windows, the scent of eucalyptus and last year's ashes struck her like a fist.

In a book on the shelf under the eaves upstairs was a packet of sonnets, nearly fifty, papers creased and brittle from the number of times she had unfolded them, from the way she'd carried them the winter before they got engaged, when Al was away teaching English in a boarding school in Wyoming. He'd written to her, he said, on a single long cold night, until his candles burned out and the ink froze in the well. The sonnets weren't about her; they were for her. She could sense all he'd poured into them, even when she wasn't entirely sure what all of it was. It made her want all that poured into herself.

She had been a lazy student, enrolled in summer school at UCLA when they first met, but she was ardent in her letters. By the time Al came home for Christmas break, he wanted to marry her and take her away from California, to France, to Dijon, where he'd been awarded a three-year fellowship. The first time they kissed, she'd fallen against him, the ground beneath her swaying like a ship. She was twenty-one.

France had been a fairy tale, an adventure, an extended honeymoon. Al was a student, and so there was no money but what they accepted from her parents, Rex and Edith. There was no time to be what Al was studying to be, a writer. Perhaps that was why one shouldn't spend one's time studying to be something rather than being it; there was only so much time.

It was to the summerhouse in Laguna that she and Al returned after Dijon, and where they'd first met Tim and Gigi.

There had been a minor earthquake. When it passed, they'd tumbled out to the pebbled lane to find Gigi, the ties of her madras sundress flapping against her bare neck. A downed power line snapped and flared behind her, and when she started toward them, it was as though she'd been cracked into motion with the whip of it.

Mary Frances felt Al stand up straight beside her; she stood up straighter herself.

"Dear god, California," Gigi said. In her hands, she held the pieces of a china dog she let chunk into the dirt. "Dillwyn and Gigi Parrish."

But there was no Dillwyn. The three of them looked behind her to the latticed porch she'd come from. "Timmy!" she called.

The Parrishes had been their constants ever since. They were renting the house next door while Tim worked on several others they owned, one in Laguna and one back in Laurel Canyon. He was older, an artist, he'd run a restaurant, he'd published a novel years before, and illustrated a handful of his famous sister's children's books. He knew people in New York and Hollywood; he'd hire Al to paint a fence, and they'd end up plotting a screenplay. Mary Frances remembered the evenings they talked over a bottle of wine or two, with the fire in the hearth and the wind whisking outside and Gigi like some kind of crystal chandelier, suspended overhead. She often felt she started writing just so they wouldn't forget about her altogether.

But after a stretch of painting fences, she knew Al was relieved to be part of college life again when he got a job at Occidental starting in the fall. It had been months since they'd seen the Parrishes, since the end of summer, when they'd moved to Eagle Rock.

Mary Frances had missed this house. She had been raised, truly, at this long table by the sea; all the parlors and cooks, the teas and socials back in town, all that balanced by a summer spent scrabbling along the rocks with her sisters, Norah and Anne, their feet black with tar, their bellies full of fish their brother David pulled from his nets. The Kennedys' Laguna. She had come here hoping for some sense of what this place might do to fix her now.

She took the path from the weathered porch through the sage and down the cliffs to the ocean. It was not warm, and the beach was curved around itself and empty, the broad neon sign for the hotel winking on and off up the coast. She sat on the bottom step nearly in the sand and watched the sea beat itself against the shore.

Behind her, she heard footsteps and turned to see another couple she knew from the summer. Every afternoon they'd sit on their blanket, the man in a short, tight bathing suit, the woman dressed like his nurse, rubbing his thick brown back with oil. Now passing her on the bottom stair, they let their conversation drop, to be picked up again once they were alone.

In summer, the man had watched her as she came from the ocean, his forearms draped over his bent knees, squinting after her into the sun. Every day he watched her pass their blanket for the stairs, her wet bathing suit somehow making her more than naked, and his eyes so constant. One day she looked back, met his stare, held it. Then, from behind, the woman rose and nipped the fat part of his hand with her teeth the way a bitch directs a pup, and he laughed, turned to the woman, smiled, spoke. Like a distant light, Mary Frances had snapped out.

Now the man walked along the water's edge, just outside the spray, and the woman followed a half step behind, her arms folded against her gray buttoned coat. After a while, she reached out and brushed some fleck from the shoulders of his sweater. Mary Frances no longer walking past their blanket, the winter, this chill, this season had not really changed them.

Soon Mary Frances would take the steps back up the cliffs to her narrow bed beneath the eaves and sleep, and then tomorrow she would return to Al, her face windburned from this morning on the beach and fresh enough to hide behind. She would make supper, the simple kind of meal they used to eat in France, then the last of the good cognac by the fire. Al would pick up the book they were reading, *Moby-Dick,* and the great white whale would take them back to the sea.

It was just a night she had insisted on, with her willfulness, with her shoes in her hands. It was just a night, and back in Eagle Rock, she would feel her life nip her into place again, blurring at the edges so that she could not say if she had meant for such a night to happen or just to come close enough to watch it pass by.

Back in Eagle Rock, Al was writing the same he'd been writing for almost their entire married life together. He went to class in the morning and came home for lunch, a bottle of milk, a fried egg on rye, a kiss on her cheek before he went to his office, and that was what she saw of him until dinnertime.

She followed the rhythm of his typewriter around the house. She washed the dishes, hung the laundry, took a bath, the tap of his keys coming over the transom from his desk next door, a vibrant whickering, so loud and bright. She was afraid of what would fill her head if not this brightness, if not the clip of his typing, the crank of a fresh page.

In Dijon, Al had seemed to be thinking all the time, and even when they were first married, she never knew what he was thinking about. He could be perfectly still for minutes, his lanky legs folded under his chair, looking out the same window she sat in front of. His black coffee, his pipe, the still keys of his typewriter, and his long stare right through her over the mossy rooftops of the city. It was worse when he worked in their rooms. It was worse to see how far away he was, right next to her, than to imagine him at the café in the *place,* not seeing strangers around him, not even the pretty girls.

She'd slip off her velvet house shoes, cross her legs high, and wait for him to notice. She'd tap the tip of her pen against her teeth, the wet pop of her lips in the silence. She'd turn her face to the sun, arch back against her chair, and close her eyes, but she was nearly screaming in her own head, innervated, willing him to turn her way. Finally she'd snap out of her chair, the novel open in her lap clattering to the floor.

Finally, then, Al looked at her.

"Darling," he said, reaching into the breast pocket of his coat. "It's Thursday,

35

isn't it."

And he'd press into her hand some tiny gift he'd picked for her in the market, a pair of ivory buttons, a lavender sachet, a tortoiseshell comb for her hair. He gave her something every Thursday to mark the day they first met, and turning the bauble in her palm, she would feel as if she'd forged it herself, with all her want pressing up against his lofty farawayness.

He'd smile at her, brush his fingers across her cheek, and everything was fine again.

Now she jumped at the ringing telephone, the mailman's knock. She lingered in the hall outside his study — Al's chair, Al's black typewriter, Al's poem, the last thin light faint across the desktop — waiting to be invited in.

"Darling," he said. "Is it so late already?"

He extended his arm for her to step inside. They looked at the scattering of work across the desk: the slips of ciphered paper, the full ashtray, the growing stack of manuscript that she would not ask again to read. She could throw a dust cloth over all of it, pack their bags, and go south to Mexico, back to France, return maybe in the spring. They had once spent a chilly holiday planning a trip to Algiers they both knew they would never take. She needed a plan like that now, a string of plans, the sort Al had always made with her before.

"Dinner?" she said.

He sighed, his blond curls sweetly ruffled. "Of course."

He took his place at the kitchen table, and she reached across him to strike a match for the candles, her body brisk and distant, a kite too far away to chase. It was difficult to leave his desk sometimes, to remember what she'd want from him, how to be a husband.

She pulled a small glass from the cabinet and a bottle of sherry, placed them at his elbow.

"What would I do without you?" he said, but she did not turn around.

Al pressed the palms of his hands against his eyes. He liked to listen to Mary Frances in the kitchen, the rasp of the knife against the board and whatever thunking vegetable she was taking down. It was a habit they'd begun those last few weeks in France, their apartment so small and cold that Mary Frances had prepared supper in her overcoat. They didn't talk — later, huddled together in front of the coal stove, they would read to each other, they would talk then — but when Al had spent the day at his desk, to be in the same room with her was often overwhelming.

He'd never seen such company between his mother and father. His mother boiled potatoes and slabs of meat, and he'd never seen his father sit and watch her, never seen him sit without doing something else: reading the paper, listening to the radio, eating, and then moving on. His mother had her hands full with himself and Herbert, brothers for whom food was fuel. And then there was his father's church, the parishioners, the handfuls of people in and out on any given day. The community. The community had always been important to his parents.

Al felt without one now, only himself, Mary Frances, and her family.

"You know," he said. "Larry says Fay's boy is less a terror since he's been talking more. More words, less screaming. Perhaps we can have them back around."

Mary Frances laughed. Larry was their oldest friend. "But what about Fay?"

"You love Fay."

"I love Larry. I like Fay."

Mary Frances sectioned an orange from its membrane over a bowl to catch the juice; the quick feathering motion of her wrist. The kitchen filled with oranges.

"I doubt they'll have more children," Al said.

The rhythms of her knife broke, began

again. "Oh, doesn't the world have children enough? Clearly, Fay has her hands full."

Al didn't say anything.

She turned.

"Clearly," he said. He spun the sherry in its glass.

In his mother's letter yesterday, she said the X-ray treatments had done little for his father's pain, less for his cancer. Blood was the most efficient conduit. And Herbert was still in China; it was unlikely he would ever take a wife and come back home.

The evening slipped away outside the kitchen window, the candles finding the underside of Mary Frances's profile, her straight, true jaw. She'd paused when he mentioned children, but the mention was so buried, he couldn't tell how to read her best. It was up to him, he supposed, to bring it up again.

He stood, pulling his shirt free from his pants. "I'll get cleaned up," he said, and left for the bedroom.

In the skillet, fat burned, then blackened. Mary Frances snapped to it, nudging the pan with a dishtowel. She wiped out the skillet with a piece of newspaper and began again, this time screwing her attention tight. She browned onions and garlic, and from the pot on the windowsill, chopped a few winter-sad leaves of tarragon. The smell was green and strong, and she thought of spring.

Spring in Dijon, when she and Al would hike into the mountains with the Club Alpin, the old women forever chiding her tentative steps, her newborn French: *la petite violette, violette américaine.* She would turn back to Al, annoyed, and he would laugh. Hardly his delicate flower. When they stopped for lunch, it was Mary Frances with the soufflé of calves' brains, whatever was made of liver or marrow, ordering enough strong wine that everyone was laughing. The way home, the women let her be.

If she wanted calves' brains now, she wouldn't even know where to begin to look or how to pay. She and Al seemed to be living on vegetables and books, tobacco, quiet. She blanched a bunch of spinach and chopped it. She beat eggs with the tarragon, heated the skillet once again. There was a salad of avocados and oranges. There was a cold bottle of ale and bread. Enough, for tonight.

Her own mother had relied on cooks, on the larder and the icebox, on there always being plenty, but in France there had never been a place to store plenty, and Mary Frances had learned how to manage day to day. She supposed Al had learned too, not necessarily how he might expect to be cared for, not meat and potatoes, coffee and cake, but rather something back and forth, give and take. A conversation. She took up the dishtowel again and slid the skillet beneath the broiler. Such a conversation with Al might be the safest kind these days.

He returned to the kitchen asking if she wanted to go for drinks at the Parrishes.

Mary Frances steadied herself against the edge of the stove. He held the invitation in his hand.

"Isn't Gigi out of town?" she said.

"I'm sure she's back by now. A welcome home?" Al snapped the card against his palm. "We haven't seen them in too long."

"No," she said. "We haven't."

She had been so stupid. Of course, there would still be parties. There would still be drinks and dinners and movies and card games with the Parrishes, and whatever sparkling thing that used to happen when she caught Tim's eye across the table would never happen anymore because she had been unable to leave it at that. Because she could not leave well enough alone.

There was a fast slip in her thoughts, and suddenly Tim's skin against her palms, as real as if she'd touched him, and then only her hands again, fishing for the last knife in the dishwater. The simplest responses failed her. She pulled the frittata from the oven, sliced wedges of it for herself and Al, dressed the salad, cracked the ale, and laid the table. Al bowed his head in thanks; what was there to do but what they'd done before? They bent to their meal, and ate.

Across the valley, dinner was already cooling in its plates. Gigi had made soup, silvery dumplings of fat floating on the surface of the bowls, a hunk of something still smoking in the kitchen. They had almost laughed, it was so bad, and called dinner off completely. Tim was too hard upon the gin to really care.

In the living room, Gigi sat at the piano, plinking out a song she was supposed to learn for the Busby Berkeley picture, the next one where she would play a girl with legs. It was the best Tim could figure it; she had no lines, no part in a story, but she and ninety-nine others like her would all put their legs together and call it a dance number. He tipped the gin into his mouth. She couldn't play piano either. She was twenty-two years old. What difference did it make if she could sing and dance? He loved her, god, and he was sorry about Mary Frances.

The thing was, Gigi wasn't sorry. Gigi was finished.

He went to the kitchen doorway and watched her stuttering between the singing and the playing. Her hair was lifted off the back of her neck and held with a comb. The song was about being shy.

"Here," he said.

He rested his glass on the bench, his arms coming around her, and she accepted his closeness as she might a seamstress or a nurse. She watched his hands at the chords, her small voice free now to do the rising, and she filled her lungs, almost proud. She found the chorus, how her words were in her heart, and Tim held the last notes with her as long as she was able.

She leaned back into his chest for a moment, and thanked him.

"Can't we talk?" he said.

She was already gathering the music, gathering herself away from him. They had talked so much these past few days, but Tim still thought there was something else he could offer her. Just one last thing.

She didn't look at him. "I've got early rehearsals tomorrow. I need to get to bed."

She leaned from the waist and kissed his brow. If he'd worn a tie, she'd have straightened it. He remembered her suddenly as just a girl with her braids in her mouth, bent over her primer, painfully reading to him in Latin, her foot beneath the table atop his own. She was always touching him, petting him, but he suspected now it was something she did without meaning to.

But she was sure, of course she was sure. Of course.

"We can work this out," he said. "If you —"

"But I won't. We can't." She put a hand to his cheek; there was a kind of pleasure in her voice to tell him no. "And anyways, I was thinking how you won't be alone for very long. The men you know are not alone. They all have wives."

"Gigi —"

"You'll find another one."

She backed away, butting against the piano bench, jangling his empty glass. She passed it to him, wiping the ring of sweat with her hand. "You should call the ice man in the morning," she said. Her exit then: a swirl of skirt and green perfume.

John Weld was a screenwriter or a stunt-man, maybe both. He and Gigi had known each other since the spring before, and she was not ashamed of herself in the least. It couldn't be helped who you fell in love with, she said. Which was the excuse of a child, he said, and when would she ever grow up. But he'd made it all the easier for her, what with Mary Frances.

He took the last of his drink to the French doors, the night garden visible through his reflection in the panes, the woolly arm of a juniper, the floss silk tree and its bulbous trunk, near-monsters from where he stood. A stuntman, for chrissake — a man who did dangerous things other people took credit for.

He let the night grow late, and kept his glass full.

He woke in daylight, late morning, Gigi standing in front of his chair like a woman on the edge of a diving board.

"Everyone is still coming for drinks," she said.

"Yes?" Tim sighed, looked out at the terrace, the short shadows of the neighbor's palms. He felt as if time shimmered out there somewhere, had failed to pass the way it usually did. Goddamn Laurel Canyon. "Everyone?"

"The Fishers, the Sheekmans. Nan and whoever."

Gigi wore an apron over her blouse, printed with apples. She held a wooden spoon by the bowl instead of the handle and looked at him expectantly. When had she become this person who wanted him to break? She turned back to the kitchen, her house shoes clapping loosely on her small feet.

"I'll go for ice," he said, and left by the terrace door.

He was just coming home hours later when the Fishers' Chrysler pulled beside him in the drive.

"Old man," Al said, and Tim turned around, a bag of ice dripping on the dark canvas of his loafers. "What the devil are you doing?"

Al leaned across Mary Frances's lap to speak through her open window, and she put a hand to his shoulder, her left hand, her wedding ring suddenly so plain. They were friends, for god's sake. They'd all been friends for years.

Tim smiled at them. "Hello."

He looked different to her now, his face handsome in its angles and shadows, his face above her in the half-light of his bedroom, as she would always see him now. He leaned against the window talking to Al, his mouth making sounds she could not seem to collect into words, his hands cupping the

46

doorframe, his long fingers. Her insides reeled.

"Are you all right?" she said finally.

Tim looked at her and spoke, and she supposed he answered her question. He smiled, and she laughed, and Al did the same. Tim slapped the door of the car and stood, walking away, waving over his shoulder as he disappeared behind the house.

Mary Frances felt the breath she was holding give out.

"Good lord," Al said. "What happened to him?"

"What do you mean?"

"He looks awful. He looks run through. I mean, really. Do you think he's ill?"

"Ill?"

Al glanced at her, and Mary Frances closed her eyes, her mouth, the parts of her not to be trusted. "You didn't notice?" he asked. And then, "Darling. You must learn to pay attention."

She shook her head. The next few hours seemed impossible, literally impossible, like boulders to be thrown uphill. But then Al opened her door, she took his arm, yanking on the thumb of her short black glove as he raised his hand to knock, and she was headlong into it.

Gloria answered, Gloria Sheekman now.

She was squealing glad to see them both.

"You know," she said. She braced Al's back with the flat of her hand, exceptionally strong for her size, her hair the color of snow today. "Timmy's disappeared."

"Ah. Not really," Al said.

"Really. Gigi said he went for ice, but his car's still in the drive."

"Let me get you a drink, Gloria," Al said. "Introduce me to your latest husband."

"You're such a grouch, Al." She leaned to kiss Mary Frances. She smelled of roses and gin. "Get yourself a drink."

She made like they were taking coats and butted Mary Frances down the hall, talking, talking. The lights were on in the master bedroom. "And Gigi is a flutterby, in and out. She's wearing an *apron,* for god's sake."

"Gloria. I wear an apron sometimes."

"Not when you've spent the last two weeks in a tin can with twenty other girls, you don't. Something's fishy." She looked off absently. "Maybe she's pregnant."

Mary Frances swallowed. "You just want somebody else in dutch with the studio."

"Studio, schmudio. I've got a new daddy now."

The Love Captive had been in the theaters for weeks; Gloria played a hypnotized ingenue, wandering around the screen for

48

an hour until her fiancé broke the spell. The papers had slayed the movie and made Gloria sound as if she were well accustomed to mindless wanderings herself. It didn't matter; it was her last picture with Universal. Hollywood was changing. There were rules now, laws even, and reputations like Gloria's had become problematic; starlets didn't divorce. Still, she seemed to have landed on her feet. She couldn't quit talking about this Busby Berkeley showstopper, mostly because Gigi had a part too, a smaller one, a chorus girl.

"She's had the longest girlhood in the history of girls," Gloria said. "Does she think she'll be a girl forever?"

Mary Frances lifted her shoulders to say she didn't know, and then there she was, Gigi, around the corner from the foyer, the hem of her apron balled up in her hand. Underneath the apron, she wore a slender dress of blue crepe that rustled as she stopped and started again toward them.

"Gloria, you stop making fun of me," Gigi said. She leaned close to press Mary Frances's cheek. "How nice to see you."

"Oh, Gigi," Mary Frances said. And then, "You know I don't believe a word."

Gloria sighed. "I'm just jealous, darling. I was never so young as you."

Gigi patted her hair back from her face, her smile a flashbulb at close range, and Mary Frances felt dizzy, caught in their stutter-step. She remembered Tim saying how he told Gigi everything, everything. Then Gloria called them all her little birds and butterflies, and wasn't it time for a drink.

"I'll be right along," Gigi said, and passed through toward the bedroom.

"Oh, damn," Gloria whispered. "How much of that should I take back?"

"All of it," Mary Frances said. "In fact, let's just start over from the top."

Gloria stuck a long finger in her side. "What's wrong with you?"

"I need that drink. And two more just like it."

"That's my girl." Gloria flung her armful of coats onto the drafting table in Tim's studio and ushered them to the living room. A half-dozen pink poinsettias filled the hearth. The holidays.

Tim pulled a candy-colored V-neck over his head, a sweater Gigi had given him last Christmas because she said it made him look as if he played golf at the club. He didn't play golf at the club and never wore the thing, but she was right, the light peach made his skin seem as if he hadn't been drinking five days straight. He'd cut himself with the razor and tried to think it wasn't because his hands were shaking. He pressed a pad of toilet paper to his chin. He couldn't stay in here any longer.

When he opened the door to the bedroom, Gigi was curled over herself on the end of the bed, her face swollen and wet. It was the first he'd seen her cry since he'd met her at the train station, about all of this, the first time.

"Dear," he said. "Please."

"Please what?" Her voice was cool.

"I can send everybody home, Gigi. I can bring you a cup of tea, and we don't even have to talk about it. We can sort it all out in the morning."

As he offered this, he felt the pressure in his head lifting like weather. He realized how much he wanted her to admit this was hard. How much he would enjoy going to the living room and dispatching everyone back to their cars. Gigi has a headache. Gigi has a touch of something. He loved her so much in this moment, more than ever before, and how cruel that was.

"I'm fine," she said. "Truly. I'm better."

She pressed her small white hand to her cheeks, one and then the other. She

51

smoothed the coverlet away from her hips, smoothed her smooth blue skirt. He could see her drawing herself up, her back straight, her face finding the light. He waited; her pride could still push her either way.

"I don't know what came over me." She smiled, and he knew how they would present themselves for the remainder of the evening. She hadn't even asked where he had been.

And in the living room, somebody played the piano badly. Somebody delivered a punch line, and laughter broke. There was the delicate *ping* of ice to glass, and into this came Tim in his candy-colored sweater. The men shook his hand and clapped his back, and some of their wives leaned to kiss his cheek. Some of those wives were Gigi's friends. Tim wondered how many of them knew what was going on.

He could see, suddenly, the invisible map-work between these people, like the paths through this neighborhood between the houses of men and their lovers. He thought of Mary Frances, not his lover really, but now something more than what she had been. He watched her through the arches of the doorways, her voice bustling with the others: her prim, private school features, then her laughter like a low-cut blouse.

Where did women like her get made?

She saw him, too; she held a glass in front of her as one might hold out a hand in greeting. He waved, and she came to sit beside him at the piano, a little too close, but what did it matter, really. Perhaps she had been drinking too.

"Your advice, Dr. Parrish?" she said. "Editorial or otherwise." She rested her elbows on the fallboard and surveyed the room, her lips pursed, her brow inclined.

He could not rise to the occasion. "I have no idea what to say, Mary Frances."

"All right," she said. "First of all, you should have told me to go home."

She was being deliberately smart, painfully so, and Tim scrubbed his face with his hands. He wished he had not waved her over. She was going to keep talking.

"It's too late for that, though, isn't it," she said. "Second of all? I don't have a second of all."

She looked away, across the party. He studied the sheet music, the same song Gigi had been playing for weeks, studied the seam of Mary Frances's stocking where it left her shoe. She began to hum, and then to sing the horrible, horrible song about hearts.

"Gigi has fallen in love with someone

53

else," he said.

"Tim." She smiled. "That's not funny."

"She's fallen in love with a man closer to her own age, and she wants to be with him. She wants a divorce."

"Well. I hear they're all the rage at Paramount."

Ice rattled in her glass. It would have been worse if she said something mild, if she said something kind or comforting. "I haven't told anyone, obviously —"

"You're serious? Christ," and now he could hear the bleed of liquor in her voice, each word too carefully placed.

"Yes. Well."

"Oh, Tim. We ought to find me a conscience. There must be one of those around here somewhere."

He put his head into his hands. He wished, suddenly, he could talk to Al, tell him everything, and also that everything was something else. Mary Frances was right, of course. He should have told her to go home, he should have been true to his wife, this was all his fault. He turned to her again, and in the second before she could collect herself, he caught a glimpse of whatever raw, throbbing thing she was trying to cover up, and his chest came loose entirely.

"I'm sorry," he said. It's all he seemed able

54

to say anymore. "I'm just so goddamn tired."

Al watched as Tim walked toward the back of the house. Mary Frances looked after him, and Al tried to guess what had been said from the wry little twist to her lips. Six years he'd watched her face, and he'd seen a thousand things stand in for surprise. It was as though she thought to be surprised would be a weakness.

Of course, Tim was in trouble. People always sent for Mary Frances when they were in trouble. Her sister Anne during her divorce, her mother when she had the flu, even strangers; in Dijon, there seemed hardly a midnight in the house on Petit Potet that didn't bring a mincing knock at their door, the landlady's delicate son whispering about some maudlin Prussian too full of brandy, some hysterical Czech who refused to put her clothes back on. It didn't seem to matter that Mary Frances's German was weaker than her French, they sent for her. And when she returned, later that night, early the next morning, she never did tell Al what the fuss had been about. He was beginning to understand there might be legions of things she managed not to tell him. Her writing had cut a small window into that.

He was grateful for Tim's attentions to her writing, her anecdotes and sketches. Al had seen Mary Frances through the art classes and the tutoring, the days when she carved table legs; this would run its course as well, and he wanted her to be happy. Tim could make you feel brilliant when nobody else seemed to care what you were doing.

But Al didn't think they were talking about writing tonight. If he had to guess, he'd say it was Gigi.

Truth was, Gigi was too young for Tim. Around the living room, her friends were easy to spot: glossy hair, glossy dresses, so much skin. He thought of his students, nearly Gigi's age, the young glossy-lipped whores in Dijon. Al had liked to talk to them, to watch their pretty painted mouths at work.

Mary Frances was standing now, draining the last from her cocktail glass. Soon someone else would draw her into conversation. She was always in the midst of something: stories, admirers, audience. Those afternoons in Dijon, he remembered her waiting for him at the apartment, before she made friends or started her art classes. The cold walk from the university, he would think of her powdered and dressed, perched on the edge of the bed, then pacing to the window and back, waiting just for him, looking just like she did now.

He wanted to take her home.

He checked his watch; they couldn't leave, not with the awkward way the evening had started. But she was still looking across the room, her mouth wet from the last of her drink, and he thought of what he could do if he took her home now. He wanted to take her home now.

Where the hell was Tim? And Gordon, long gone from Gloria's clutches, still drinking his way out of a paper bag. The rate things were going, soon there would be nothing for him at these parties but to watch.

He crossed the room to Mary Frances. "Ready?" he said.

"Now?" But she was already backing down the hall to Tim's studio for her coat, and then they were on the road to Eagle Rock.

Al pulled her close on the seat, feeling the warm stretch of her thigh against his, and the darkness. They could ride like this for miles, he thought, east into the desert. They had never lived in the desert. Another country.

She looked up at him, her face waxed in

moonlight, in nerves, tender with concern and maybe something else. Al wanted to cover her eyes with his hand, cover her mouth. He could see her pulse hammering in her throat, and he wanted to press it still. He pulled the car off the highway and dragged her leg across his lap.

She made a gasp and settled down once, twice, the stir in his cock already gone, yet somehow here was where the sex began: Mary Frances curled around him, her knees on the seat, her skirt around her waist, and her hand working between them. She pantomimed her part so well, her fluttered breath, her voice trapped in her throat, a small cry against their rocking. Al held her tight. There was no way, he knew there was no way, but he couldn't let her pretend this by herself.

When it was over, Mary Frances slid off his lap. Al fastened his pants. The quiet was shatteringly complete, as though someone had just stopped screaming.

Al started the engine and pulled back onto the road.

They had once been timid with each other and full of love, the prospect of sex. They had not waited for their wedding night.

The invitations had been engraved, addressed, and all her mother could talk about was which punch bowl, how much standing rib. It seemed to have nothing to do with them; they easily slipped away. They borrowed her father's Auburn roadster and drove to Laguna, stopping along the roadside where a Mexican was selling iced-down beer and watermelons. They scooped the cold flesh with their fingers, licked their mouths, then each other's. They took a blanket back into the trees, opening their clothes just enough to fit themselves together.

In the end, it was so fast and blunted, she felt as if she had not paid close enough attention. But then Al sank his face into her neck and wept, or something close to weeping, and she was moved by his tenderness. He kissed her jaw, her ear, whispered how he loved her and asked again and again if she was all right, watching the side of her face as they drove on.

"Of course, I'm all right. I'm happy, and soon this whole mess will be over."

"This mess?"

"I mean the wedding, the party, whatever it is Edith's making. It doesn't matter. Soon we'll be married. And French."

"Oh." Al put his eyes back on the highway, and fell quiet.

It had been wrong to be so casual, to leave

that place where he'd wept for her so quickly, and she'd stung him. Al was sentimental at his core. She would do well to remember that lesson, the dark ride home.

Al took a long time in the bathroom. She listened to the pound of his shower, steam curling into the hallway from beneath the door. She thought of the burlap sacks full of snails they'd gathered in the woods above Dijon, their meat extracted and boiled, their shells scrubbed clean; the kitchen could be such a brutal place. They had been the finest snails she'd ever tasted, and the first. So much of what she'd done for the first time she'd done with Al.

When he finished his shower and came into the bedroom, she pretended to be asleep. He stood over her a long time, her breath even, eyes closed. He reached down to smooth her hair back from her cheek, his touch light and lovely, and even then she did not stir.

"Darling," he said finally. "You've inspired me. I think I'll get a little work done now."

She sighed and whispered all right, and he snapped out the light as he left the room. She could hear him strike a match in the study, imagined the soft pant of his pipe, and soon the clip of keys, whatever Al was thinking stretching out across the page, then facedown atop the last and all again. That, he could do for hours.

She rolled over to the nightstand, her pen and notebook. She wrote down *snails, Papazi, their little bodies starving in the night,* not even turning the light back on to do it.

In Dijon, they'd eaten snails, tripe, livers, brains, meats rotted and roasted, pâtés ten years old and better under clouds of fat, sliced and spread on toast. The air smelled of *pain d'épice,* honey, cow shit, and the wine was red, the winters cold. Mary Frances wore woolen stockings, bloomers made of challis with elastics at the knee that Al liked to snap; they would pile the blankets onto the bed and crawl beneath. She wished, sometimes, they'd never come back to California, and other times that they'd not gone to France. They might have been happier to never know the difference.

She could not stop thinking about Tim.

It seemed impossible that Gigi would leave Tim for another man, even more impossible that Tim would talk to her about it, without pride or temper, without anything to shield himself. She hadn't known what to say, and she'd done a bad job pretending she did. She was ashamed of that.

But the truth was, Gigi leaving changed

61

everything. It would continue changing once Tim told Al about it, which he would want to. The Parrishes were their closest friends, and Tim and Al confided in each other, or at least they had once upon a time. Gigi leaving would change everything for all of them.

She had begun to see how her own life might divide. Her closet became things she would take and things she would leave. She imagined what she would tell her mother, what Al would tell her mother, their friends. She thought about it so much, it was as though it had actually happened; she would pass Al in the hallway and be surprised to feel him squeeze her hand and smile. She went to the market, did the laundry, read her books and exhausted herself with her thoughts, both invented and recalled, until all she wanted was to rest for a while against the mindless tasks before her in the course of a regular day. She didn't always have to do it to know how it could be done. There was a comfort in that, she thought.

She set the table, poured what was left of the wine, and Al wandered from his study, a man in from a storm.

"What's that I smell for dinner?"

"Oxtails," she said. "For tomorrow."

"Not tonight?"

"They'll taste better tomorrow."

Al lifted the lid and breathed deeply over the pot, licked the spoon. "Where on earth did you find them?"

"It might have been cheaper if I raised the cow myself."

The market had been empty, eerie, the shelves furry with dust and not a single shopper other than herself. She needed something to make for dinner, and she'd borrowed from the larder at her parents' house the week before. She couldn't ask again; Edith would start to worry. She'd rounded the corner to find a crateful of carrots, their long fingers reaching from their stacks, cheerful against the lumps of potatoes and squash. She filled her basket, as many as she could carry home, their green tops sticky in her hand. One thing she had decided, she would not ever waste a chance again.

Now Mary Frances lifted the lid on a pot of carrot soup.

Al sighed. "When I was first married —"

"All those years ago?" This was a game they played. Her part was to egg him on.

"Yes, yes, to a *wonderful* girl, we lived abroad in France. We lived in a boarding-house with a strange and very French fam-

63

ily, and we ate at their table every night. Meals made from air and sawdust and whatever Madame found at the bottom of her shopping cart."

He went on, rhapsodizing: the *blanquette de veau* and legs of mutton marinated for days in wine and juniper, Madame's oxtails, the first oxtails he ever ate, and how the smell of them would wake him from his afternoon nap, hours to wait until supper.

"And I would turn to my sweet wife, sitting by the window in her chair, a novel open in her lap, and I would think . . ." He turned to her now, his face soft and suddenly young.

"You would think?" she said.

"Someday she might make oxtails for me. Someday we might have oxtails of our own."

She turned back to her pots.

"I never thought you'd make me wait like this," he said.

They weren't playing anymore, and they weren't talking about dinner. "I'm sorry," she said.

"But you won't change your mind."

She could hardly believe what she was hearing. This would be the story now, that Mary Frances didn't want to have a child, not that Al couldn't perform long enough to make one, that Mary Frances wasn't ready, that she was distracted, immature, or worse — that she didn't want a child because she wanted to spend all her time writing, as though that would ever amount to anything as fulfilling as motherhood.

Where did he think babies came from? What would happen now if she grabbed the collar of his shirt, if she swept the dishes from the table and pulled him on top of her? Her mind flashed to Tim, his full weight bearing down, and the pot she was holding slipped from her grasp.

They both watched the bright orange fantail cross the floor, splashing her apron and skirt, her stockings, everything hot and clinging. It felt, first, as if she'd been slapped. Then her hands began to shake over all the mess and burn; she couldn't tell where to wipe them first.

Al scooped her up beneath her knees and shoulders and carried her to the bath, flipping on the cold water, filling the tub. He said things — he was scared — things she could not hold in her head, and there was this awful panting sound. Was she making that sound? The water rose, muddy with what leached off her clothes.

"Darling, darling." Al cupped the water in his hands to pour over her legs. His face was so tight, it hurt to look at him. What on earth were they going to do?

"I'm okay," she said.

They peeled off her clothes, the stockings first, then her apron, her skirt. Her shoes were ruined.

"I just feel so very dumb." Her arms went around Al's neck, and he held her. It was just an accident. He was sorry, she was sorry. He loved her, he was a good man. What difference did it make, what she said about children. It was easy to want something. She wanted things all the time. She could say she wanted a child if it made him happy; it did not mean they were going to have one.

Later, they ate. Her legs were still tender, the splash of burn marks livid on her shins, but the oxtails, delicious.

Fridays, Mary Frances took the electric train into Los Angeles and spent the morning at the public library. She loved the great hall, its Spanish arches scrolled across the ceiling like rosy bones. She loved flipping through the card catalog, then wandering the stacks, plucking this old history and that translation and the next, and they smelled so good, and they weighed so much in her arms, the weight of what had come before.

But today she chose a table and reached

into her satchel for a sheaf of compositions from Al's class to grade, a simple way to start her pen to paper. Later she would get around to working on her own book. Once she had cleared her head.

Her book, too, had changed, or maybe it had never really been her book to start with, just a handful of essays about the history of food, the Greeks, the Romans, the French, slipping in bits and pieces of things she remembered, things she knew. She'd always written to show Tim. She wanted him to see her as wise and experienced, the woman she wrote about like some kind of veil she let over herself, or maybe something she peeled away. But too, the work was something they could talk about, just the two of them. When he'd asked for more, she'd written more, and when he said she should write a book, she said she already was. She had no idea how to begin that conversation again now. Maybe it was just another thing that didn't really matter anymore.

Then Tim pulled out the chair across from her.

His pallor was startling, even as he was clean-shaven, his hair neatly waved and white, a bright pink handkerchief folded in a four-point crown tucked into the pocket of his blazer. The library was nearly empty, and no one was watching them, but she felt nervous just the same.

"How did you know where to find me?" she said.

"You spend every Friday with Lucullus."

"You look awful."

"I am awful."

"And maudlin, I see."

"So that's it, then. Sympathy is dead. Where are the dusty books, the tomes you're so concerned with?" he said. "Those look like first-year compositions."

"Second."

"You waste your time with someone else's busywork."

"You'd do it, if Al asked you to."

"Ah. Yes. I would."

And there they were again, at the heart of it. Tim leaned forward, his face unfocused, one square hand folded back against his cheek, idly rolling a marking pen across the tabletop. Her skin prickled, waiting for whatever he had come to say.

"I never told you about the tearoom, did I?" he said.

"No."

"When Gigi and I first came to California, it had been my thinking to open a *thé dansant,* like she and I had loved in Paris before we married."

He'd followed Gigi to Paris after her mother had discovered them without their lesson books, Gigi's braids unraveled and her head in his lap, and it hadn't mattered that he wanted to marry her. Her parents took her that night. It was a week before Tim could find a way to follow. He was a younger man then, France still fresh in his mind from his tenure in a field hospital, bearing litters, boxing coffins, moving effects from one wet pallet to the next and wasting away from hunger. Since the war, he'd written a novel, he'd taken up and put down his paints, he drank too much to measure, and then one day there was Gigi in her father's study, her braids and red ribbons, her naughty smile. She hadn't cared to hide it, or hadn't known she should have, too young to conceive of consequences until they struck.

In Paris, the *thé dansant* had been an easy dodge; an afternoon dance sounded wholesome and cultured, even in light of the fact that Latin studies had once seemed wholesome too. Tim met her chaperone at the door with a box of chocolates and a ticket to the talkies, and found himself with two hours of Gigi's time, whenever he pleased.

She was a beautiful dancer, tiny and lithe. He liked the attention they drew, his hair already white, Gigi barely more than a girl. Her dresses had been her sister's and hung loose on her frame, her feelings about undergarments ambivalent, and so Tim was left with the velvety rasp of too much fabric beneath his hand, and her wide blue eyes tipped up at him.

"Marry me tomorrow," he would say. "Marry me tonight."

She laughed, her eyes slipping closed; everything she did seemed like she was doing it for the very first time. "What's the hurry? And we have tickets to the opera anyway."

"We can go to the opera, too, if you like."

"Oh, yes, Timmy. You come tonight. I'll sneak away and meet you in the lobby, and you can whisk me off to the catacombs in the cellar. You can keep me prisoner. You can make me sing for you."

"Will you meet me tonight?"

Gigi laughed. "Of course."

But she always said that, and there was only so much she could do. The potted palms cast long shadows across the floor of tiled stars, the whole idea of afternoon disappearing in wafts of smoke and La Baker on the phonograph when the orchestra took their set break. Tim led Gigi to a little table in the darkest corner and a waiter brought their tea, a cart piled high with frosted, jammy tarts. Gigi with her sweet tooth, her mouth tasted of cream. The war dissolved, and France was beautiful again.

It only seemed natural they could do the same in Hollywood.

"At four o'clock," Tim said, "the band would break and I'd warm a long row of teapots on the bar. These friends of Gigi's would sit still for tea. It was like watching a herd of gazelles, a school of fish; they changed direction suddenly and held."

Now his hands hovered above the table, mesmerized.

He reached into the breast pocket of his coat and pulled out Mary Frances's typescript she'd left the night they spent together, his notes scrawled across the page in blue ink.

"I remembered those gazelles, reading this. That tearoom. What you've written is good, and not because you understand history or the importance of Lucullus and what the Romans put in their wine. But because it's about you."

He held her gaze.

"A moment in time," he said. "Arrested, at the table."

"Thank you," she said.

But he waved her off, reaching for Al's

papers and the marking pen. "You, write," he said. "I can do this as well as you can." He opened the composition on the top of the stack.

Mary Frances closed her eyes, pressing the heels of her hands against them. He spoke so easily of his life with Gigi, and what he made of it, what he'd lost, without shame or anger, without anything to cloud his story. They weren't negotiating some new lesson or exercise, but talking like equals. Which part of all this made them equals?

She looked down at his notes, lines underscored and crossed out, the questions he asked: why this and not that, and how much is enough? He urged her to be specific and clear, the fine dots and points of his handwriting filling the pages. But as she reread the essay, it was clear the person on the page was a dim version of her now, Mary Frances from before. She wanted to seem smarter than that, confident and unflappable, and she could seem any way she wanted.

She took out a clean sheet of paper and began again.

The first kitchen she'd known was on Painter Avenue in Whittier, before Rex and Edith moved to the Ranch on the outskirts of town. The first time she'd had that kitchen to herself, her parents gone for the evening in a cloud of smoke and French perfume, her sister Anne left in her care — that first dinner, Mary Frances made eggs.

She conducted the meal from beginning to end, eggs boiled and cracked on the countertop, peeled and sliced into a casserole dish with a measure of her grandmother's white sauce, a sauce the flavor and consistency of paste. At the last minute, Mary Frances had spotted the curry powder in its dark green tin, and she didn't think about her grandmother's recipe anymore but added the curry to the white sauce until the scent of it filled the kitchen.

When they ate, she and Anne, young enough to still wear pinafores, were set on fire. They drank enough milk to make themselves sick, ate enough eggs to escape being scolded for wasting food, but blisters rose inside their lips, and Mary Frances spent the rest of the evening promising a great deal of chocolate in exchange for Anne's silence. But she had learned about pride. She learned about respect for things you knew nothing about.

Across the table, Tim leaned over some girl's musings, his eyes squinted at the paper as though to better discern her point.

"What happened to your tearoom?" she asked.

His face lifted to hers as if she'd struck him.

"I couldn't keep it going," he said.

"Oh. I'm sorry."

He nodded. He seemed to be trying to remember what he'd just been doing, and she felt a stroke of jealousy for Gigi, for the history they'd shared, and the pain it was causing him to lose it.

She stood, began to gather up her things. She felt herself, inexplicably, smiling.

"Mary Frances," he said. "I need a favor."

She sat back down. "What now?"

The collar of his shirt was frayed; if he asked, she would mend it. She would throw herself at him again and again until he caught her. She couldn't stand to feel this way.

"There's a lunch counter around the corner. I'm famished. Aren't you famished?

"I can't think."

"So we'll eat something. I've done too much thinking myself."

He unfolded himself from the table and held out his hand for her satchel. His gesture was easy and elegant, but she took his arm and felt her touch go all the way through him, as if he were made of feathers and air, no more next to her than a ghost.

A few days later, Al took Tim to the station for his train to Delaware and waited with him on the platform. It was the earliest train back east, and all along the platform there were couples parting: mothers and children, men and women, some of whom bore the same studio features as Gigi, near glimpses of her everywhere.

Al reached into his breast pocket for his handkerchief and offered it to Tim.

"I'll be fine," he said.

Al had never seen a man cry like that before, just the steady fall of tears down his face as though he were standing in the rain. "You have your satchel? You didn't forget anything? I can send it to you, just let me know."

Tim put his arm around Al's shoulders, and Al could feel him catch his balance. He would let him know, Tim said, and Al racked his brain for something else to offer for comfort. He stared out at the empty tracks and let Tim lean his weight on him, neither of them talking now, and the bustle of other people going past. Al had never stood so close to another man for so long before, and it seemed somehow right to do it for Tim. He could not imagine what he must be going through.

The train whistled down the tracks, and Tim turned, putting both damp hands to Al's face. It was so very cold this morning.

"You don't need to decide right now," Tim said. "Think it over, and drop me a telegram. Talk to Mary Frances. I want all of us to agree."

"You and I agree," Al said. He would have said anything. "That's what matters."

When Al returned to Eagle Rock, he wouldn't take off his coat, the morning broken cold and yet to warm, their little house prone to drafts. Mary Frances had made herself three cups of tea, each forgotten in a different room. She put the kettle back on the stove and went to him.

"He was crying," Al said.

She put her cheek against his shoulder. The coat was his heaviest; he hardly ever wore it anymore. In the lapels, she could smell the chimneys of Dijon.

"Devastated." Al sounded amazed. "He had nothing with him but a satchel. He's leaving all his canvases, his paints."

"When will he be back?"

He didn't hear her, and she stilled herself against him, mindful of her stroking and patting, her rhythms of distraction. Behind

Al's shoulder was the armchair, the mahogany table, a cup of tea left there. She was no good at waiting.

Al sighed. "He asked a favor of us. Really, it's a generous offer, but you know Tim, and how he puts things."

She did. Tim had asked her first. At the lunch counter, neatly devouring a stack of ham sandwiches to the crusts, as though he had not eaten in days. He drank glass after glass of milk, put his head down on the counter, and spoke in the direction of the floor.

"I'm sorry to put you in this position."

"You don't have to be so polite. Please."

"But I do." Tim cleared his throat. "I need your help."

"It's all right," she said.

"I've telegraphed the lawyer in Delaware, and I'll file papers when I get there, but the process is not quick. Things like this, time is of the essence. If word gets out —"

"I'd never say anything, Tim. Of course not."

"But the other girls at the studio, they'll go tattle-telling as soon as they even imagine something is fishy. They've all signed morality clauses, very cut and dry. Her contract might survive the divorce, handled quietly enough, but an affair . . ." He laughed here almost, a sound that cut. "Gigi would be one less girl in the next picture."

He looked at her, and Mary Frances sighed.

"It's all she's ever wanted," he said.

"Not all, evidently."

"I owe her this much," he said.

The afternoon grew long outside the window. Mary Frances had to be home soon. She took another sip of her coffee, thick and bitter. He might never return to California. Why would he ever return?

"I'd like your help, too," she said. "With my book, when the time comes."

He looked back at the floor, saying of course he would, of course, it would be his pleasure, and she hated herself for asking. It sounded as if she were taking advantage of him, and maybe all of it would come to sound like that. She had seduced a man who was in love with his wife, and everything that happened afterward bore the echo of that fact.

Now in her living room, her conversation with Tim seemed discrete. She could be here and there, knowing what Al was about to say and at the same time having no idea. She closed her eyes against Al's shoulder, breathing the damp coal smell of his coat, and long ago in France. Part of her had lived through this already; she was just looping back again.

"Poor Tim," she said. "Of course."

They would move into Tim's house after the holidays, to live with Gigi while Tim sought a divorce quietly back east. They would just say they were keeping her company while Tim was out of town, and no one would suspect otherwise.

"Too," Al said, "there are some complications."

"Like?"

"The kind with proper names, I suppose. It's not my business."

"None of this is our business, Al."

"Tim wanted me to ask you. It was important to him that this was amongst friends."

She wrapped her arms again around his neck. The less space she had to cover, the less hollow she felt.

"The family has a lawyer Tim's talking to back east, and when the time comes, he and Gigi will just go to Sam Goldwyn and say what's done is done. Once it's all over, Goldwyn won't care anyway."

"Why would anybody care? It's not like that's the worst that happens over there."

"Mary Frances. It's still Gigi."

"But it's not." And she realized then how completely she felt this. "It's not Gigi any longer. It's just not."

She sounded as though she were about to cry, and maybe she was. Regardless of what Gigi needed the studio to think, she was now the person most likely to tell Al everything, if she was bitter, if she wanted revenge. The thought of living with her seemed at once a disaster, and the only way to keep her quiet.

Al patted her back, offering that good people made mistakes, that it was not our place to judge, and Mary Frances let him go on thinking she was upset by yet another of her friends splitting up.

"Come on now," he said. "Look at the bright side."

He would be tutoring after the first of the year, the children of the conductor of the Philharmonic, who lived above Laurel Canyon in the hills. Living amongst all those rich neighbors, they might pretend they could afford their lives for once.

"That's what you like, isn't it?" He was smiling, but Mary Frances could feel his meaning, the hard feelings underneath.

"I like our little house. I like our privacy."

"Of course you do." He unclasped her wrists from his neck, straightened the lapel of his coat as though she'd mussed it.

"Aren't we off to the Ranch for family lunch?"

"I mean it, Al."

"I know. I know."

He was finished talking, already walking away, and she knew this would burn through the afternoon with him, especially in front of her parents. Al often found it easier to put distance between them before afternoons at the Ranch, when it became so clear how tightly she still fit to her family. Today she was relieved as well. Now she had something tangible to be responsible for, which was a whole lot easier than pretending things were fine.

In the long, low-lit kitchen at the Ranch, her sister Anne looked thin and frayed. She and the baby had driven down from San Francisco, and Sean was still squirmy and drooling, a tight bundle of new energy. Anne held him in her lap and tried to spoon him oatmeal, most of it clotting on his cheeks, his waving hands. His hands were everywhere.

"Oh, Sis," Mary Frances said. "Go take a nap. You're exhausted."

Anne made a sacrificing smile. "I'm fine."

"I can watch him. Mother's upstairs."

Mary Frances took the spoon and rested

her chin on the block next to Sean's bowl of oatmeal. He was laughing, round and white, a baby like dough. She dipped the spoon toward his mouth once, twice, the whole thing like trying to daub honey from a pot, and Anne began to cry.

It was almost embarrassing, how fragile Anne seemed since the divorce. She dithered and sighed; she rarely had anything nice to say. Mary Frances could not imagine surviving a life where she spent so much time with her face in her hands. Perhaps it was better not to live with your mistakes, or at least not to let them out into the open for everyone else to live with.

Mary Frances snatched Sean onto her hip, oatmeal now on her blouse, in her hair, which she'd just washed and set the night before. She plugged the sink and put him in it, clothes and all. He squealed.

"Let's give him something he might really like, Sis. What do you say? Let's give him applesauce."

Mary Frances handed Sean a jar and watched him feed himself, the first bite strange and tart, everything he thought about it happening right there on his face. She tried to remember the last time she'd tasted something for the first time, but that comparison failed quickly, as Sean was new, and new to everything.

"I don't miss him," Anne said now, and they were back to talking about her husband. Maybe they were always talking about her husband. "I don't. I'm just so tired all the time, Dote. It's too much."

Mary Frances took back the jar of applesauce and watched as Sean fisted the soap toward his mouth. She didn't miss Anne's husband either, a brute and a boor, and thank god Anne left him, but she wasn't sure that was what she was supposed to say now. She lifted a palmful of warm water over Sean's head, and he sputtered, Mary Frances twitching back to keep from getting wet.

"I'll do it," Anne said sharply.

"It's all right. It's just water."

Mary Frances tugged at the buttons on Sean's shoulder, his wet jacket and undersuit, unpinned his diaper, the clothing slapping to a pile on the floor by her feet. She held his wrist to keep him from slipping away.

Out the kitchen window, Al sat beneath a lemon tree with an open book he was not reading in his lap. Mary Frances wanted him to look up, to see her wrestling with Sean and for it to make him laugh, but he kept looking at the book, and the moment passed.

"Mother's coming," Anne said, and she pushed off her stool, making her way out the back door to the garden before Edith could see her crying. She passed before the lemon tree like a shade.

"Oh, Mary Frances, let Liesl bathe him," Edith called. "You're going to be entirely soaked."

"Liesl will be getting lunch, Mother."

"She wants you to clear out of here anyhow for that. Where is Anne?"

Mary Frances shrugged her shoulders.

Edith's face turned tight. "I keep hoping she will wake up from this mood she's in. That's ridiculous, isn't it? She was married for three years."

"We could just pretend it never happened."

"Of course it happened." Edith moved to take the baby in his towel. "We have Sean here to show for it."

"I was joking, Mother. I meant to be funny."

"Your Dote," Edith said to Sean, who had a firm grip on her earlobe, "is a ninny."

In the garden, Al still sat beneath the lemon tree with his cheekbone balanced on his fingertips, his ankle across his knee. She

84

could see the worn-out sole of his shoe. What happened, what didn't happen, what you wished to happen, and what you pretended not to, what you worried was about to happen. It was hard for Mary Frances to decide where to place her care anymore.

Edith called her from upstairs. Where were the baby's clothes?

Everyone gathered at the long walnut table in the dining room, and Rex opened a bottle of wine, beginning the patter of luncheon conversation, raised glasses, gentle compliments to the food and company. No one mentioned Anne's husband or the strike in San Francisco, the drought, or the fact that Rex needed an editor at the paper. Her younger siblings Norah and David were home from school in a week, and they'd have the holidays together at the Ranch; more of these gatherings, less that could be talked about. Over her father's shoulder, Mary Frances could see the broad globe of the fishbowl in his study, the shimmer of movement in the late light.

She would just say it; that would be the most natural thing to do.

"Al and I are moving to Laurel Canyon, after the holidays." She looked at Al, and he stepped in to explain.

"A delicate situation, really," Al said. "It seems —"

"Delicate?" Rex rested his glass beside his plate.

"Nothing at the college, sir. It seems, well, you remember the Parrishes, from Laguna?"

Mary Frances bit the inside of her lip to keep quiet. It was taking so long for Al to get around to it, she was stuck here, waiting for him to say the wrong thing. She was sorry she'd brought the matter up at the dinner table. She could have just told Edith, let her pass it on. Rex shook his head; he was a midwesterner at heart, and no one from Indiana got divorced.

"You people," he said, picking up the delicate cage of the hen's breast. He closed his eyes to take a bite.

"Us, Daddy?" Anne said. She could not abide to be judged wanting.

Then like a door slamming, Sean wailed from his cradle by the fireplace, and Anne sprang up so fast her chair tipped back onto the floor. Al reached down with one long arm and righted it, still nodding his head at Rex, whatever Rex had to say. Anne called for Liesl in the kitchen and Sean's bottle, the afternoon turning back so easily toward the baby's needs and satisfactions, their announcement seemed gone as quickly as it had come.

After lunch, Al was ready to go home.

"I need to get back to my study. I have notes." He jabbed his book in the air like a prophet. "I thought we were just going to stay for the one thing."

"Mother wants to take me into town. Can we stay just an hour?"

"For what?"

"It's almost Christmas." She turned to brush out her hair. It was silly to be so vague, she knew it, but she couldn't seem to stop herself. If she said they were going shopping, Al would draw up like a sponge. "You could sit in the garden and read again like this morning. That would be quiet."

He didn't say anything.

"Please, Al." She dropped her hair around her shoulders and turned to face him, but he was already stepping back, determined to keep their distance as it was.

"What difference would it make if I refused?" he said. "Go ahead. Have a nice time."

She laughed as if he were joking and turned back to the mirror. Rouge, a dab of Vaseline on her eyelids to make them shine. When she opened her eyes again, she was relived to see him gone.

Edith was waiting in the foyer in her

sensible shoes.

"Shall I bring the car around?" Mary Frances said.

"We can walk. It will do us good after that meal."

"We're not going into the city?"

"Your father's money is spent right here in Whittier these days. He supports this town in thick and thin. And I need the constitutional."

Anne arrived on the stairs. "You sound like Grandmother."

"And you sound disrespectful."

Anne's expression could blacken like a cloud. "Mother."

"Here we are then," Mary Frances said, holding one arm for Edith and the other for Anne.

Edith was having one of her days of resolution; they would walk because she wanted to, and perhaps it would improve her mood. Rex walked to town every morning. He said it was better than church for clean living, and god knew he never went to church.

Whittier was a Quaker settlement, and Christmas was no more or less holy than any other day. But when Mary Frances was a child and they lived downtown on Painter Street, Christmas morning she and Anne

88

would run to the sleeping porch and crawl into bed with Rex, Edith already gone to sing with the Episcopalian choir. At dawn, a trumpet played "Joy to the World" from the steeple of the meetinghouse, chilly, trembling notes in each direction. Mary Frances thought of the pale, church-bound holidays in Dijon, she and Al shivering in their apartment, waiting for the peal of bells. It had not been much different: the promise of a child's holiday to come.

Somehow today didn't seem as much like Christmas as it might have when they were children. Part of it was Norah and Dave off at school, but too, as they passed into town itself, the shops were quiet, some of them with the windows papered over with the *Whittier News.*

Edith stopped to read the dates, full of tut and bustle, one hand twisting at the other. "Your poor father."

"He didn't close the hat shop."

"But he sees it, Dote. And I know it kills him."

And here her mother headed into the version of Rex-as-pillar-of-the-community. People of Whittier looked to him for solutions and responsibility, had always looked to him, but especially now that times were hard and jobs were few. Anne rolled her eyes and turned away, but Mary Frances liked this version. Rex was a great man; Rex was her father.

"I saw an old woman, a woman my age," Edith said. "Down in the orange groves by the Ranch with a pack of hungry children. I don't think they were even her children. I told her to pick all the oranges she wanted."

Edith was intent, and clearly Mary Frances's audience was not enough; Mary Frances could see it, and she didn't know why Anne could not or would not. It would be Anne's first Christmas on her own with the baby, and everyone was worried she was turning mawkish.

Mary Frances caught her sister by the elbow. "What will Santa Claus bring Sean?" she said. "I want to make him something. I could knit him a sweater. Herbert Fisher brought me some really lovely lamb's wool last winter, and I never did anything with it."

Anne squeezed Mary Frances's hand where it fell across her arm. "Sweet of you," she said. "You are so talented. I never have time for that sort of thing anymore. Or patience. By the time I get home from the office —"

Mary Frances let out her breath, and let her sister talk.

■ ■ ■ ■

Edith bought Mary Frances a dress of deep russet silk, the skirt fluted and biased close, with a bracelet-length bishop sleeve and a keyhole tied at the neckline. The color set off her skin, her eyes. The dress cost as much as a week's rent for the house in Eagle Rock, and Mary Frances could not remember the last time she'd worn something so pretty.

Anne laid the flat of her palm against Mary Frances's hip, nudging her around to model. She was not trying on dresses herself.

"It's just right, Dote," she said, and she kept spinning her until Mary Frances stumbled and laughed.

"You buy one, Anne."

"I need so many things before a new dress. Besides, who would I wear it for?"

"Oh, come on, now."

"You'll see someday. You and Al will have a child, and then what you want will be different. Or god forbid, you won't know what you want anymore. . . ." Anne wandered to the curtain at the edge of the dressing room and stared off theatrically.

Mary Frances didn't know if she could

bear to hear her go on like this. A baby didn't make you smarter, or a humanitarian. Without really thinking about it first, Mary Frances blew right into the middle of Anne's speech to say she wondered if she and Al would ever have a child anyway.

The talk stopped. Anne's fingers played the base of her throat. "You mean?" she said.

"I thought maybe I was pregnant last spring, but frankly I was relieved to be wrong. Anyhow, I'm not sure it's for us."

Anne was quiet. The quiet rang through the dress shop, out to the settee where Edith waited with her tea, and beyond. They had talked often about Anne and Ted, but Mary Frances had never offered anything about her own marriage in return, and in one deep breath she'd drawn back the curtain entirely.

Anne touched the top of Mary Frances's head and left the dressing room. Edith would know in a matter of seconds, and later Rex, and then Nora, eventually even David. Every Kennedy knew everything about each other. She reached around herself to unbutton the dress, its skirt slicking to the floor, and she wanted to go with it. There would be no one she could ever tell about what she'd done with Tim.

She looked at herself in the mirror. There were carolers on the street, and she could hear them singing about good kings and laden boughs, probably for money, or worse, for food, and here she was about to take a silk dress from a shop because her mother still bought her clothes. She turned to see the shabby edge of lace along her hem, her second pair of stockings, not her good ones, held at the garter with a pin. She fingered her slip at her shoulder where she'd stitched it, just the touch drawing that particular evening to her mind again, and she whispered *no no no* over and over to herself. This was not her life: this dress, the move to Laurel Canyon. These were not the things she could afford.

It happened when he was tired. Al had been reading Keats's letters, then scanning the page, no longer registering words as they were written but rather as they occurred to him, and suddenly he slipped into some kind of liminal space between reading and writing that felt weightless. *We take but three steps from feathers to iron.* Connections clear and essential, slipped together in his thoughts with a sudden loop of language, until the thump came loud from overhead, and he was himself once again, in a chair, in the Kennedys' parlor, Alfred Young Fisher, Al.

He looked around: the English antiques, the portraits, the sheer size of the place — you could not see the end of the property from the windows. Rex wanted a dovecote, he built one. He wanted a new car, he bought one. Al wasn't sure how he was going to pay for the gas they needed to get home, but it had been important to Mary Frances to come here today, and he hated to tell her no. He looked at his watch. She'd only been gone an hour.

These long afternoons at the Ranch were always tedious — Rex ensconced in his office like a resident dignitary, and Mary Frances shopping with her mother, or canning fruit, or carting David and Norah somewhere, or performing some other task that could not be done without her presence, or at least her say in the matter. Edith wasn't feeble, but she required Mary Frances. Since the divorce from Ted, so did Anne.

Through the ceiling, he could hear the trip-stop of the baby running from the cook, laughing. Not that Ted was such a good guy, or that people didn't do it all the time, in one way or another, but you could not lose a child the way you could lose a wife, and Ted was an idiot if he thought so. Look at Mary Frances; look at Al here now. The

Kennedy family was as much a part of his life as if he'd married them all, and there was no real way to divorce yourself from that.

He thumbed the pages of his book but couldn't concentrate with the patter overhead, and found himself taking the wide oak staircase two steps at a time to tell Liesl to keep the boy quiet. The day did not have to be a total wash.

The door of the nursery was cracked, and Al stopped with his hand on the knob.

It wasn't Liesl on the floor with the boy, but Rex in his shirtsleeves, rolling a blue spotted ball and watching the boy chase it back. He was completely taken, laughing nearly as much as Sean. Al could not recall having ever seen him in the nursery, let alone without a coat and tie, kneeling. He tried to back away, but the floor groaned and Rex looked up.

"Sir," Al said.

"Are we disturbing you, Al?"

"Not at all. I was just curious."

Sean clapped his hands, his face intent upon his grandfather. And Al thought an invitation might follow, that Rex might call him into the nursery, onto the floor, to play with this baby as if this baby were his concern as well, but Rex just laughed and

95

rolled the ball again.

Al backed into the hallway, pulling the door closed. He would have declined anyhow.

The clock chimed. Next to the clock, an étagère. On one of the shelves, a framed photograph of Mary Frances when she was in high school. Her dark hair was pulled back over her ears, her dress falling loosely from her shoulders, and all that cleverness in her face Al had first been attracted to when he met her in the library. Only in this photo, it was the promise of such a woman, rather than the shifting fact of who she had become.

Al could not guess what she was up to at the library these days, leafing through old books, taking careful notes. In Dijon, she'd started a potboiler mystery novel, a sketchy travelogue, and countless articles for *Ladies' Home Journal,* all abandoned at some difficult point along the way. She wanted to write something important, he could see that, but it was a little like watching a kitten with a mouse, fast enough to catch it, but without the instincts to do what needed to be done next. Maybe she would get lucky and find something she wanted to say. But maybe she would lose interest and go back to knitting socks. Now, especially, without

Tim to encourage her.

He slipped the photo from the frame and slipped the frame into the bottom drawer of the étagère. There were so many portraits of the children in Edith's house, he doubted anyone would miss it. Downstairs, he tucked the photo into the back of his book, turned to the front page, and started reading what he'd been trying to read all afternoon, the *thwack* and patter sounding from overhead, each line repeating, repeating once again.

He was nearly beside himself when the women finally returned, but Mary Frances pretended not to notice. He stood from the chair he'd taken by the fireplace, his books already gathered under his arm. She asked if he was ready to go, and he rolled his eyes.

Anne brushed past them, tugging off the fingers of her gloves. "Sean?" she called. And then, "Good travels, Dote. I'll see you both next week."

Al reached out for Mary Frances's shopping bag.

"I have to see my father," she said. "I have to say good-bye."

"Fine, Mary Frances. Whatever you need to do."

"Thank you."

Rex was back in his study with his typewriter and a cup of coffee, the closed-up room rich with man and dust and book leather. Edith was forever trying to shove the cleaning woman through there, but Rex protected his schedule. His hours at home were few. He sat with his feet propped up on the desk, his glasses slipped down his nose and his arms thrown back as though he might solve whatever problem you presented, but that was just how he relaxed.

"Do you ever think," he said, "if we'd not had those Sundays in Laguna? The ocean, Dote, such a magnificent balm. Without it, we'd have shot each other."

Mary Frances went to him and pressed her lips against his head, his great big brilliant head. Sudden tears leaped to her eyes. She did not want to leave him, ever.

"I went to the house a few weeks ago," she said.

"Oh? You didn't say."

"It was a secret mission."

"Mary Frances Kennedy." He put his feet back to the floor and looked at her. He seemed about to say something else but took her hand instead, pressing a fold of bills into her palm.

"For your missions," he said. "Or whatever else arises."

"Daddy. You embarrass me."

"Then you, my dear, need a thicker skin.

That there is mostly enough for a night on the town. A girl needs a night on the town, a new frock. These things don't stop because you get too old to take money from your dad."

"Al's waiting," she said.

"He's been waiting since he got here, by the looks of it."

Mary Frances tried to laugh.

"It's all right, Dote." Her father patted her hand where it rested on his shoulder. He could always read her deeper currents.

"I don't think it is." She shook her head. "It's not."

"We were all young once, dear. If it were so difficult to survive, we wouldn't be here now."

And she knew Rex meant to sound glib and cheery, but she found herself wondering what he'd given up or turned away, what inexorable choices he'd made beyond Edith and his children. Rex was barely fifty; how far was this life from the one he once imagined?

In the driveway, Al shook Rex's hand, kissed Edith, opened Mary Frances's door. In the flurry of remembrances for the holiday — Mary Frances would bring the Baltimore relish she had put up at the end of the summer, and Edith needed plenty of help with the goose — she said good-bye and fell silent.

She tried to remember if Al had always been this impatient with her, or if he only seemed so now because she knew he had the right to be. Her anger in return also seemed convenient. She thought of Anne in the dressing room of the shop, the willowy unhappiness she flounced like so much veil. Anne had done the thing that was supposed to make it better, she had left her husband, and yet she had not been able to quit the display of wanting to leave that had sustained her for so long. Her freedom seemed to leave her with nothing to push against. Her freedom, it seemed, had made things worse.

Mary Frances knew she would do anything not to end up like Anne. Even now she felt herself dividing, some false bottom giving way, making room for some other kind of life: there would be the truth of what she'd done, and she would keep that to herself, for herself. Then there would be the things she would do to keep it, and that could make a marriage. Couldn't it?

She slipped across the seat. Her hand fit neatly in the pocket of Al's trousers.

"Oh," he said. "Would you look at this?"

She could feel his thigh clutch as she

pressed her palm against him. She tried to say something with that pressure, but he kept his own hands on the steering wheel, and she couldn't think of what to do next.

When he stopped the car in front of their house, the sun was low in the sky and terribly gold beneath the brow of clouds: Al looked handsome, and she told him so. She took his arm to walk inside. She led him to the sofa and sat on the edge of the tufted seat before him, her legs crossed primly, looking up. She imagined all his schoolgirls, their smooth young faces upturned, who must find him so handsome every morning at the lectern, their notebooks open and ready, pens in hand.

"Read me your poem, Mr. Fisher," she said.

He laughed, but not as if she were funny. "Mary Frances."

"Please."

She stretched back and let her arms go long overhead, closed her eyes, and now the delicious sound of all that fabric upon itself, the catch and glide of her stockings to her skirt, her blouse pulling free at her waist. What was it the schoolgirls wore these days? She pushed one knee loose from the other and imagined Al standing between, the balance tilting her way, and god, she had hope.

She imagined they were people who would do this, who would ravish each other come an early evening at home. Maybe if they were fast enough, they could sneak past all of it, wind up on the other side of these days, sweaty, spent, and somehow knit back together. It seemed possible. It seemed as if it were going to happen, and Mary Frances whispered, just once, his name, *Al.*

Nothing.

She opened her eyes, and she was alone. The room seemed suddenly bright with sunset. She pushed herself up, smoothing the back of her hair, her blouse. She heard the cupboards in the kitchen open and close, then Al with a sandwich in the doorway, three huge bites already gone.

She felt herself smile at him, surprised at how easily the pleasantness came to her. It closed many of the conversations of the day.

Later, she woke hungry, and slipped from her covers for the kitchen. On the counter was the crate of avocados they'd brought from the Ranch. She split one along the pit and took the saltcellar and a spoon, stood in her nightdress in the window's blue light, scraping the flesh from its skin and sprinkling it with salt. She ate two avocados that way, and in the icebox, there was cold milk, and in the pantry, a big wedge of Edith's

102

cake, enough to fill her up, to send her back to bed. But it wasn't so much about being hungry as it was about being alone.

She thought of that winter in France when it was so horribly cold, she'd never left their rooms, the long days waiting for Al to return from the university. She'd discovered tangerines. They could not be peeled too carefully, each velvety string stripped away, the bright sections left to dry atop the radiator on yesterday's newspaper while she took her bath and brushed her hair. The tangerines filled the room with their perfume, and when they were tight to bursting in their skins, she opened the window and nestled them into the snow piled on the sill to eat when they were cold, changed somehow for all the care she'd spent on them. And not to serve or share, but care she'd spent for herself. Alone.

She found her notebook on the table and wrote this down.

She wondered if Tim had gotten to Delaware, and how long he would stay. She hoped, suddenly, for him to stay forever, just slip off the other side of the country where he came from. But then she remembered the flare of his match as he touched it to a cigarette, his quick draw of breath beside her in the darkness. She turned to him, the smooth hammered skin of his chest (she could not remember his bare chest, but her mind rose up to make it for her now), and she put her mouth down, his smoke still languishing in the air, in his hand, they would do anything not to talk, moving against each other again, the sheet tangled in her feet, and she wondered how much more of this night she had to remember and reinvent and relive until it would at last be over.

That she wrote down too.

Years from now, she will find these notes when she and Norah are gathering her papers; the library at Harvard wants everything she's got, and there are letters to publish, the diaries to edit. She sits at her high-piled desk and pages the old notebooks, the cat curled in her lap, a glass of cold vermouth set aside, anything to steady her hands now, which always seem to shake. The notebooks are full of little gems she never knew how to set, and she loses herself to them constantly, whole afternoons slipping away. She reads this page, and here suddenly is Tim. He comes back to her full force, and even as she hasn't had a new lover in what seems like decades, that night comes back to her complete. The first.

She has written about Tim for years now. Hasn't she always written about Tim? He haunts her, and she lets him, she writes him into places he never was: beside her, all around her, her one true love. And because she can make Tim anything she wants, their coming together has always been cast as fated and clean, as inevitable as daylight. She has not left room for complicated feelings.

Norah lays a thin hand to her shoulder now, exchanging her vermouth for a cup of tea, so attentive these days, so good to try to help sort through it all. Her life has made so much paper, which seems as though it should be weightless until it overwhelms.

"Not this one," she says. Norah puts the notebook on the growing pile that will never go to the library or the publisher, the notebooks and letters and scraps of her life they will burn when they are through here. For a moment it's amazing to her that with everything she's already written, there's still this stack of things she cannot, will not say.

When Al found her in the kitchen the next morning, all the cookbooks were open, and Mary Frances sat disheveled amongst the stacks of them with ink on her cheek, making notes. He crouched down, and she startled.

"Sorry, sorry." He held out his hands. He looked happy, or was he making fun of her?

She closed her notebook, pulling her bathrobe tighter around her waist. "I couldn't sleep," she said.

Al spun a cookbook to read it, the cover open to an old inscription: "Improve each shining hour."

"My grandmother's. Her brother gave it to her on her wedding day."

"Another little essay for Tim?" he said.

She shrugged. "They're not really *for* Tim. Tim reads them. You could read them, too."

Al held her eyes a moment longer, then stood. She remained looking at the crease in his charcoal pants. She felt he was about to pass his judgment, and she would not bow her head for it.

"We should go out for dinner tonight," he said. "Why don't I make a reservation in town? Why don't you put on something pretty? Would you like that?"

"Yes. I'd like that."

"Of course you would."

She knew there was no money for this kind of evening, no money but what Rex had given her, but she couldn't come out with that now without causing a fight.

Then in Al's fingertips, there was a clean white envelope, slit at the top, addressed to MFK Fisher. "This came yesterday," he said.

She tore into it. *Westways* had paid her thirty-five dollars for the story about Laguna, more money than she'd ever made in a month. She sprang into Al's arms, and he was laughing too.

"We'll go shopping," she said. "I want to spend it all on treats for us. And Mother and Rex. Oh, this is so good, Al. Just perfect."

"MFK Fisher," he said, looking at the check in her hand.

"Thirty-five dollars," she said.

He searched her face again, wanting something she couldn't find to give him. "I'll get a bath right now," she said, and she stacked her books back in their basket.

She was excited to go out, Sardi's perhaps, they could call Gloria and Mr. Sheekman. She felt like a party. She had been paid.

She washed quickly and slipped back into her robe, "Stormy Weather" on the radio, *keeps raining all the time.* She went back into the bedroom to get dressed, and in her bare feet, Al didn't hear her coming.

There he was before the bed, his fists cocked on his hips and his feet astride, as if he were surveying a field just planted. The box and wrapping lay on the floor at his feet, the new russet dress draped across the coverlet, the skirt fanned, the slender tie looped into a bow. She watched him rub the back of his neck. What was he thinking about?

She crept back down the hallway how she'd come and took a pair of stockings from the basket of folded laundry in the kitchen. She'd wear something else tonight.

After a pleasant dinner out and another glass of wine by the fire, after Al read to her from *Crime and Punishment* and she knit the gusset on a sock she wanted to have ready for David's Christmas present, after the whole evening passed easily, she returned to the bedroom and found the dress box where she'd left it in her closet. The dress and the tissue were folded back inside; Al had left no sign that things were ever otherwise.

Al packed his books into his satchel and cleared the last of his papers from the desk. The light was still good outside, and it wasn't too cold. He could take the long way back to the house at Eagle Rock for the last time.

The dean had personally extended his

apologies. It was a matter of numbers, the economy at large; Al was a fine teacher, adored by his students, respected by his colleagues, a valuable asset to Occidental. Al had known the conversation was coming, and he thanked the dean, asked about his plans for the holidays, spoke of the time he would have now for his own work. The dean was almost certain there would be a place for him in the fall, and Al hoped that was true. As the man walked away, Al ticked the months by in his head.

He had a tutoring job for the spring and summer; there were lines of men in Los Angeles waiting for jobs, for houses, for loaves of bread. He was lucky to have what he had. There would be the drama in Laurel Canyon, surely a drain on his time and patience. In the end, he would be grateful for this flexibility. He bent to check the drawers of the desk, and there was a knock at the door.

"Professor Fisher?"

It was a girl from his lecture, Miss Prescott; he tried to remember her first name but could not. The conversation would be a formal one. She clutched a composition book against her chest.

"I just had a question for you. About my essay on Keats?"

"Certainly, Miss Prescott."

She handed him the essay, and he skimmed it, not one he had graded himself. He started to explain that his wife often made comments on his compositions in his lecture classes when he realized it wasn't Mary Frances's handwriting in the margins. It wasn't a woman's handwriting, at all.

"Miss Prescott, you're sure this paper was written for my class?"

"Yes. Yes sir, on Keats."

Al folded back the cover of the book and saw his name, the room and course number. He stared at it for a long moment.

"I see you made an A," he said. "What is your question?"

The girl rattled on about a letter Al had read to them in class, one of Fanny Brawne's, and the significance of their relationship in light of "The Eve of St. Agnes." Al remembered: *My love has made me selfish,* Keats wrote. Selfish. He listened to the girl, told her what she wanted to hear, and sent her on her way. He walked home in the long winter light.

One evening last summer in Laguna, Tim and Gigi had come for dinner, and Mary Frances pulled one of her little essays from her skirt pocket, reading it almost as a toast. It had been a piece about dinner partners,

110

who made for good ones and who did not. Al remembered laughing at her cleverness. Then later, the meal spent, he found Tim and Mary Frances in the kitchen, the essay in Tim's hands now, and the two of them bent over it. Tim began speaking, and Mary Frances finished his sentence for him, taking the pen from his hand, scribbling in the margins of her paper. At the time, his only thought had been to open another bottle of wine.

It was dark when he reached the house at Eagle Rock. Mary Frances had the news on the radio, the elections in Czechoslovakia, seventy-four Nazis passing blank ballots. The house smelled of pork fat and sage, dinner that had probably taken all day to cook. When would she have had time to meet with Tim? What did she do with her time when he was not around?

"You're home," she said.

"I am." But this would not be their home much longer.

At Christmas, everyone was at the Ranch: Anne and Sean, David in his school uniform, nearly a soldier, and Norah, the gazelle, the long, lean beauty, Norah! Mary Frances tucked into her room at the top of the wide oak stairs as soon as they could be alone. She wanted to hear everything, and not with Mother or Anne there to arch their brows. Norah was shy at first, her pretty chin tucked against the fall of her hair. There were boys, yes, lots of them, and books, and ideas.

"Oh, Dote," she said. "I sometimes wish you were always with me. I see this, and this and this, and I think how you would love it. But that's not very grown up, is it? To always want your sister by your side."

"I often think about the time you lived with us in France. I never felt like you were the baby."

Pride puffed in Norah's voice. "I didn't either."

"Are you writing? Mother says you're writing."

"Not as much as you."

Mary Frances flipped onto her stomach and fiddled with the tatted edge of Norah's pillowcase. Rex had poured the wine freely at dinner, and she felt good and light, like talking with her sister as long as they both could stay awake for it.

"Did you read my article in *Westways*?" she asked.

"Well, of course I did." Norah turned from the hand mirror like a model in a magazine. Had Mary Frances ever been so flawless? "I read it aloud to my friends at school, and they all wanted to hear more about Laguna. But I started with my stories, the tar on the beach in August, how we'd climb up the rocks with our fried-egg sandwiches, and nothing was quite so good as what you'd written. They wanted to hear you tell it, Dote. And then they wanted to hear you tell it all again."

Mary Frances fell back into the pillows, laughing.

"I'm sure they did," Al said.

Nudging the cracked door open, his face had the bleary twitch of too much wine as well. "I love to hear Mary Frances spin her tales. I think she's the best storyteller in the Kennedy family."

She pushed up from the bed, searching his expression for something hidden. He was flattering her, and it fit poorly. "Don't be silly, Al."

"No. I liked your magazine story. I really did."

"You must be quite proud," Norah said.

"Oh, I am. I am." He sounded tender, and sincere. He put his hand on the doorknob and stepped back, an invitation. "Coming to bed, dear?"

"Yes. In a minute."

"All right, then."

But he stood waiting for her, or waiting for her and Norah to begin their talk again. Mary Frances studied the toe of her shoe against the wide plank of the floor, everything suddenly a measurable angle. She knew the right thing to do was to go with Al, but all she wanted was to stay.

"It's wonderful we're all together for Christmas again," Norah said. "Don't you think?"

Edith set the tone in her kitchen, and she was worried mostly about the geese. Liesl had plucked and trimmed and blanched the birds that morning and then arranged them under an electric fan, blotting the skin with onionskin paper because she swore this was what they did in Chinatown to make the ducks so crispy. Edith had never heard of such nonsense; Mary Frances didn't care. Liesl liked to be agreed with. She peeled and quartered a mountain of turnips, blotted her geese, and mumbled under her breath. Liesl's knife was steel and sharp, and Mary Frances had hardly ever seen her without it tucked into the ties of her apron. She would not be going home until after the Kennedys' dinner was served.

Into goose fat and onions, Mary Frances tipped a bottle of old Madeira wine. There were oranges everywhere; she sliced one and gave it to the baby. She sliced another and dropped it into the pot with the wine, pierced the skin of the geese all over, stuffed their cavities with oranges and thyme branches, and laced the legs closed. Edith put them in the oven. Norah stirred a pot. Outside, Rex and David roasted almonds they'd gathered from the neighbor's trees. The sun cast a long beam across the kitchen floor.

Anne sat beside the baby making pomanders, a fistful of cloves and an open tin of Edith's nougat candy on her lap.

"Careful, Anne. You'll get sick," Mary Frances said.

"I won't."

"You get sick every year." Everyone said Anne had inherited their grandmother's nervous stomach, but Mary Frances suspected it had more to do with self-indulgence than anything passed down. She had an uncanny ability to find and eat vast amounts of sweets. The sugarplums were gone already.

Edith cracked the oven to peek at the geese. "Anne," she said. "You have Sean to think of."

"Good lord, Mother."

Edith looked at her sharply, and Anne put

the candy away.

The Kennedys were a large family in celebration, but it had once been larger. Mary Frances caught Edith lingering over Grandmother Hollbrook's tea service with her cloth, even though Liesl had already polished it once. Her face, reflected in the domed hip of the pot, distorted and wistful with a passing grief. And then upstairs, Anne standing in front of her wedding portrait, the baby wauling at her feet.

"Oh, Sis. Mother ought to take that down."

"I looked thin, don't you think? Too thin."

"You're thinner now."

"No. No, I'm not. I'm better now. I feel better."

Mary Frances was uneasy with the subject. She bent and scooped Sean into her arms, lofting him high, so light, a boy made of birdstuff. He leaned out for his mother, and Anne took him automatically, still looking at the portrait.

"Do you think Sean looks like his father?"

Mary Frances pressed close and kissed her ear. She whispered, "He's a Kennedy, Sis. All the way."

Downstairs the front door flung open, the rumble of men, and the house filled with the scent of cedar, Al on the other end of an enormous tree he and David had hacked down. By the time Mary Frances and Anne got there, Rex was already in full admiration, and Edith a high twitch over where to put the thing, the past set aside. She looked at the baby in her sister's arms — the past, in brand-new form.

And late that night, after the perfect goose — Liesl had been right, the crisp skin like enamel — after midnight carols and children sent to bed, the tinsel hung on the tree and the table set for breakfast, she and Al took the wide oak stairs to the bedroom that had always belonged to her and Anne. They undressed in darkness and said good night.

But Mary Frances couldn't sleep. She felt Al not sleeping in the bed beside her.

"What is it?" she said.

"I got a letter from Tim today."

Her back went cold, the part of her closest to him. She said nothing.

"He sounds so desperate. He doesn't ask about her, doesn't mention her, but he sounds all the worse for it."

"He loves her." It was surprisingly easy to say.

"I just can't imagine what he's going through."

Al was quiet. Mary Frances hoped that was all.

"It is not lost on me," he whispered. "I'm grateful I can't imagine it."

She turned toward Al, his eyes full of devotion. They had met when they were children, really. They had seen so much through. You could not take that history back and give it to someone else, like trading a part in a play.

She remembered the first time he took her hand on a street corner, tucking her palm into the crook of his arm and holding it there, the way she could feel his heart slamming in his chest. She remembered their train from Cherbourg to Paris, the crumbs of their first baguette scattered across the tablecloth, married three weeks but finally knowing she was married, that her life was about to begin. She remembered the first time he'd looked at her this way, and it was not so long ago, and not so different than now. She only had to make herself remember.

She watched the first pale bands blue the sky outside her window.

She whispered, "Can you hear it yet?"

"Aren't we too far from town?"

"Listen," she said. "You can still hear it."

Together, they strained their ears for the tinny peal of joy on the trumpet. Mary Frances could feel her chest filling with anxiety, all that was to come in the months ahead.

"I love you, Al," she whispered, and he said he loved her too.

LAUREL CANYON, CALIFORNIA
1935

When they arrived, the driveway was empty. They stepped into the foyer, found a note on the table by the telephone: Gigi had a screen test this afternoon, and then an event at the studio until late. They should make themselves at home. Mary Frances's relief was all too clear.

"Are you all right, dear?" Al said. "You aren't sick, are you?"

"The car was too stuffy. I'll be fine."

She looked down the long hallway to the bedrooms. She wondered how long she would have to stay in this house before Tim was the second or third thing she thought about when she looked down that hall, before that night faded entirely.

There was another letter for them on the hall table, propped against a vase of chrysanthemums as big as baseballs. Tim's handwriting was slanted and loopy, elegant, familiar. Mary Frances reached for the envelope, thinking of his blue ink across her pages. If she wrote him back tonight — though that would be ridiculous, desperate, what would she talk about, his empty house, his wife? — if she wrote him back tonight, there might be a reply by Saturday.

She handed the letter to Al, and he tucked it away into his breast pocket, left her standing in the hall.

She lit a cigarette. Her hands were shaking. She looked out the sidelights at the Chrysler parked in the driveway, everything they needed packed into the back, their lives, their boxes and bags. There was almost nothing they could not leave behind. Damn California, damn all of this.

There was no ashtray in the hall. She could not stop shaking.

"You want a drink?" she called. "Al?"

"A drink? Now?"

"Or not." She could get one herself; she was perfectly capable.

The kitchen was big and white, a refrigerator hulking in the corner. She opened the door to a gasp of ripe air, ice furred on the freezer box: a quart of milk, two eggs, a sack of oranges with a Christmas greeting printed on the label. She quickly closed the door again. It was almost as though she'd made a knot in time. She was going through Tim's house to find something to do, something to start and finish and direct herself upon, but all she kept coming up against was how there would be no Tim here, not anymore, not to eat these oranges or peel these eggs or make her a goddamn drink.

She closed her eyes, and when she opened them, Al leaned against the counter, chewing on a swizzle stick.

"Where'd you get that?" she said.

"Tim's studio. He's got a whole collection of them."

"Are you going to work in the studio?"

"I hadn't thought about it. I don't know."

Al said this heavily, as though she were asking some kind of existential question instead of a logistical one, and maybe she was. It remained to be seen which of them would lay claim to the space and time and materials of being a writer. Something had changed when Mary Frances got paid for her article about Laguna, but neither of them had said what, or how.

Al left the swizzle stick on the counter, went back out to the car, and brought their suitcases inside.

Later that evening he stacked all Tim's canvases to face the walls of the studio, their framed backs to him, cleared a space on the worktable, and opened the case of his typewriter. His manuscript to the left, clean paper to the right, his notebook open and ready, but Al stood at the window, looking out.

He could not stop thinking of his father, the cathode ray treatments; his mother said the skin on his neck was sloughing away. When Al was a child, he'd had scarlet fever; when his mother lifted him from the bed, the skin from underneath his arms came off in sheets, and he could not remember a greater pain — surely he'd felt one, but now his mind was working to find something empathetic in his father's illness and would not budge.

Nobody knew, really, what happened inside the human body. It wasn't as if mucking around in there taught us anything more than what we could see, the parts moving, beating, holding everything together. It was a glorious design, perhaps impenetrable. And yet everything the doctors could think of to cure his father's cancer was virtually invisible.

He sometimes thought *The Ghost in the Underblows* had begun like that. Al would arrive at the Café de Paris after morning classes, order his cassis, and sit to write. He wrote until his fingers cramped, and the poem was always pushing, grabbing all his thoughts for itself, and you couldn't see it, but god, it ate time. He would look up from the page to find his cassis untouched, the lunch hour come and gone, and he would run back to Mary Frances.

She would have something waiting for him in the little tin oven, and after lunch he would kiss her — the passion, too, it came from the poem, from the lunch, from the streets outside their tiny rooms that were as old as the first streets ever made by man — and he would promise to come straight home from afternoon classes, straight home. She would cling to his hand, laughing, telling him to hurry, telling him to write some more.

He had not felt that way in a long time, and he had no idea if he ever would again.

He reached into his breast pocket and took out Tim's letter. He was planning to leave Delaware this summer for a trip through England. He needed to clear his mind, he said. Shake off the darker perspective. Such a luxury, Al thought, to be able to leave your life behind and keep leaving it.

The letter was also for Mary Frances. Tim asked for her essays so that he might show them to his older sister, Claire. Tim and Claire had written and illustrated a half-dozen children's books together before she'd moved on to Harper and a string of novels you could find in any bookshop across the country. Tim thought Claire might be of help in finding Mary Frances a publisher for her work.

Al stared out the window of the studio, into the scalloped landscape of the backyard. He needed a new perspective, because lately all he was thinking about was money and how he didn't have it, his father and how he was dying, his ardor and how it had dried up. He had time, three weeks before tutoring began, he had paper and ribbon for his typewriter and space, a wife who didn't ask much of him. That had been his hope in the beginning of their marriage; Mary Frances was always able to entertain herself. He had admired that once, but it seemed suspect now.

He shut out the light in the studio. The door was cracked to the hall bathroom, and inside, Mary Frances readied herself for bed, her hair held back from her face with a ribbon, cold cream white along her jawline. She bent to fill her palms with water, the curve of her hip silhouetted in the sheer fabric of her nightgown, and he wanted to press himself against her, to feel all that humid, furtive rush he remembered from those afternoons in France. He stood watching her a long time, but nothing came to him.

Mary Frances woke to a great banging racket. It took her a moment to find herself in the darkness, the unfamiliar room and the sounds coming from corners she could not place. She tilted her watch from the nightstand; it was two a.m.

She rolled over. Al's eyes caught hers before he pretended to be asleep again, and so she had no choice but to go, as she always would have, and see what was the matter with Gigi.

The kitchen was a crime scene. The refrigerator door stood open and dripping, a tempered glass container of leftover yellowness shattered on the floor, puddles of soapy water, ammonia. The faucet was running, overspilling a bucket placed beneath the spout, but Gigi sat at the table in a pretty pink dress, high heels, her hair waved back from her face as though she were preparing for an evening's entertainments, not just returning from them. She was smoking a cigarette, tapping her ash into a tented gum wrapper on the cherry print cloth.

"Oh, I'm sorry," she said. "I didn't mean to wake you."

"It's all right. I was up." Mary Frances

126

bent to pick up the pieces of glass at her feet. The yellowness on the floor was thick and curdled.

"I'll get that," Gigi said. "I'm just so clumsy tonight."

But she sat with her hands clasped against her pink skirt, her stagy poise pronounced enough to read across the room. Mary Frances caught a bank of perfume: verbena, lemon, heavy flowers. Gigi thanked her for coming to her rescue.

"I think this will be exciting. Don't you?" she said. "Like a pajama party. It was Timmy's idea, of course, but immediately I could see the bright side. I owe you a great deal."

"Oh. Al and I are happy to help."

"But you" — Gigi reached out and put a hand to her arm — "you have made this so much easier."

"Given time, everything gets easier."

Gigi smiled. "Please. Make yourself at home."

Mary Frances wished she would not say that again; this was not her home. But now it wasn't Gigi's either. Her perfume was overwhelming, and Mary Frances went to shut off the faucet. She pulled two juice glasses from the cabinet. She reached into a cabinet beside the sink for a pint of apple

127

brandy that had been tucked away under the dishtowels, and from the pantry, a sleeve of Saltine crackers, a tin of pâté.

"I see Gloria visits here, too," she said.

"With her strange bottles and jars of, I don't know, stuff. What is that anyway?"

"*Alouette, gentille Alouette.* It's skylark."

Gigi propped her brow on the heel of her hand. Her cigarette was out. Mary Frances poured her a short brandy, herself a larger one.

"You're so smart, Mary Frances. Just so *smart.* The glasses, the food — you know where everything is, how to find just what you're looking for in my house."

Mary Frances felt the blood in her face; she could not stop it. Gigi drew on the dead cigarette, then studied the unlit end, her expression horribly opaque.

"In my house, for goodness sake," she said.

Mary Frances knew she ought to apologize, to thank her for her discretion or maybe burst into tears, but her mind had turned cold and quick in another direction. Gigi knew, she would tell others, and the truth would run like a ladder in a stocking. It was only a matter of time, and if there was a shape Mary Frances wanted this to take, the time was now.

"I can't stop thinking about him," Mary Frances said.

Gigi came fast across the table, her face bleary and willful and no longer remote, coming up on her elbows, the pink bodice of her dress gaping open. She upset the glasses, brandy rolling and dripping to the floor, and took both Mary Frances's hands into her own.

"You know it's not that you did what you did, right? Whatever you did. Whatever you did . . ." Gigi was shaking her head. "If I wanted him, I'd still have him. I could have him back."

"But you don't."

Gigi laughed sharply. "What are you talking about?"

"Want him. You don't."

Gigi smirked at the overturned glasses, her scripted moment already spilled out.

"I feel sorry for you," she said. She pushed herself up and away, the swish of silk and the taps of her heels steady down the dark hall.

Mary Frances looked at the mess on the table, the mess on the floor. She was sure Gigi did feel sorry for her, and angry and betrayed, but also exposed, frightened, and passionately distracted herself. Someplace in all that, Mary Frances thought she could find her sympathy. At the least, her sense of pragmatism. If Gigi sought revenge with Al, she and Al would leave her here alone, and this little arrangement to save her standing at the studio would fail; but Mary Frances knew the most dangerous thing she could do would be to say so. She balled up the cherry print cloth, took the bucket from the sink, found the mop. If she didn't do it now, she had the feeling it would just be waiting for her in the morning.

Driving down the canyon, she passed men walking the berm of the highway, their caps pulled low against the florid sunrise, their hands in their pockets. The radio went on and on about the hitchhikers, the police officers dispatched to the state line to keep the tides back, but that didn't seem to change the fact that people were there, and needed work, and would walk to where they thought they could get it if nobody would give them a ride. Still, Mary Frances couldn't stop. She was alone, and this wasn't Whittier, where everybody knew her father.

The city pushed itself out of the valley, a sleek web of boulevards and date palms and oleander, insistent, overdressed, a city like a nervous widow. She drove slowly, circling, the streets still empty of cars.

The farmer's market was on Third and Fairfax; it gave off the stink of cows. There were knots of people, the kind who bartered for bruised tomatoes, neck bones and pork rind, their rosy children clinging to their skirts. Men leaned against the open tailgates of their trucks, smoking hand-rolled cigarettes, dogs circling, and low clouds overhead, blackening with rain. She could not shop in a place like this without thinking of Dijon.

The way Al lost himself, first to his studies, then to his teaching job, his poem, she had lost herself in those market stalls, her lists, her basket clutched in her hand, her endless questions of what to do with how much. In that, Al had been the perfect companion, her fellow traveler.

The market smelled of hay and roasted nuts; she bought a newspaper cone of almonds from a woman stirring them over an open fire. She bought thick sandy leeks, a rope of garlic and a pound of tomatoes; she bought a long *batard* of sourdough bread, a dozen bluish speckled eggs, a jar of cream, because now she had a refrigerator and could keep such things for more than an hour or two. She lifted the paper lid of the cream and tasted it, wiping her mouth with the back of her hand; she remembered

131

the pillowy clouds of Gruyère grated onto her piece of waxed paper at Les Halles, the cheese maker young and handsome and milk-fed himself; he tried to teach her the French for being in love with him: *mon cocotte, mon chouchou, ma petit lapin, Madame, s'il vous plaît.*

She walked the stalls, and on the edge of the market, a fishmonger laid out his catch on two blocks of ice: strange curled squids and spider crab, silvery piles of sardines, their eyes still sparkling, thick slabs of some white-meated fish, its head as big as a dinner plate.

"What is that?" Mary Frances asked.

"Is fish," the man said. "Fish that swam in the sea this very morning. The fish that is the most fresh. Here."

He took a knife from his pocket and opened the blade, spinning the fish head along the ice. He wedged the blade into the gill, sawing a clean half moon into the cheek, slipping his thumb between the flesh and skin to pull free a small pat of meat. He made a thin slice, squeezed a bit of lemon over it, and passed it across to Mary Frances on the tip of his knife.

"Eat, eat," he said.

She took the bite. It was tender and sweet; it felt clean in her mouth. She made a sound, and the fishmonger echoed her.

"What you like?" he said, and she gestured at all of it.

There was no coffee in the pot when Al got out of bed, and the house seemed empty, the women gone. He cracked ice into a glass and filled it from the tap; there was nothing else for breakfast. The ice tasted rotten, and he poured the glass back down the sink.

He caught the flutter of a hem on the terrace.

He had not seen Gigi since before Christmas, before all this broke out, and he walked to the glass, expecting some kind of markable change in her. Perhaps she would seem less attractive because of what he knew now; it was not the sort of thing he knew about very many women. After Mary Frances came back to bed last night, he had lain awake, trying to imagine the tenor of their conversation in the kitchen from the sharp tones he'd overheard. It embarrassed him to be this curious, but it didn't really matter if he was embarrassed in front of Gigi anymore. After all this was over, they would never see each other again.

He opened the French door. "Good morning?"

"Yes," Gigi said. It was all she seemed

133

capable of. Her frame was draped in a kimono that fell low over one small breast, she wore dark glasses, her hair wrapped back in a turban. She made no move to cover herself, and Al looked at the ground. There was an open bottle of aspirin there, a soda siphon, and a bottle of Peychaud's bitters.

"Oh, dear," Al said. "That sort of evening?"

Gigi sighed and turned, the kimono shifting. Actresses. He stuffed his hands into his pockets and waited to be dismissed. Sometimes, polite conversation eluded him; he settled for countdowns instead, backward in his head from ten.

"Al," Gigi said. She pushed her dark glasses on top of her head. Tired, without her makeup, her face still looked like porcelain. "My father died shortly after Tim and I were married."

"I'm sorry to hear that."

"I hadn't seen him in years, and I didn't go east for the service. I didn't even hear about it for two weeks after it happened. Heart condition."

Her voice had the faintest tremble in it. He leaned closer to hear her.

"Anyway. Tim told me you were having troubles, and I just —" She tried again. "I just wanted . . ."

"Thank you, Gigi," Al said.

Her hand skimmed his pant leg. Al stepped back.

"I know Mary Frances must be such a comfort now. She's so close to her family, I'm sure she understands. But if you want to talk, or if you need anything."

"Thank you, Gigi. Thank you." His fingers beat time on the frame of the French door.

She studied him a long moment as if sizing him for a suit, then looked away, waved her hand. He felt, at last, dismissed.

His papers and typewriter were just as he had left them, but he couldn't shake the feeling somebody had been touching his things. He missed his study in Eagle Rock; he had grown used to working there, and now this house would be full of distractions it would take weeks to rise above. Gigi on the terrace, half dressed, Gigi's friends — they were all so young, and lately youth only made him feel impatient.

He needed to clear his darker thoughts, like Tim. He needed to go somewhere, but Mary Frances had taken the car.

He left on foot. The winter sky was angry and gray, and the air damp, his head bent to watch his long strides, one after the other.

He enjoyed the rhythm of a long walk, and let his mind loose to it. He could walk all day.

Up into the hills, he walked to Otto Klemperer's house, the man whose children he'd be tutoring. Without thinking about it, he knocked, and as though he were expected, the servant led him into the ballroom, where a black-coated man bent to the piano.

"I am sorry, Mr. Fisher," Klemperer said, without raising his head from his work. "You find me on a day I am composing."

"Please excuse me. I was in the neighborhood —"

Klemperer held up his hand. "A moment, Mr. Fisher. Feng, please show Mr. Fisher to the . . ." He waved his fingers. "The veranda, yes? Lunch, Mr. Fisher?"

"Well, yes. Thank you."

Al was starving. He hadn't really eaten since yesterday. He followed Feng through the French doors, the veranda in the shade of an enormous Morgan fig tree. Below, a rippled swimming pool; in the distance, the reservoir, the HOLLYWOODLAND sign, as though he might forget where he was.

Feng brought him a cup of coffee, the door to the house like the opening of a vacuum, music rushing out to meet the air and then sealed in again. This was a familiar rhythm too; Al thought of those mornings at the Café de Paris, the way time accelerated and collapsed around his poem, his work. This is how it had felt, if not sounded: a day composing. He could have those days again. He took his notebook from his back pocket, his pencil to a blank white page.

He drank another cup of coffee before Klemperer joined him, and Al left his notebook folded open, a mark of who he was, a writer.

"Thank you, Mr. Fisher, for your help with my children."

"Of course. I look forward to meeting them."

"And you are living in the area now? Your letter said you were moving?"

"Yes. My wife and I are staying with friends for the next few months."

Otto Klemperer lit a cigarette, his sharp face, his round black eyeglasses bearing down. He stared at Al in such a way that Al kept talking.

"The wife of a friend, she's in the movie business. He is . . . traveling."

Al felt the stupidity of this topic settling around them now, Klemperer's first impression of him, the tutor to whom he would trust his children.

"Ah," Klemperer said. "I have been married for twenty-two years. Traveling is often a part of life."

He smiled then, a quick, well-guarded flare, and Al felt welcomed into a kind of confidence he was not prepared for. He had always valued his relationship with older men, the precision of their opinions. Tim was like that for him, a good friend but also counsel. He missed him now in a way he had not yet permitted himself to understand.

Feng came with the plates from the kitchen, slender curls of ham wrapped around white asparagus, dark bread, a soft, runny cheese, and a bottle of *pinot blanc,* three glasses. He opened the wine and poured it, Klemperer looking back toward the house.

"So," he said with a clap of his hands. "We will not wait. Enjoy, Mr. Fisher."

And carefully, with exacting care, Al watched Klemperer eat every bite on his plate, and then every bite on his wife's. He drank her wine, he discussed Amelia Earhart and how she had just landed the first flight from Hawaii to Oakland, and did Al know Oakland, and did he know Amelia Earhart? Klemperer did, and he liked her intelligence. His daughter, Britta, who was twelve, loved to fly. Christoph, eight, loved milk shakes and the idea of being buried in a tomb with all his earthly possessions. Klemperer wanted to buy them a dog while they were here in California, a big hairy dog. What were the hairiest kinds of dogs in America?

Al looked out over the deep green swimming pool and answered Klemperer's questions: he did not know Earhart, he'd never flown in a plane, he liked Airedales, but they were more fuzzy than hairy and they probably had those in Germany as well. The sun was warm, the food good, and Feng seemed to magically appear whenever Al's glass was empty. This life seemed so evenhanded — vital and civilized at the same time. Al was very comfortable.

"May I ask you a personal question, Mr. Klemperer?"

Klemperer crossed his fork atop his knife and sat back in his chair. "Of course."

"Do you think a man ought to encourage his wife's creative pursuits?"

"Her hobbies?"

"No. If your wife, say, wanted to conduct an orchestra, or play music professionally. Do you think it's suitable? For a woman to be an actress, or a writer."

Klemperer turned the handle of his fork, considering.

"Do you have children, Mr. Fisher?"

"I don't, no."

"I wouldn't have thought so."

Al feared he would ask why not, but he didn't say anything, and the silence settled and split open. Al had never been judged for not having children, not by his parents or by the Kennedys. He felt something petty begin to simmer in his chest.

"It is not for everyone, I suppose."

"No, sir."

Klemperer pushed back from the table. He suggested a schedule beginning in February where Al would come to the house in the afternoon and instruct the children for four hours, Monday through Friday. He reached into his wallet and extracted several bills.

"A retainer."

"It's not necessary, Mr. Klemperer."

"But it is. You would not have come all this way for lunch."

Al's face flushed. He would leave the job on the table but for the fact it would be their only money this spring. He'd leave the job on the table but for the fact he could not live his life without it, his life such as it was these days, his life as Gigi's keeper, as a teacher without a class, a poet avoiding a poem. And how easy for Klemperer to take a day for his composing, the bills from his wallet, there was always more for some people. He told Klemperer he could show himself out.

In the ballroom there was a woman lolling in a slender gabardine skirt, her oxfords perched on one of the long white sofas, her wavy red hair fanned along the back. She was smoking a cigarette, the ashtray balanced in her upturned hand. This woman could not have been the mother of a twelve- and eight-year-old, nor did she seem particularly bothered that she'd missed lunch. She trilled her fingers at Al as he was leaving, her long freckled arm extending from her slouch with all the snap and lash of the tail of a cat.

On the street, Al took his notebook from his pocket and started with the pages he'd written on the veranda, peeling them from the binding and holding them to the wind. When he had been a student at Princeton, he'd once destroyed a thesis he'd worked on for a year and a half; sometimes there was no other way to free yourself. He did not follow where the pages fell, just kept peeling them away until he felt better, purged of the afternoon's illusions.

Back at Tim and Gigi's, he found Mary Frances at the stove with a dishtowel tied

141

around her waist, her hair damp and curling at her temples. From a long board, he watched her rake a pile into the stockpot: tomatoes and garlic, orange peel and bay, the heads and spines and tails of a dozen sardines. She plunged a knife into a spider crab and split it in two, tossing it after. She hadn't noticed Al standing behind her.

He cleared his throat, and she swung around.

"Oh, goodness," she said.

"You've been busy."

She held to his face a mortar of green pounded herbs and garlic, a rouille so sharp it made his eyes water. And then a hard loaf of bread, white fish steaks translucent as china; she put a salted almond in his mouth, a crust dipped into the stockpot, her finger. She was giddy, beautiful, his wife.

She poured the stock through a strainer, pressing on the bones and shells with the back of a wooden spoon. She poached the fish steaks, some tiny rings and tangles of squid, picking out the mussels as they opened; she toasted bread; she warmed a Delft tureen with boiling water. She set the table, handing a cold bottle of white wine from the refrigerator and a corkscrew to him.

"There's so much in this kitchen," she

whispered.

"Is Gigi here?"

"No, not ever, I don't think. But she's got every kind of gadget. Look at this. Do you know what this is?" She held up a Bakelite-handled comb with a dozen tines.

Al waited.

"It's for slicing cake," she said.

"How'd you figure that out?"

"Who needs to slice cake like that?"

"I don't know." She was transfixed. Al sighed, and opened the wine.

The bouillabaisse was rich and red and spicy, as good as any they had had in France. They bent over their bowls, blowing and slurping and adding dollops of rouille, more bread, more wine. It was a meal to serve a dozen people, a feast, and Al was already full, so much food left over. Mary Frances could be so extravagant. He could feel the impatience welling in him again.

He said, "I need to see my parents in Palo Alto before tutoring starts."

She put down her spoon. "We just got here," she said. "We're supposed to keep up appearances, yes? We can't just turn around and leave."

"I've only got a little more time. You could stay, though."

"By myself?"

"I saw Klemperer today."

Al put twenty dollars on the table. They stared at the money. She could not account for the panic such a trip caused in her, but she did not want to go, and did not want Al to leave her here with Gigi, or explain why not. The air in the kitchen went from humid to thick. Mary Frances tried to imagine that it was Rex, sick. Would she ask Al's opinion of anything?

"I don't know," she said.

Al said nothing, still looking at the money.

"Whatever you think, Al."

The front door opened, Gigi home, the tarantella of her bracelets, her keys, her high heels across the floor.

"God," she said. "What is that smell?"

It was hard to say if her question was a positive one. Al folded the money and put it away. Mary Frances rose from the table, pulling out a chair, setting a place between them. Gigi hadn't eaten all day. And she was bubbly and bright and smiling as though the night before, the morning after had never happened, the three of them suddenly historyless and clean.

She picked a shell from her bowl and tipped the mussel into her mouth.

"Everything you do is like an advertisement, Gigi. Al, look at her. It's amazing."

"You eat beautifully, Gigi." Al didn't look up from his plate.

Gigi smiled. "Tim says I am to tell you to stop being polite."

"I'm sorry?" Mary Frances said.

"You're supposed to send him your stories. He wants to show them to his sister, and he can't if you won't send them. He says he mentioned it."

Mary Frances put down her spoon. "When?"

"In his letter?" Gigi looked at Al. "I left a letter . . ."

"Oh yes," he said. "His letter of the other day. Yes, he did."

Al went back to his bowl.

The phone rang, and Gigi pushed back from the table to catch it. Her voice became like music in the other room, detectable only in the higher registers. Mary Frances couldn't look at Al any longer. She stood up and began clearing dishes, running a sink of water, anything to make noise of her own.

She wondered what Tim had said and how. The letter had been addressed to both her and Al; Tim must have assumed Al would be pleased, proud, excited. She finished the dishes and wiped down the table and counters. She swept the floor. She had not been thinking of a publisher, only of Tim, only of Tim's attention, only of what she could keep of it now.

Al sat with his hands folded over his plate. It was not unreasonable for her to ask for the letter, but he'd gone quiet since Gigi left the room, and Mary Frances hesitated to break that. She thought about everything twice now with him: once as his wife, and once as the woman capable of what she'd done. She wondered if that would ever change.

Finally she asked, "What did Tim say?"

"I'll find it for you. I just forgot."

She tried to tease. "I don't want to be rude."

"Of course not." But he didn't get up for the letter either.

In the hallway, they heard Gigi hanging up the phone. Mary Frances turned back to the sink and sunk her hands into the dishwater. Behind her, Al bagged the trash and took it out to the can.

"Oh, I might have done those dishes," Gigi said.

"It's all right."

"But I don't expect you to cook *and* clean."

Mary Frances turned. Gigi was inspecting her nails. She stopped, and met Mary Frances's stare. There was no point in pretending that either of them did anything around the other without making calculations anymore.

"I wish you hadn't brought that up in front of Al," Mary Frances said.

Gigi smiled a harmless smile; she had an amazing number of smiles at the ready, and Mary Frances had no idea how to defuse an anger so carefully played out, so costumed.

"We wouldn't want to bother him," Gigi said. "With our little bargains."

"I don't have any bargains with you. Or Tim."

"Then I guess I have no idea what's going on here. Because where I come from, that's exactly how a girl gets a part."

This moment will return to Mary Frances again and again. She'll try to write it from distances near and years away, angles droll and poignant, but she'll never get it to seem on paper the way it feels right now — the room filled with fuel, somebody's fingers at the match.

Even when she sits some forty years later with her sister Norah at the round table in the kitchen of Last House, amongst the open notebooks and stapled drafts, the cartons of paper she's made over the course of her career, she thinks to try it once again.

147

There's one more book here, if they can find it.

But she's too old to start new work now; they'll have to find it in what's already been written. Her mind feels thinner, lacy; when her eyes get too bad to type, she reads. When they get too bad to read, she cooks. She is already thinking of the tomatoes ripening on her windowsill, how she'll scoop them out and bake them with crumbs and anchovies and Parmesan cheese. She could eat tomatoes like that any time of day, and she would suggest lunch now, but Norah is determined to make progress. In the chair opposite, she holds her slender, knotted fingers in the spines of several books, flipping back and forth, her reading glasses low on her nose. Norah, always so steadfast.

The new book should be about places, they've decided: touchstones, lodestars, sanctuaries. Norah turns again to the story of Gigi's kitchen, the Bakelite-handled comb, the sudden, frank address.

"There's too much to explain," she says, "about the three of you living there together. But it's good writing, and familiar. It feels like something you would do."

"It is something I would do. I did it."

"But that's what I mean, Dote. You'd hardly have to touch it."

Mary Frances perches her chin on her folded hand. "Which version do you mean?"

Because in the notebooks, the drafts, she's ended this evening several ways.

In her favorite version, she tells Gigi to fuck off. Conversationally, without a pause or second thought, in an even voice, she tells her to fuck off, and she leaves the soapy water in the sink, the dishes, whatever stew is still left in the tureen, brushing past Gigi's shoulder in the doorway as she goes. She speaks that way now, in curt four-letter words she probably said only in private then. Oh, so useful — the fuck off.

Or in another, Al returns to the kitchen, the women still circling, their tempers flared as fans. Mary Frances looks at Gigi, finding a harmless smile of her own. "Tell him whatever you want," she says, the bluff laid out to call.

Or she says nothing. She just walks out, leaves the house and all her things in it, this life already lost to her, a fact she should have known since the moment she set foot in Tim's bedroom. She's become someone else — two people, a thousand. She's become every version of herself she'll ever write about, all capital letters and abbreviations: MFK.

But in truth, this conversation never came

149

to anything. Eventually, the silence in the kitchen grew too long to be supported. Gigi uncrossed her arms and turned back down the hall to her bedroom. Mary Frances looked toward the terrace. Al had been gone a long time for just taking out the trash.

She pulled out her notebook but couldn't find a pen, not in her pocket or hooked to the neckline of her blouse, not on the countertop or in the drawer full of odds and ends. But in the foyer, beside the vase of chrysanthemums, there was Tim's marbled Parker. She'd seen him with it a thousand times, the pen he used when he marked up her work.

It was heavy in her hand, the fine nib scratching at the page, formed to Tim's script and now forced to hers. She tore the paper, tore it once again, and put her notebook down, finishing her thought on the palm of her hand, Tim's blue ink across her skin now. Down the hall, she heard a door slam and her chest pounded suddenly, once, and then returned to its own tempo. What on earth was she doing here? What on earth had she done.

Anne fought with Edith. First, the letter came from Anne, how she was not a child or a wife any longer, how she wouldn't listen to Edith at all but for the fact she and Sean needed her allowance to make their monthly bills. And then the letter from Norah, how Edith could hardly get out of bed she was so blurry, so low and upset. Anne was being a stubborn pill, but she always listened to Mary Frances, didn't she, wouldn't she? And then Norah wandered off into a long ramble about the trouble with studying Latin on an empty stomach. It seemed everyone expected intervention.

Mary Frances called out to the Ranch to try to soothe Edith's nerves.

"Anne is proud of herself, Mother."

Anne was living in a tiny apartment in the Russian Hill neighborhood, leaving Sean with a nurse during the day so she could take dictation for some president so-and-so, and this was not what Edith had raised her daughters to do. What was all that with the debut at the Hacienda Club, the weddings, college? Edith started crying. She was not a young woman anymore, and she was disappointed.

"Do you want me to come home?" Mary Frances said.

"I know you're busy."

"Not that busy. It's all right, Mother."

Al walked out of the kitchen and stood in the hall watching her. He let a handful of peanuts into his mouth. He did not try to hide the fact that he was listening.

"I could come home," Mary Frances said. "Norah said you were a little blurry."

Al shook his head, shut out the kitchen light, and headed down the hall to the bedroom. Mary Frances watched his shoulders disappear into the darkness.

A flurry of telegrams, and Al made plans to go north to Palo Alto on the weekend. His brother Herbert would meet him at the station, home from China on some kind of medical leave, dysentery, but maybe just another ploy to get out of trouble over there. Mary Frances folded white shirts into Al's valise, knowing his mother would unpack them and notice how neat and how worn. The evening stretched long before his train, and she tried to stuff down her anxiety at being left behind.

"I will miss you," she said.

"Really?" He turned to her, mildly surprised. "I thought you might be looking forward to some time alone."

"An afternoon, perhaps. A trip to the Ranch. But much more than that, I start to lose my footing."

"My dear," Al said, squeezing her hand once. He turned back to his shaving kit, counting out enough spare blades for the time he'd be away.

In the living room, Gigi dealt a hand of solitaire.

"Gin?" Mary Frances asked.

"I'll get it," Al said, going to the bar.

The women looked at each other, and Mary Frances laughed. "I'll deal," she said, and held her hand out for the deck of cards.

She held a run and a set, but couldn't remember which they were playing for. Some sort of violin whined from the radio; it had been too early for dinner, and now she just wanted to keep drinking. Even as their glasses were not empty, she asked if Gigi would like another.

Al stood from the loveseat where he'd been reading to refresh their cocktails once again.

Gigi pressed her hand to her mouth. "Sleepy," she said. "But I have to meet Doris and Nan soon. We're going to see that Bette Davis picture, at the Pantages."

She sounded seventeen, announcing her plans and asking permission at the same time. She'd left the night before around this time, and the night before that. She folded her cards and snapped them against the table edge. She'd been winning, Mary Frances was certain; she trailed her fingers through Gigi's hand to fan it.

"Gin," Mary Frances said. "You won."

Gigi smiled. From inside her skirt pocket, she pulled a letter.

"Don't wait up for me," she said.

The letter was from Tim, postmarked from Delaware, addressed to Mary Frances alone; it had come in the mail, but Gigi had taken it upon herself to deliver it as dramatically as possible, full of both subterfuge and flourish. The room seemed to contract in a breath, to pant. She folded the envelope in her hand.

Al bent over a book on the loveseat. She tucked the letter into the waistband of her skirt and passed behind him for the hallway. She stopped. There, in his book, her face — the portrait her father had commissioned on her sixteenth birthday.

"Oh, Al," she said. "Not that. Where did you find it?"

He didn't answer her. "You were so lovely. And still, of course. But you know it for yourself now."

"I was just a child."

"Well. Not anymore." His gaze stayed fast into his book as though their conversation were as idle as it seemed. She let her hands rest on the back of the loveseat for a moment, her nails rasping at the barkcloth as she turned away.

He wished she had not caught him with the portrait, but it was bound to happen sometime. He'd moved it from Keats to Milton, found himself studying the fringe of bangs across her forehead, the open way she gazed at the camera. He would've loved to have been the object of that brand of scrutiny, and maybe he once was. He couldn't remember anymore.

He had lived so long in other people's houses. As a child and then a man, a husband; in boardinghouses, at the Ranch, the summerhouse in Laguna. Now here, in what increasingly seemed like a foolish arrangement. Down the hall, the women were opening and closing doors, running water, sliding hangers on the closet bar. He could sit still and imagine what they were doing. What did it matter if he could watch over them or not?

He liked Gigi, he always had, but what she was doing to Tim was hard to stomach. She was no more going to the Pantages with somebody named Doris than Mary Frances was, and she didn't seem to care if Al knew it. She was a woman on her way out of this house, and the motions came to her naturally. He looked back at the portrait and wondered what Gigi had looked like at sixteen. Though she was hardly older than that now.

She sashayed from the hallway, checked the sidelights by the front door, and drained the last of her martini. At the piano, she played the chords of a song, humming in the highest registers.

"What's the part?" Al said.

Gigi let her hands fall back to her lap. "I don't think I'll get it."

Al wasn't sure how to respond. To encourage her seemed wrong, but he didn't know anything about who got what and why. He felt suddenly, irrevocably sad. He returned to the Milton in his lap.

"Isn't school out for you?" Gigi asked.

"I read for myself."

"Of course. Timmy used to say that, too. If only I could act for myself, I'd get out of all these lousy auditions."

She spoke of him so easily, as though Tim had died years ago, or been lost at sea, some disappearance she'd made peace with rather than asked for.

"Work is hard." He sounded frosty; he heard it himself.

She sighed and looked away. Her profile was so elegant, almost defiant, the lift of her chin, the tilt of her nose in the air. He looked back down at his Milton, hoping she would just leave.

"The song is fine, anyway," she said. "They can train you to sing." She closed the fallboard on the piano. "What I really worry about are my legs."

She stepped in front of him now and lifted her skirts past the tops of her stockings, the high arch of her garter belt around her shaven sex. She was looking at herself, tilting her heels so her skin would catch the lamplight. Al felt a sickening rush and lifted his gaze to meet hers.

They heard the car in the drive that Gigi had been waiting for, the engine at an idle. They heard Mary Frances cut the water in the bath. Still Gigi stood there with her skirts around her waist and Al, paralyzed. Seconds beat past. From the driveway, a tap on the horn, and she smiled, and let them fall.

It was a flat card, not a letter; he said he'd been reading an article in a magazine the other day that made him think of her, a little piece about the sand and the sea, an artist's colony of sorts. He had found *Westways* at the library near his mother's house. The piece was very good. He hoped she was proud. She turned the card over. A single line:

Write to me.

It was more haiku than conversation; he offered her nothing more in these few words than what she could make herself. But still, he'd gone to the library. He'd looked up her essay and taken the time to tell her as much.

She took off her clothes and climbed into the tub. She could hear Gigi leaving, the front door slamming as she rushed to meet whoever waited in the driveway. She sank back into the water, Tim's card still clutched in her hand. *Write to me.* She had been. She did, all the time she wrote to him in her head, of what had happened and might still happen again, of what she saw that made her think of him, his razor left in the bathroom cabinet, and pulling the open blade across the soft hairs at the back of her hand, seeing his white shirt, crisp and hanging from the laundry, and burying her face in the empty chest of it, hoping for his smell, his chlorine and wet pavement and grass. The ink bloomed across the card-stock, and what rose in her gave way to that thing that tried to figure out how long, how much she would give him, now that he was asking. Now that she was here, and Al was going away.

His departure was early, and they dressed

in darkness; Al whispered they could share a coffee at the station.

They did not notice the blue Hudson blocking the drive until they'd already started backing out.

Al checked his watch. He cranked around in his seat, gauging his options, and then turned back to the steering wheel. Mary Frances didn't know what to say. She folded her hands in her lap as if she were waiting for the light to change.

"I can't leave like this," Al said. "I can't leave you here alone."

She looked back at the Hudson, as if for confirmation she was not alone.

"Your train, Al."

"I can't."

"They're in love, aren't they?" she said. "People in love are completely full of themselves. You're not going to stop any of this, obviously. Nothing will."

He was still looking at the wheel. She suddenly had the feeling they could sit here for days and not get past this moment. She patted Al's shoulder as you would the flank of a good horse.

"Cut over the lawn," she said. "You don't want to miss your train."

When she got home, the Hudson was gone.

Gigi's door was ajar: on the nightstand, a cup of coffee and the newspaper collected from the front porch. The sheet was low on Gigi's back, so slight Mary Frances could trace the basket of her ribs, a long scar, thin and red as a whip of candy, disappearing over the arch of her hip. Mary Frances had seen Gigi in bathing suits and harem costumes and had never seen this scar. She wondered how hard she had to work to keep it covered.

Tim would have known every curve of it, of course. In a strange translation of time and space, Mary Frances knew that the time Tim had taken with her body the night they'd spent together was his habit, was what he gave Gigi as a matter of course, and she stuttered there at the door. To have that all the time. To walk away from it for something else. Or maybe every person met another on their own fresh terms, and what happened between her and Tim had never happened before. She couldn't say, and she was surprised by how little she cared.

In the studio, Al's manuscript was still stacked beside the typewriter, his clean paper, a fine film of dust collected there, and the paintings stacked against the walls, like children made to face the corner. She trailed her fingers along the top edge of the canvases smeared with red and ochre, tipping one back against her leg: a flurry of shapes and colors. Another, and another: they were all bright, dodgy, difficult to understand upside down and backward.

Tim had never showed her this work. There were paintings he'd made all over the house, landscapes and portraits and studies of small objects, paintings his cousin had made of Tim and his sister when they were children that you could now buy on greeting cards, and none of them were like this. She pulled out a canvas and hung it on a tenpenny nail across from the worktable.

It seemed to be a view through a scrim, the wavery aspect of water. She had the feeling her eyes were adjusting to the light in the room; which room exactly she could not say, the studio or the space in the painting, but after a while, a man's face appeared, angular and strong, a bright stain of rouge or red on his cheek, as though he'd been kissed there and rubbed it away, as though he'd been slapped.

She pulled out a stool and sat down, cranked a clean page into the typewriter, and opened her notebook.

Lucullus placed a live fish in a glass jar in front of every diner at his table. The better the death, the better the meal would taste.

Catherine de Medici brought her cooks to France when she married, and those cooks brought sherbet and custard and cream puffs, artichokes and onion soup, and the idea of roasting birds with oranges. As well as cooks, she brought embroidery and handkerchiefs, perfumes and lingerie, silverware and glassware and the idea that gathering around a table was something to be done thoughtfully. In essence, she brought being French to France.

Everything started somewhere else. She thought of Tim's note: *write to me.* He didn't want to hear about Lucullus and Catherine de Medici; but she loved her old tomes and the things unearthed there, the ballast they lent, the safety of information. She spread her notebooks open across the table. There was a recipe for roasted locusts from ancient Egypt, and on the facing page, her own memory of the first thing she ever cooked, the curry sauce and Anne's chocolate. A conversation rising between the two, her own voice at the center of it all.

It was hours later when Gigi knocked on the studio door.

"I'm late," she said. "Did Al get off all right?"

Mary Frances turned on her stool. Gigi wore an ivory coat that gathered and buttoned at the waist, a pert hat pushed forward over her sleek curls, and Mary Frances wanted to excuse her same white blouse, her same blue skirt and oxfords. But Gigi was staring at Tim's painting.

"I didn't know he kept that," she said, her expression skipping like a record.

"There are stacks of them."

Gigi tried to make a sentence several times, her pretty mouth discarding the words before they'd begun. Finally, she turned to Mary Frances.

"You know that's a picture of him."

Mary Frances looked at the painting again.

"He had a collection of mirrors — old mercury glass ones, cracked ones, some that were ruined with age. He used the mirrors. Sometimes we'd have to stop —"

"It's just nice to have something to look at."

Gigi let her gaze settle on Mary Frances.

"He used to let me help, give me little chores around his studio," she said finally. "He was always very good at making you feel important."

"He's probably still good at those things."

She laughed. "Of course. That's not what I was saying. Only that I'm familiar with his methods." She gestured at the typewriter.

Mary Frances turned back to the page she'd written. She felt exposed the way she had playing cards, Gigi passing her Tim's letter like contraband. She thought of the pale fish twisting in the jar, and she listened to Gigi walk away.

Without Al, Mary Frances discovered what she did alone. She liked to cook for herself, to assemble a meal of things he would never consider worth a mealtime — shad roe and toast, soft-set eggs, hearts of celery and palm with a quick yellow mayonnaise, a glass of wine, an open book in her lap, and the radio on. The elements that mattered most were the simple ones: butter, salt, a thick plate of white china and a delicate glass, the music faint, the feel of paper in her hand, and the knowledge that there was more, always more book to read, more wine if she liked it, some cold fruit in the refrigerator when she was hungry again, and the hours upon hours to satisfy herself.

She wrote. She wrote when she got up in the morning, straight on the typewriter or with her notebook in her lap, a cigarette lit but unsmoked, coffee poured but turning cold. She wrote while she did the breakfast dishes, while she swept the kitchen floor or hung the laundry, while she unpacked the refrigerator, wrapping everything in wet newspaper to keep it cold while the freezer box dripped into a mop bucket inside the open door. She wrote mostly when she was not writing; she wrote mostly when she looked as if she were doing something else, and then she typed late into the night in Tim's studio to have another manuscript to send to him, another way to keep their conversation going.

She stayed out of Gigi's way. Her friends came to the house, other chorus girls and actresses, all of them as young as she was, slender as switches, their hair every shade of blond imaginable. They passed around eyelash curlers and lipstick, cinched and beaded dresses, draped their clothes around the living room as though it were a costume closet: somebody had a date and needed a sweater, a skirt, a pair of stockings without runs, it came off another girl's body, as if one were as good as another. Mary Frances lingered in the kitchen just to listen to them talk.

The talk was constant, wrapped in nudge and insinuation. This director was easy, this one hard, the production code would be the death of all of them. Roles were being cut because of it: embraces that lasted too long, hips that shimmied too long, the moll to the devil who didn't get his due, and suddenly movies they thought they were playing in belonged to someone who'd kept their sunnier side up. One girl, Nan, was sad there would be no more kissing.

"Not the way there used to be kissing, at least. You know, like kissing so that maybe you got a date later."

"No more bad girls." Doris's voice was whiskey-burned, and she liked to take the dim view. "No revenge in modern times. I mean, just think about that. What kind of stories are you going to tell without revenge?"

"I think that's the modern times part, Doris," Gigi said. "I think revenge is just old-fashioned."

"But it's human nature."

"What isn't?" And they laughed.

Tim had been right; they loved their scandals: who was too fat, too thin, and what that might mean about their habits, and what would happen if the studio found out. Once a subject was open, it always seemed open. Nan was having an affair with someone famous; they referred to him only as the King, and with a great deal of whispering and giggle. They all thought Tim was out of town.

It wasn't long before Gloria heard that

the Fishers had moved to Laurel Canyon.

She appeared late one afternoon, still wearing her backless lace gown from whatever scenes she'd shot that day, its fishtail hem dragging on the slate. She was stunning. One of the girls in the living room gasped when Mary Frances opened the door.

Gloria took Mary Frances's hands and kissed her cheeks. Her stage makeup was frighteningly dark, as if her features had all been underlined.

"I want you to move in with me," Gloria whined. "What do I have to do to get that? Al?"

"Al's gone to see his father in Palo Alto." Mary Frances slipped her arm into Gloria's and turned her toward the living room.

"So it's just us girls?" She shot a gleaming smile over her shoulder, and Gigi seemed to wilt.

The actresses fell away for her entrance. She swept into the love seat, her skirt flung wide, perching forward for a cigarette from the box on the table. She waited for someone to light a match, and Nan fumbled through her purse.

"Would you like some coffee?" Mary Frances said. "I was just going to make some. Coffee?"

Gloria was suspicious already; her imagination followed only one direction, down a path she'd taken herself many times and so was familiar with the scenery. When Mary Frances returned from the kitchen, she was still digging at Gigi, Doris and Nan hanging on every word.

"He went home to Delaware without you?" she said. "Are you working? I mean, that's a long time for you to be working."

"And Al did the same thing to me," Mary Frances said. "Just last week, he took the train north by himself and said I could keep Gigi company."

"Well. It's an epidemic!"

"I wouldn't be surprised if they planned it together. I haven't heard from Al once, but Tim and Gigi talk every day. I've never seen a man more in love."

"They are *adorable,*" said Gloria.

"Oh, more than that, I'd say." Mary Frances looked at Gigi, her face coloring over her cup. "I'm jealous."

"Who isn't," said Gloria, and then, "I heard the fixers had to drag somebody's wife out of the House of Francis yesterday."

Nan looked nervous. "Whose wife?"

And they rolled on to other matters, finger waves, and how to lose five pounds in three days, and a woman downtown who fit corsets as if she were giving you a whole new rib cage. Gigi smiled and laughed and flattered Gloria, but when Mary Frances returned to the kitchen with the coffeepot, she'd followed her inside.

"That Gloria," she said. "I never —"

Mary Frances said, "Gloria has been my friend for as long as I can remember."

Gigi looked small and suddenly tired, dark circles beneath her eyes beneath her makeup. Everyone had lives they lived outside themselves, and altogether separate ones within.

"I'm sorry," Gigi said quietly.

Mary Frances understood then that maybe their fight was over, debts paid. "I'm sorry, too," she said.

"Show me what you're doing here. Even I can learn how to make coffee."

Mary Frances measured beans into the grinder and turned the handle. Gigi filled the pot. In the other room, Gloria's spangled laughter led the others, and neither woman found herself particularly eager to return.

Mary Frances sent Tim the piece about Catherine de Medici and waited. She no longer pretended she knew what she was doing; her sense of reason seemed to have

169

evaporated in favor of another letter, and then the next. The postman arrived in the morning and returned most afternoons; she knew his schedule by heart, shuffling through the envelopes before she'd even closed the door. She wanted her exchange with Tim to be as immediate as what she carried in her head, but a week went by, ten days, the time it took a letter to travel all the way across the country and another one to travel back, and there was little for her to do but imagine what he might have written, and then imagine it another way again.

Your writing is beautiful, Mary Frances, and it lingers with me long after I have put your pages away. I planted a small garden in the cold frame here and went this morning to work in it. The seedlings are still tender, but by late spring, I should have lettuces and peas, a radish or two. Your essay was on my mind, and I thought of how in France there was a time a woman might have been as flattered by a bouquet of lettuces as she would have been with roses. I read the piece a second time, and I think you might —

Enclosed was her essay and Tim's blue notes across it, careful and precise, a record of his time, his interest in her. A second reading, she thought. At the end of his letter, he thanked her for sending her work and asked for more, dear god, more.

She found Gigi on the terrace, basking. She wore a bird's-egg blue hostess dress, the organza tie at the waist flailing against the flagstones like something that had lost its wings. She had slices of cucumber over both eyes. Mary Frances asked her if she wanted the bitters.

"Just tired," she said. "But aren't you sweet. I was out late with Nan. It seems she's making a surprise move to San Francisco."

"She has a picture there?"

"A nine-month engagement, so to speak."

"Oh."

Gigi rolled her head along the back of the chaise, letting the cucumber fall into her open palm. She looked at Mary Frances from underneath her long, long lashes.

"She's Catholic. And he's married, maybe to two women, it's hard to say. Nan's lucky, really. The fixers only come into the picture if you're worth something to the studio. Otherwise you have to work these things out for yourself."

They were resourceful girls on the whole, the studio girls — they knew how and where to get things done, and when the fixers wouldn't help, they helped each other, getting money together or a place to stay, the name of a doctor in another town. Circles were small. A dozen pretty girls with long legs and good voices, and one became Jean Harlow or Joan Crawford, and everyone else was like Nan. So when someone did pick you, took you aside and told you that you were more than pretty and long-legged and good, it was hard not to get carried away.

Mary Frances thought of Tim's letter, what a beautiful writer he said she was. It was easy to say those things from the other side of the country. It was easy to send them, to send anything on paper.

Gigi said, "I don't think Tim can father children. It's the kind of thing we used to talk about on the train, late at night with the other girls, when we talked about troubles. I didn't think Tim and I would ever have a family. But I'm certainly thankful not to have one now."

"Is that why you left him? Do you want to have children?"

Gigi faltered, then pretended otherwise. Mary Frances could see her draw a sense of gravity over herself, her posture in the chair shifting, her face veiled with something new.

"It was hard for me to make the decision to leave Dillwyn," she said.

She never called him Dillwyn. Mary

Frances pressed her hand against her temple, and Gigi went on.

"I think John was even surprised I did it. We wanted to be together, of course, but it didn't seem possible. It didn't seem possible until it was."

Gloria was like this too, a billboard of interior thoughts, without a shred of self-protection. It must be what the camera so loved about these women. Too, she knew her lines, and how to deliver them.

"I doubt you can understand it," Gigi said, "unless it happens to you."

Still, Tim said, *still, I love those moments where you reveal yourself. I love to hear what you want in a dinner partner, in a kitchen, your wooden spoons and copper pots. (There is a beautiful set I left at the house, undoubtedly going green. Please use them, take them. They're yours.) You are the center in these stories. And everything about you, your wit and passion, your sensualism, your fine arched brow, is clear and true on these pages. I can close my eyes and see you now.*

In the cupboards, she found the pots, French ones with heavy bottoms and a thick patina of disuse. She scrubbed them with a lemon dipped in salt, buffed them with mineral oil, arranged them on the stove: a

173

stockpot, a large sauté, and a saucepan. She would keep them for the rest of her life.

In Last House, they are really all she needs. The newspaper people come, the magazine reporters, soon someone from the library at Harvard to take away her cartons of paper, which seems strange to do while she is still alive, but there is so much she's glad to be rid of. They come, expecting a meal with her, the pleasures of her table such as she's described them for some fifty years and counting. In the past year, she has made nearly three hundred meals for visitors of some professional stripe or another; she keeps a tally for the tax man at Norah's insistence. Everyone wants their piece.

Norah has gone back home for the weekend, another grandchild soon to be born, her family still growing and expanding, still lush in a way that needs to be tended. And Mary Frances can entertain her guests alone. It's how she prefers to meet new people these days; the labor of bringing her old life to their expectations too great. Instead, she lets them do all the heavy lifting for her. All that seems to be required is an arch of her brow, some cursing in French, and a good, honest meal.

In the deep sauté, she has made a stew:

eggplant and tomatoes, onions and summer squash, a sort of ratatouille, *tiella, samfina, pisto,* there are as many names for it as countries, and she has stopped caring for all the names of things. She has made stew, and there are ripe peaches and cream for dessert, a few bottles of wine to choose from. She does not know when the librarians will arrive. Her marmalade cat rubs at her ankles, hungry too.

She pours him a small saucer of the cream, takes her cold vermouth to the fan-back wicker chair on the balcony that looks toward the mountains. Night will come soon enough, and her skin is so thin, she won't be able to keep herself warm out here. But for now, she looks out across the vine-yards, the thick smell of her stew wafting behind her, and she feels content to wait.

When Mary Frances saw Al get off the train, she hardly recognized him. Travel could do that to a person, and grief, but it was still shocking, the gray sag to his features, the smell of his mother's house that clung to his clothes.

He pressed a dry kiss to her cheek. "Have you been waiting long?"

She shook her head. They made their way to the car, through the cluster and press of people coming and going, people standing around with their hands out. He let her drive, resting his head on the back of the car seat. He seemed to be balancing something that required all his concentration; he had nothing left for questions or talk or an easy expression on his face. Mary Frances could hardly bear it. These days apart made his silence feel like an accusation.

"How is your mother?" she asked, and she thought Al had not heard her, so she asked again.

"Last night I found her at the laundry sink. She'd been scrubbing my father's sheets. Her head was stopped against the canning shelf above the faucets, sound asleep."

"Oh, Al."

Mary Frances reached for his hand. She thought of Rex, his ink-stained fingers prying back the flesh of an orange, his graveled laugh filling his office. He was steadfast in her thoughts, a fortress of security, but Edith could fall to pieces any minute. She felt her palm begin to sweat in Al's and pulled away.

She drove him to the house in Laurel Canyon; he went to their bedroom and lay down atop the coverlet, his coat, his shoes still on. She stood at his elbow, her hands twisting at her skirt.

"Can I get you anything?" she said.

"I'm tired. It was a long trip."

"A glass of juice? A cup of tea."

"No. Thank you."

She lingered at the bedside, and he could not think of what she wanted now.

Al's father was the kind of sick that looked like death would be a blessing. His mouth hung open vacantly when he slept, and he slept all the time. When he wasn't sleeping, he was frightened, and that was worse — all the years he'd comforted others, all the years he'd preached about milk and honey, but the fear was there, beneath his pallor and his dull eyes fluttering closed. He was afraid he didn't know what came next. If Al's father didn't know, who would?

The whole house smelled of rot and fear and probably would forever. His mother moved constantly from room to room. She slept standing up. Herbert had hopped a boat the afternoon Al left, back to China for another tour. There seemed nothing left to do but to wait for the inevitable.

When Al woke, Mary Frances was perched on the edge of the bed, her shadow looming over him. It was nearly dark outside.

"Oh." Al sat up. "The time."

She looked out the window as though it

had just occurred to her as well. "It's not so late," she said. "We could have dinner."

Al thought of the two of them across from each other at the big table in the dining room, some carefully simple plate and full glasses of wine, maybe some music: the very antithesis of his father's house. She would want to hear more. He remembered the feeling he used to have leaving his office at the end of the day, working his way back to her, and the weight he felt now was tenfold.

"Let's take in a movie, shall we? Eat some candy bars and laugh."

Relief flickered on her face, too. "Marx Brothers?"

But *Night at the Opera* was not playing close by, and they ended up in a movie neither one of them knew anything about. A young woman from some pastoral, daisied homeland was whisked away to the big city by a handsome, wealthy benefactor. Over time they fell in love, a fact signaled with the clasping of her hands to his heart and singing. There was lots of singing, a few jokes with a terrier named Milo, and a very happy ending. Mary Frances looked over at Al, his head lolled back against the seat and the light from the picture catching the sharp parts of his profile. He laughed when he was meant to, and the darkness took care of the rest.

Sunday afternoon, and Gigi had been out all weekend. Mary Frances worked in the garden, Al on the patio behind her, turning the pages of the paper. They had been outside for the front page and half the city section, a sheaf of iris blades gathered at her knee. He was not really reading; the sound of the newspaper clapping back against his body from the breeze marked the time.

"Al," Mary Frances said, "can you take these for me?" Her basket was full of clippings from the garden.

"Another way to earn our keep?"

"I enjoy it," she said.

She enjoyed everything. Around the corner of the house, he dumped the basket of Mary Frances's clippings by the rubbish pile and caught the flash of that long blue Hudson. He edged closer to see Gigi and her stunt-man. Gigi lingered at his car door, her pale hand to her throat, and suddenly it seemed pornographic, that she had to linger here, in her old life, house, with himself and Mary Frances looking on, linger at the car door, so desperately.

Do it, Al thought, please just do it, kiss her, something. But instead he watched the two of them for full minutes, staring at each other.

If everybody saw, could he and Mary Frances just go home?

He walked back to the patio. Mary Frances was still kneeling by the flower bed. She could kneel for the longest time.

"Gigi's back," he said, and she looked up, startled. She brushed her hands on her skirt, faint green streaks left behind.

"I'll make supper," Mary Frances said. "Did she bring a friend?"

And because Al was not himself, because Al was looking for a fight or a distraction from one, he took long strides back around the side of the house and called across the yard. "Gigi, dear. Bring your friend for dinner."

John Weld was a nice man. He was tall and tan, had won swimming contests when he lived in Kansas City. His teeth were straight and white. He came from a newspaper family, had worked in Paris after the war, and wrote screenplays and novels. There was plenty for Mary Frances and Al to talk with him about.

And yet they didn't. John Weld folded his long legs over themselves, and Al jingled the change in his pockets, and Gigi smiled,

180

drinking her vermouth too fast. John Weld was not the one responsible for all of them being in these circumstances; they were adults and had made their own decisions, yet there he was, in all his bright and shining strength. And he looked half Tim's age.

"It's a lovely home you have, Gigi," he said finally.

Al stopped his pacing. "Oh, you haven't had the tour?"

"No, I haven't."

"Let me tell you about this house, then. Are you a fan of architecture?"

The house had been built in the last five years and wasn't architecturally significant from its neighbors, really, but Al started in with a history of Laurel Canyon as a development, Wonderland Park and the trackless trolley, which didn't even run anymore. He was lecturing. He had John Weld standing at the patio doors and looking out into the garden as if the view were a mappable one. Gigi stared at the Parrish painting of Tim and his sister that hung above the piano, looking bored or desperate, it was hard to tell.

"I don't think he plans to buy the place, Al," Mary Frances said.

"Everything's for sale, for the right price. Isn't it, John?"

Mary Frances excused herself to the kitchen.

Supper for two was now supper for four. She pulled the rabbit from its brine, heated a lump of salt pork in Tim's copper pan. She plugged the sink to fill with water. Al followed moments later.

"I was being funny," she said. She kept her voice light and even, but she did not look at him, and she did not laugh. "What possessed you?"

"I don't know." He rubbed his face, stared at a spot on the linoleum. "I was angry. I felt like embarrassing her."

"She's not embarrassed, Al. What are you talking about?"

He didn't answer.

Mary Frances turned back to the stove. He could no sooner embarrass Gigi than drown a fish. She could hear her laughter in the other room, the rattle of ice in a glass, and low talk, and Mary Frances thought of how long it had been since she'd been to a dinner party. She missed the sounds of people gathering for an evening.

She turned the flame up under the rabbit and gave it a good shot of brandy, poured a quick glass for herself. Some stock, more herbs; she put a lid on her casserole to simmer and went back to the living room.

Gigi and John sat close on the barkcloth love seat, the record skipping on the player.

Mary Frances picked up her cocktail, her resolve slumping.

"What happened to Al?" she said.

Al had gone to bed. He had meant only to rest his eyes, but the thin afternoon light was leaching away, and he began to think of his father, their last conversation, which had happened in his dim bedroom at the back of the parsonage in Palo Alto. He had wanted his father to tell him something profound. But the drugs he took for pain made his mind glassy, his mouth dry. Speaking was a challenge, and he had trouble holding his head still, the room stale and airless, the edge of the bed sagging beneath Al's weight. Finally, it was just his father's hand lifting from the sheets in his direction, a kind of benediction, and the request for a glass of water before he left.

In the other room, Mary Frances was flirting, telling one of her stories — he could hear the race in her voice if not the words. His father had wanted him to marry one of the Lassiter girls from his congregation, Alice or Annie, a girl with milkmaid skin and round shoulders, a girl who'd never finished high school and never left California and never had a boyfriend before she was introduced to Al.

He didn't regret marrying Mary Frances. But he was filled with regret now nonetheless, a great current of it pulling him, and there was nothing to do but let it have its way.

"What are you doing?" Mary Frances stood at the end of the bed. "Al?"

"I'm tired, Mary Frances."

"But you can't leave. Dinner's almost ready, and then we'll sit down, and what will I tell them?"

He didn't open his eyes but turned onto his side, wrapping his arms around a pillow. She was still talking to him, still shrill, but it didn't matter. He wasn't getting up. He wasn't going out there, and she couldn't browbeat him into it. His conscience was clear. Sleep rolled him like a thief.

Mary Frances sat at the piano bench in the living room and stacked her pages on the music rest as though she might begin to play, and in a low voice, she read aloud. If there was a way to trim a line from a paragraph, a word from a line, a simpler tense, a clearer example, she drew her marks and began the piece again. Soon her pages were covered with notations, and she could recite them with her eyes closed. They began to feel like rhythms more than words; they began to feel smooth.

She opened Tim's studio. It didn't look as though Al had been there since he'd come back, and he would be tutoring all afternoon. She turned fresh paper into the typewriter and began to type. She wasn't hiding what she was doing, but neither did she want to have this conversation again, about what belonged to whom.

The front door opened and shut. She had three more pages to type, and she beat the keys to go as quickly as she could, as if that would make a difference.

"What are you doing?" Al said.

She stood from the typewriter and gathered her pages. She was acting as if she'd been caught, but she couldn't make herself stop. He crossed the room to his manuscript, still stacked beside the typewriter, where it had been since they moved in.

"I'm sorry," she said. "I needed the typewriter."

"This isn't for you to read, Mary Frances."

"I didn't read it. I wouldn't."

He seemed to be talking to the room, to himself. "Of course not, dear. I should never have left it out. It's not for reading. It's not for anyone else."

"I'm sorry," she said.

He didn't answer her, looking around the room for a place to tuck his manuscript away. For the thousandth time since Al returned from Palo Alto, Mary Frances thought how weary he looked, as though something in his person were dimming. She should be more careful with him. She slipped her pages into a manila envelope and left the studio, closing the door behind her.

Al sat in the chair before the typewriter, still clutching the stack of manuscript. He could not account for how uncomfortable it made him to find Mary Frances sitting at his typewriter, or when he'd come to think of it as his typewriter, but he felt the violation in his bones. This was serious work, the kind you did alone, not some glorified travelogue or recipe card. He would have to make Mary Frances understand.

Across from the workspace, she'd hung a painting of Tim's that Al could not make heads or tails of. The color seemed off, sour, garish. What had Mary Frances liked about it?

He spooled a clean page into the machine, turned the last page open to see what he'd been doing, turned another and another. He couldn't remember the last time he'd tried to write. Gently, he put his head down on the keys and closed his eyes, exhausted. He'd forgotten to tell her about the tickets Klemperer had given them for the show.

Al put his hand to the small of Mary Frances's back and guided her to their seats. The night and the canyon rose up around them, the bowl of sky full of stars. The crowd pressed in, its hum enough to take the place of conversation, and Mary Frances was relieved not to have to try. His hand slipped away, she smiled at him, and they turned their attention to the band shell below, lit from inside, a hive.

A woman stepped forward on the stage in a long black gown, her eyes fast upon her conductor. Her white skin and red curls, the delicate way she arched to the music drawing up in her — even at this distance, she was beautiful. Klemperer raised his baton, and the orchestra let loose its opening plumes of sound. The redheaded woman opened her mouth and sang.

Mary Frances had loved opera since she was a child, and tonight the music unfurled its full way up the sides of the canyon, notes rose and fell, stumbled, rolled and then spun off under their own sail into something unexpected and fast. Her own breath came fast in her chest with it. She listened often to recordings, but she'd never heard sound like this before.

Al leaned down and whispered in her ear; it was all she could do to keep from snatching herself away.

"Yes," she said, and she smiled tightly. "Beautiful."

The first aria ended, she glanced up, and he was gone.

Perhaps he hadn't whispered about the music, perhaps he'd said something else altogether — she hadn't paid attention. She gathered her sweater and purse and slipped out of their row, back up the rough-hewn stairs to the parking lot. She would retrace their steps and find him. He wouldn't just leave her.

In the parking lot, Al leaned against the Chrysler, smoking a cigarette. The soprano's voice vaulted all around them, the bright lights from the band shell pinking the sky. Mary Frances felt suddenly less sure of herself.

"Al?"

"I said I'd be right back."

"Are you all right?"

He didn't say anything, jetting a stream of smoke from his nose.

"Do you want to go home?"

"Home?" He laughed. "We told Gigi we'd be out until late. God knows what we'd walk back in on. That's the interesting thing about this life we're leading, darling wife — we can't just change our plans. We can't quit holding up our corner of the sheet."

She leaned against the car fender. Al was frayed and brittle, and she knew some of the things that weighed on him, but she could not bring herself to say the words *father, job, poem,* or even to think of the rest of it. She leaned next to him, and waited for him to go on.

"I feel so trapped," he said.

The orchestra began a new song, but Mary Frances knew they would not be returning to their seats. And too, this was a kind of call and response; Al needed her to say the next thing.

"Come on. If you're ready to go, we go."

She let herself into the car, and Al turned to watch her, stubbing out his cigarette on the heel of his shoe. He needed her bluster in these moments; he needed her not to care about propriety and rules and manners as much as he did. He needed her to act, and yes, it felt good to do something right.

They found the driveway empty, the house lit up. At the dining room table, dinner had been served. The candlesticks placed, napkins still tented neatly, a bowl of lemon-colored roses in the center, and dear god, Gigi had cooked. But the plates were hardly touched, as if the meal were still waiting for grace. One bite taken from a lamb chop, squarely cut away with knife and fork, the slender frenched bones, the pink skin of new potatoes, thickly waxed with butter. Mary Frances plucked one and ate it in two bites. Good food, wasted on new lovers.

She gathered the plates into the kitchen, wiping the melt from the fridge and setting things to rights, just for something to do with her hands.

"Don't worry about that," Al said. "Gigi will get it. She'll be home soon."

They both knew that wasn't true.

"Do you remember," Mary Frances said, "how we used to celebrate the tiniest thing with dinner out? Our one-month anniversaries at Aux Trois Faisons, the gifts you brought me every Thursday."

Al looked at her, a strained kind of melancholy on his face. "Of course."

Aux Trois Faisons had been the first truly French restaurant they loved, the place they learned to order, and eat, together, all those years ago in Dijon. Mary Frances found her notebook in her purse and a pen.

"What are you doing?" Al said.

Mary Frances looked up from her note-book. "I'm sorry?"

"You're writing that down?"

"Yes."

Al shook his head. "Honestly," he said. "How can you use such things."

Mary Frances finished her thought. *Use* was an interesting word, the word for tools, talents, whores. She wanted to say, *At least I'm using something,* but she looked at his face, and she couldn't.

"It's just my notebook, Al. I don't want to forget."

"Ah," he said. "I doubt you're at risk for that."

In bed, they read their novels, Al with a pencil in his hand and his own notebook open on his lap. She couldn't concentrate and studied the side of his face: his sandy, ruffled hair, the true lines of his features still so boyish.

"I'm sorry you're unhappy," she said.

He made a dismissive sound, not lifting his eyes from his page. It was a frustrating book he was reading, and somehow he'd managed to read the last stanza three times. He snapped the book closed. Maybe he would quit reading, too.

He hadn't read Mary Frances's essays; he had no idea what they were about really, beyond food, eating, dinner parties. But he knew she'd been sending her manuscript to Tim. He watched her checking for the mail, her eyes always flicking to the door, the quick way she jumped from her chair. He knew she was waiting for some kind of verdict. And he knew he'd made it impossible for it to come from him.

"Al," she said, "are you awake? I was thinking we could go to the reservoir tomorrow for a swim. It might be a nice day. Al?"

"Yes, dear?"

"How about a swim tomorrow?"

It was as though she'd handed him a teaspoon and a coffee can, asked him to dig the reservoir himself. He settled farther into the bed, making the same grunt of adjustment he'd heard from his father all his life.

"Whatever you'd like," he said.

The Santa Anas came whipping through the canyon from the high desert like something on horseback, dragging the smell of fire, dust, leaden heat behind, bearing down upon the three of them, sometimes four, in the little white house in the hills. Al left for the Klemperers in a pair of mirrored sunglasses he'd found in one of Tim's drawers, returning hours later chapped to the bone, a fern of sweat blooming on the back of his shirt. Lunch was soup and crackers, ham and cheese, sometimes just Al standing over the sink with an orange, Mary Frances at the table with a cup of tea. She fit sentence to sentence, paragraph to the next while she mopped the floor, made the beds. She would not use the typewriter in front of him again if she could help it, christ.

The newspaper said the winds made people do crazy things, made them violent and nervous and sleepless and sad. Al read the articles aloud from the front page: this woman in Racine strangled her cat, this father disappeared, this girl was beaten and pushed from a moving car, that girl threw herself into the sea. The canyon on the other side of the reservoir was on fire. After he left for the afternoon, Mary Frances typed her headful of paragraphs, as surely as if she were taking dictation.

"Did you two have a fight?" Gigi asked.

Mary Frances was knitting, a long tube of lace and counting. "We didn't fight," she said.

"Okay. It's just that —"

"Yes, I know. It will pass."

"Maybe you need to do something to make him jealous."

"That has always seemed to me the most ridiculous idea. Don't men get jealous well enough on their own?"

"I like a little nudge once in a while."

Gigi's hair was slicked back tight against her scalp and fringed at the nape of her neck. She'd been wearing a wig; Mary Frances could see the scrim of glue along her forehead, the dark gloss of stage paint still beneath her eyes.

"You look like Clara Bow," she said

Gigi sighed and folded herself into a seat at the table. "Everybody looks like somebody else these days.

"You sound so jaded."

"It's just not fun anymore, all the rules and regulations, and everybody's nervous. Somebody follows the girls around the set with a bathrobe, like what happens on the set might get us canned. I think I'm done with being an actress anyway."

"You're joking."

"I think it's time for a change. Don't you?"

No, she didn't. It had always been a comfort for her, to think about the things that couldn't be undone, that only moved forward. And here they'd spent the summer, she thought, salvaging the one thing Gigi wanted from her old life, her good standing with the studio. The whole awkward press of the summer, for nothing. Mary Frances felt dizzy.

"What will you do?" she said.

"We'll marry. We'll move away. I'll take another name."

"Your given name, it's Katherine?"

"John calls me Katy. Katy Weld."

Mary Frances rolled the name in her mouth, but could not bring herself to say it. She remembered Tim and their night together again, how he'd brought her a spool of thread to fix her slip, and a pink satin pincushion embroidered with initials not Gigi's. "Her name is really Katherine," he'd said. "Her brother called her Gigi. Not really her brother, even. She was adopted."

He'd watched Mary Frances make her fast, looping stitches, one ankle tucked beneath her hips and the wet spot of what they'd done darkening the sheets between her legs. The sun was not yet up; it was the longest night she could remember, and she was grateful for that and anxious at the same time.

"What will you say?" he asked.

"I'm a decent seamstress."

"I didn't mean that."

She didn't answer him, breaking the thread against her white teeth. "I'm driving out to Laguna for the weekend. It's been months since I've seen the ocean. Would you like to come?"

He told her no, he was sorry, he couldn't get away, even as he took the pincushion from her hands and eased her back again.

And even now, all these months later, the air drew tight around her like a robe to think about it. She had to physically shake herself free, and only to arrive back here, across the table from Gigi. She could not believe she'd allowed herself to do the things she'd done — that night, this summer, any of it.

"Christ," Gigi said. "I need a shower."

And when she stood, there was that drawing tall of her limbs, the pull and lift of her shoulders, her chin, the crown of her head as though she were a deck of cards stacked into place. She knew Mary Frances was watching her. Could she stop being an actress? Could Mary Frances stop being a writer? Was it like stopping being somebody's wife? If there was one thing she doubted she was capable of, it was knowing when, and how, to stop.

Tim had read her story about the fifty million snails: *I remembered a summer in the south of France, the whole coast beset with heat, a kind of dust and burn. There was nothing for it but to lie in the darkened room, or brave it. One afternoon, walking outside Hyère just to feel the air move, I saw peasants harvesting grapes in baskets on their backs. They had set a stand of grass on fire, or maybe it had combusted in the heat, but as I came across these bent, brown people, they were gathering the roasted snails from the ashes for their lunch.*

He would be leaving soon for England with his sister. Perhaps they would go to France too; he had been thinking a lot about France lately, because of her. He would give the full count of her pieces to Claire so she might read them while they traveled. *It will be harder to tell you so while I am gone, but you know my thoughts never seem to stop circling the things you write. If only we could talk without our skulls and fingers in the way.*

She took his note to the patio and stretched out in the chaise to read it again. She wanted to have seen that roadside with him, to have tasted the ashy snails. Her imagination was without distraction; she wondered if she could keep this temperature if she saw him face to face.

We might have spent the day together in Hyère, in the shuttered afternoon of your rooms, she wrote. She untied her blouse from where she'd hitched it around her rib cage, and in her mind, he watched as she loosened herself further from her clothes, the room green with heat now, a jungle, the slatted light cast across the floor. It was only the bed and the room; she conjured them slowly, not yet that sunbaked field, that roadside set on fire. *I can imagine it,* she wrote, *from what you tell me here. I find of late I can imagine almost anything you say, and everything you don't.*

She could imagine them meeting again, and their days together that would follow, their lives together full of writing and talk and skin against skin, their lives full and yet fitting neatly into her head now, complete in miniature. She could live their lives in an afternoon's time, in an hour or two, in her dreams, in private, and she had no expectations beyond that. This little bit was enough. Or perhaps it was that more seemed terrifying.

A telegram came, first thing in the morning, the dew still painting the slate of the front walk. Mary Frances answered the door, and there was the boy and his bike and cap, so much shiny red. He looked at Mary Frances's shoes as he held out the ink-blue envelope, so intently that Mary Frances looked at her shoes as well. The lace on her oxfords was frayed. Her fingers trembled. A telegram. She scanned the window for her name, and her hopes fell, once for herself and again for Al.

She called back into the house and went to fetch a nickel for a tip.

When Al saw her with the telegram, he turned around, back down the hall to their bedroom. Mary Frances followed. He was packing a suitcase.

"Al," she said, but he didn't stop what he was doing. "I'm so sorry."

She laid the telegram on the bed beside his case, but he did not open it or even pick it up. His face was brittle, and she felt a wave of shame.

"Shall I call the station?"

"No."

"I'll make you something to eat, then."

"Jesus, Mary Frances."

"All right," she said.

She left him for the kitchen. She sliced rye bread and split links of sausages for frying, cracked an egg and let it bubble against the meat. She toasted the bread and spread it thickly with mustard Gloria had brought them, good Dijon mustard, and Mary Frances knew she must have paid a fortune for it, and what a strange thought that was to occupy her now.

Al's chair scraped out from the table behind her; she could sense him there, wanting and not wanting her. He stood buttoning his collar, brushing at his shirtfront, his fingers moving over himself of their own accord. She split a grapefruit and juiced it into a ruby-footed glass, poured coffee, and set it all in front of him.

"Okay," she said.

He bent over his plate. His collar had been badly pressed, and she reached to smooth the crease. A crease like that, anyway, there would be no fixing it without water and an iron, without starting all over again. She was crying now.

"I'll check the train," she said.

"We'll take the car," he said.

"Of course." She wiped her face with the heel of her hand. She had not been particularly close to Al's father, and she studied her tears now for some sense of what they were for: Al's pain, of course, and his distance from her, which had everything and nothing to do with what he was going through now. The room was hot and airless; Mary Frances turned to shut off the broiler before it caught fire. There was nothing to do but pack their things, and go.

The driveway of the Fishers' house was full of cars, and women in solemn gray and navy flanked the porch, older women practiced at this kind of ministering, and Mary Frances felt for just a moment jealous at their ease, their graceful presence. Clara's roses lined the drive, and one woman held a basket and shears, carefully clipping rose upon rose for an arrangement. Al nodded to her, to the other people waiting outside, and Mary Frances understood him to be home. He had been the right reverend's son here, and now he was the right reverend's son come to pay his respects.

He opened her door for her, and Mary Frances could hear his mother at the piano inside. She had played all her life, and beautifully, even now.

Suddenly, Mary Frances thought of her courtship, how she'd told Al she'd live in a piano box with a man if she'd loved him enough. He must have thought then of his mother's piano, of Brahms and Mozart, and not the blithe, blustery girl before him. A piano box, she remembered saying it.

Al took her arm again and introduced her to the women, the endless ropes of them, by the names of their husbands. She wondered how he did it; the Fishers had moved to Palo Alto only after she and Al were married. These were not women he'd grown up with, but maybe versions of the same, from another town.

In the parlor, Al's mother rose from the piano and kissed Mary Frances's cheeks, her own cool and chapped, as though she'd been running in the wind.

"I am so grateful you came, dear," she said. "Al needs you by his side."

She looked then at her son with a kind of pain Mary Frances had never seen before. Al's head bent, his body slackened, and for the first time since she arrived, Mary Frances felt as if he were actually present, and it was horrible to stand there next to him and not know what to do.

She began to cry.

Clara patted her back and cooed to her, some of the women flocking close now and patting too, and Mary Frances felt so foolish, so greedy.

"The room in the back," Clara whispered. "Al will take your things, and you can freshen up. There are so many people here."

She said it as if they would need to be organized, arranged, but all around her the women bustled with their own discrete jobs, filling, fluffing, sweeping away. She was being kind, trying to make Mary Frances feel needed even at a time like this.

Mary Frances followed Al through the parlor down the hallway, his long frame seeming to fill all the space in front of her.

At every doorway, a cluster of the mourning women, and somewhere in the house Mary Frances did not want to look, the body rested.

Al closed the door and sat on the edge of the tall iron-frame bed, one of Clara's coiled rag rugs at his feet. Mary Frances stood before him. He reached for her wrist, but did not direct her closer or away. She wished for something to say, but nothing came.

Al sighed. "You smell like smoke."

"I smoke."

"Not here."

His face tipped back then, and he appraised her, cool, remote. He took his handkerchief from his pocket and brought it to her mouth, blotted the red of her lipstick, turning the same careful attention to the print it made on the cloth. He folded a clean, white square over it and returned the handkerchief to his pocket.

"Not today," he said.

What might have seemed funny at any other time now resounded between them, as sharp and sure as a slap to her cheek, and Mary Frances reeled backward in her heels.

"Al," she said.

His thin smile fought to turn it, and she let it go. This dying, this end, was like a klieg light. It made everything clear.

Driving back to Los Angeles, Al announced he no longer wanted to teach at Occidental. They had no choice, of course, they needed the money to live on, but he was through with that, as soon as he could be.

"I understand," she said. "You need some time now."

"It's not about time."

"Then grief, Al. I understand."

"What do you do," Al said, "that you would rather not?"

The silence hung between them bitterly. She seemed so oblivious to her good fortune, her entire life of relative ease. It was more than he could stand right now.

She said, "Gigi told me she would be leaving the studio anyway. She says she and John Weld are going to get married, and that she's done with acting."

Gigi was another thing he could not deal with anymore, the way she required an audience. There was something wrong with her that Tim was lucky to have slipped; he was only now realizing that. Perhaps these things happened for a good reason sometimes. Perhaps all this was happening for a good reason.

"You could have your study back, in Eagle

Rock," she said.

"Yes," Al said. "The study."

"We'll go back to how it always was," she said. "Couldn't we?"

He glanced over at her and reached across the seat for her hand.

"Oh, let's stop in town for dinner," she said. "Let's go to Don's. I've got some extra money tucked away in here."

She began digging through her purse. She wanted a drink. She wanted to be in a crowd, not to be alone with her husband, not to have to talk so much. She wanted to stop the car and call another couple to meet them, but days like this before, the number to call would have been Tim and Gigi's.

"We'll find something else," she said. "We'll go away again. We're good at that."

"I think we should adopt a child."

Mary Frances stopped digging in her purse and looked at him. It was the closest he had ever come to admitting they might not be able to have one naturally.

"I think we should find something else, and I think it should be a family of our own. It's time, Mary Frances. It's time to put away our distractions and live our lives."

His voice was even and firm, his eyes fixed ahead as he said it. It was insane, of course. He'd just finished saying he didn't want to work the only steady job he'd had in the course of their marriage, but he was ready for a child. He was in so much pain, he wasn't making sense. She would have said anything to change the subject.

"I'll think about it, Al. Perhaps you're right."

"You will?"

"Of course I will."

"Well, that's fine," he said. "I'm relieved to hear it."

He put his hands back on the wheel, and they rode into Los Angeles with the words still vibrating between them, too charged to continue or touch again.

At Don's, Al ordered a dozen oysters, and they talked about the grizzled men at Crespin's in Dijon, their blood-flecked hands, the green shells prized open in their palms and pearly pale inside. Mary Frances had to work to keep her face clear; she felt like a wall that had rotted through, plaster turned to slurry inside.

She would pack their things this afternoon.

The house at Eagle Rock had not rented that summer or fall, and they took it back. It looked as they had left it, the bedsteads draped in muslin, the kitchen coated with a fine film of sticky grime. Mary Frances pulled out the rags and brooms and did some satisfying work, but Al wandered the rooms for days, an engine sputtering to catch.

She left an atlas open on the coffee table in front of the fire, but the pages never turned. She suggested books and movies, a drive down to the coast, and he would nod his head, tell her to go get ready, but she'd find him napping in his armchair half an hour later. She asked him if he'd talked to Larry, to Gordon, anybody at the college, but his answer was always no. She spent a lot of time watching him when he was lost in thought, and she stayed up late to write when she was alone.

For the holidays, they went to the Ranch. Anne was secretive and snippy. She took at least one private phone call in Rex's office and came back as flushed as if she'd been sprinting up and down the stairs. Mary Frances knew she must be seeing someone, but she wouldn't say, which meant she had a reason not to. She thought of Gigi's friend Nan and the nine-month engagement she was bearing somewhere in San Francisco. It looked exhausting to be single, let alone a single mother.

Baby Sean was toddling to and from any

reachable surface, babbling his sounds, and Edith kept asking when the next new baby might be on the way. Mary Frances and Al looked at each other politely and smiled, asked Edith for another slice of cake, or Rex for his thoughts on the governor's race. Deflection seemed everyone's default position, but when Mary Frances had Rex alone in his office, she explained more of what was going on.

"Al says he wants to adopt a baby."

"Adopt?"

She could not look at him when she nodded, but she had always shared everything with Rex, the privileges of being oldest.

"Your mother didn't have you the minute we were married. You shouldn't be so hasty."

"I'm not being hasty." She sat on the edge of Rex's desk, looking at her shoes.

"But someone is, if I catch your meaning."

Mary Frances shrugged. "I don't know. I don't know what you're supposed to know, what he's supposed to know."

Rex laughed. "You people spend too much time in school."

"Daddy."

"If you want a baby, Mary Frances, I have no doubt you'll get one."

"But Al has no job, no . . . drive."

"Now, now. It's the season for miracles, Dote."

She let herself be led into another conversation, but it marked the first time a talk with her father had failed her, and she knew the fault was her own. She hadn't been able to be honest with him. He'd see her differently in light of her correspondence with Tim, and whatever else she was carrying on there, and so she'd streamlined. She made a different story, one that was just as true as the real story. Her feelings for Tim were not so different from dreaming of being a writer, or an actress, a fantasy based on slender experience, slight encouragement, and the vast space inside her head to fill.

She hadn't heard from him in weeks now. He was traveling Europe. She had no way to tell him they'd left Laurel Canyon, no good address in this country or another. The one thing Tim's attention required was paper and ink, and while filling notebook after notebook, journal after journal, she realized what a flimsy requisite that really was.

Something drastic would have to happen now if they were to continue, something equally drastic as her starting a family to continue with Al. From where she stood, either prospect seemed both unlikely and necessary, vital. A rebirth.

After the new year, a letter from Tim arrived. He was grateful for their friendship, for the time they'd spent with Gigi. He understood from her that all was well and they had moved back to Eagle Rock. But he would like to repay their generosity, or perhaps ask another favor, it was hard for him to tell — but they were such good friends, he felt he didn't need to stand on ceremony. Would Mary Frances be able to escort himself and his mother on a tour of France? They needed someone with her skills in companionship and conversation, both in English and in French. Mrs. Parrish wanted to revisit the places she had loved in her youth, and it seemed like the timing would be right in February . . .

"What do you think?" Mary Frances said.

Al let the letter fall to the tabletop. "What do you think?" he said.

Al did not sit on the edge of the bed and watch her pack. Into her trunks went clothes for the ship, silks and satins, the brocade pumps of Anne's she'd admired at Christmas, Edith's fox collar coat. She packed her French dictionary, needles, and yarn; it would be cold enough for mittens and scarves, and in Paris she would buy perfume. What was she packing for, really? She knew the sort of ladies companionship Tim suggested in his letter, the long stretches of tea and cards, museums and churches, but she would have his audience as well, unbroken, for weeks. She could not seem to push her imagination past that; perhaps she was not meant to.

From the other room, she could hear the drawers in Al's desk open and close, the typewriter silent. She told herself this time would be good for him too, time to take up the poem again, but she'd tell herself anything that made it easier to leave.

He was standing in the doorway, his gaze now fastened on the spillage of slick color from the lip of the trunk.

"Your feathers," he said, his smile tightly drawn.

Her hands felt thick and clumsy. She bundled empty hangers back into the closet, like a shuffling of bones.

"Do you remember," Al said, "the summer I sent you to London with Edith? You didn't want to go, but I thought it would be good for you."

She remembered. Her mother believed the secret to a long marriage was a long vacation, but she had been crushed to leave him in Dijon, mostly because he seemed so anxious to be alone. It was then he began writing the poem. In September, she returned, and their honeymoon was over.

"You shouldn't have done that," Mary Frances said.

He braced his hand against the doorjamb, studying the frame, as if he planned to fell it. There was anger in him, but she could no longer tell if it was meant for her.

"I keep telling myself that," he said. "I know."

And so he loaded her bags into the Chrysler and drove her to the train. It was just a trip, he told himself, a last fling before they made their plans. He had not brought up the child again, but while she was gone, he would talk to some people, find out what their next steps needed to be. When she returned, she would be ready. He was grateful to Tim; they would not have this kind of opportunity again.

"You'll write?" he said. "I meant to make it easy for you. Send some stamps and envelopes." He laughed lamely. His chest was collapsing.

She reached into the satchel at her feet and pulled out a bundle of stationery bound with ribbon. She thumbed it like a deck of cards.

"One for every day, Al. Already addressed to you."

At the station, he hefted her bags from the trunk to the porter, checked her tickets, escorted her to the platform to wait. She stood tall, she was so tall, with her hand folded sweetly in the crook of his arm, pale against his suit coat. He concentrated on that hand, the pale, slender fingers, the thin gold band. When the train pulled into the station, he passed her hand to the porter and watched the body of the train for a time, imagining her passage to her compartment, her hand once reaching out to steady herself before she found her seat, and was off.

She was writing as the train left the station, frantically, so as not to watch Al's face, but god if she wasn't writing to him. She couldn't help herself — he seemed the only solid place to turn, and so she wrote him a letter then and there, how this was like a movie they were in, and this stretch of time just a memory that hadn't happened yet. She would dissolve out with the steam and then back in a month from now, and they would continue. It was as honest as she could be. She loved him still, and she was unable to articulate the transgression she was about to make beyond that. She would go, and then she would return.

And so began another kind of honeymoon in France, the sort she will take until she is too old and frail to travel, the chance to slip away and see her life grow small on another coast and with it the impossible knots and complications. What seems unfixable can be fixed, if only by distance.

These days she keeps a suitcase packed beneath her bed and leaves the specifics to Norah.

There is no man waiting for her, here or there. There's been no man for years, which has sharpened the effect of her letters and journals they've been sorting. These last several months have given her suddenly all the men at once. It will probably be good to get away from that for a time. She can feel the loose pieces rattling even when her mind is still.

The marmalade cat hears the knock before she does, bolting for the kitchen, her food bowls, and safety. Mary Frances stands, tucking the combs into her silvered hair, a smack of lipstick in the mirror by the door before she answers it.

It's a man in his shirtsleeves with his suitcase, his face obscured by the long brim of his hat. There's a familiar set to his shoulders, the peak of his chest, and the fine square hand he extends to stroke the marmalade cat, but Mary Frances does not know him. The marmalade cat pushes up to nuzzle the brace of quail he's holding.

"I stopped in the village for directions," he says. "When I mentioned your name, everyone had something they needed me to bring to you."

She laughs. She knows the hunter who saves his quail for her, and from the pocket of the suitcase, her visitor takes a jar of olallieberry jam, a paper sack of dusty white salamis, a glassine envelope of powdered spice. She fixes on the folded birds, their bodies limpid, hung the way she's told the hunter they do in France.

"How can I help you?" she asks, taking the quail.

He is from the library. He's driven a van all the way across the country for the boxes, his suitcase full of her books rather than his clothes, her books for her to sign.

"If you don't mind," he says. "And then I can collect my parcels and be out of your way."

"Oh, no," she says. "You have to stay for dinner now. Who will help me eat these quail?"

"It's not necessary, Ms. Fisher. I have a room waiting for me in town, and a long ride home."

"And I don't want to keep you working late. But still, it is a lot of quail."

He seems to consider his options, his eyes warm and brown, his eyes not familiar, not the eyes she's longing for, but still somehow related to this sifting through the past she has been doing. This man, now appeared, a kind of souvenir.

"I'd be honored," he says.

She turns and leads the way inside.

SEA CHANGE

SPRING 1936

The train would be three days to Chicago, another to New York. The seats in her compartment were plush, the window wide, a berth the porter cranked down from the ceiling every night, a little johnnie in the corner with a curtain, a sink that unfolded from the wall. Each human concern fit neatly here, and twelve deep to a car, at least six cars of sleepers. It was like a tiny, efficient neighborhood, hurtling across the country.

The film of travel settled into her skin. The train rattled and swayed, loud and drafty, then blasted with heat so that her coat was always on and off her shoulders. The passengers talked endlessly about nothing, and when she went to the dining car, there was nothing she wanted to eat, and outside the window the red desert became the measureless bitter plains, the fields beaten back beneath the swollen sky, and

217

then all was gray or darkness.

Mary Frances could hear a mother and child in the compartment next to hers, a toddler as given to words as he was to tears and thuds and crashes, and then his mother's stroking voice. She couldn't make out what was said; parenting remained something she spied on.

She swung over the edge of the berth and huddled in her nightgown, her bare feet dangling above the floor. During this interlude with Tim, whatever happened would be something discrete, a miniature life. She rolled her palms open in her lap and wished she had someplace to pray, someone to promise, but there was only herself. That hardly seemed like a promise she would keep.

Outside the window, the middle country raced by.

At breakfast in the dining car, she faced the mother from the berth next door, whispering to the boy as though they were alone. She bent to serve her son's eggs, to pass the fork to his rosy mouth. There was no man traveling with them, and the woman wore no ring. Mary Frances thought of Anne, how frazzled and overwrought she would be traveling with Sean. The boy smacked his hands against the tabletop, sending spoons flying. His mother laughed, and the steward brought her more.

Mary Frances said, "Your son reminds me of my nephew."

The woman smiled, brushing the crumbs from her lap. She spoke with such a thick accent it took Mary Frances a full moment to hear her words after she said them.

"Oh, Mum, he's not mine. His parents are in New York a week already."

"Oh," Mary Frances said. "I just assumed."

Now looking at the pair, she could chart no resemblance. But the woman beamed at the boy in a motherly fashion; she was patient, and she seemed to enjoy him.

"Have you always been his nurse?" she asked. It was too personal, but who was to say, on this train, what she should and should not do? It seemed, suddenly, important that she know.

"Since the morning he was born."

The woman smiled at Mary Frances and turned her attention back to the boy, his fists now full of his breakfast and headed to the floor. Everything, Mary Frances thought, eventually came down. Both the nurse and the boy laughed about it.

Back in her compartment, the porter had yet to make up her berth, and so she crawled back inside, folded her hands beneath her head, and stared at the glossy capsule of the ceiling. She thought about how many lives it contained, just this single car, and how fast it was going, away from home.

At Penn Station, Tim was waiting on the platform.

He was lithe and elegant, dressed all in navy blue, a fine cashmere topcoat and herringbone muffler, his white hair waved back close against his head. He looked like a knife, like a hawk, a piece of dark blue open sky. Mary Frances took his gloved hand and tried to make her mouth work to speak. She could think of only the plainest things, *hello, how nice to see you, how nice.*

He broke her wrist back and brought it to his lips, a light, true kiss where her blood was pounding, and that was all.

He directed a porter to her trunks, her trunks to a cab, his hand steering her forward at the small of her back. They were nearly the same height. She could feel his breath on her temple, and with his hand, he was all through her, and there was nothing to say, nothing that could be heard over this.

The cab took them uptown, to the Warwick Hotel where he had reserved her a room. Watching his profile, the city racing past them, she realized he belonged here, amongst all this business and metal, noise and speed, or at least the man he was now belonged here. The thought plummeted through her. What else might she have to learn about him? What else might she have made up to suit herself in all this time they'd spent apart?

"Where is your mother?" she asked.

"She naps in the afternoons. Are you tired?"

It sounded like one thing made him think the other, and she shook her head, turning to the window. What if she was making a horrible mistake?

The taxi pulled to the curb, and Tim paid it, a fleet of doormen descending upon the car, her steamer and satchels full of books. She stood where she'd been escorted and watched her things stack up; why had she brought so much stuff? She needed the help of so many people.

Inside the hotel: the bellmen and the elevator operator, the examination of the room, tips passing hand to hand. Tim ordered tea to be sent up, and then finally they were alone. Mary Frances stood by the windows, her purse in her hand. Tim studied her, and she tried to meet his eye but lost her nerve. She had thought about this mo-

ment for months on end, a thousand different ways. Maybe the moment itself was tired
now. She laughed.

"What?" he said.

"Oh. I suppose I am tired. Completely."

"It's all right. Really." He did not cross
the room. "My sister has a party planned
tonight, for you and Mother. She's been
looking forward to meeting you."

She was still looking, distractedly, anywhere but at Tim.

"Mary Frances?" he said.

"Of course."

She felt as if she were waiting for something to crest between them, but Tim
seemed so mild, so easy. It was never going
to happen. She took a deep breath.

"Of course," she said again. "I'll meet you
in the lobby, and your mother. We can all
have a drink before we go, several drinks
perhaps. Oh, Tim."

She tossed her purse well shy of the desk,
and Tim laughed. He was so much stronger
than she'd remembered. He placed her key
on the dresser.

"It's all right. Get some rest," he said, and
he left.

She drew a bath. The tea came, and she
took a cup, a pretty pastry with her to the
tub, resting it on the lid of the commode.

She poured yellow oils into the running water, the scent of violets. In a few weeks, she would have a few weeks behind her, and she would be in France.

On another floor of the hotel, Tim took the box from his pocket and set it on the secretary in his room. He lit a cigarette and sat before the window, the afternoon sky lost in the shadows of the buildings around the hotel, the trolleys clattering in the streets below. He had all this energy and nothing to do with it, energy enough to run laps in the street, to run flights in the stairwell. He just wanted to spend it, for chrissake, spend everything: his money, his time, his hard cock chafing in his pants. It had been a year since he'd seen her, and he had not accounted for the composure that year had made necessary.

The door to his mother's room opened.

"Well?" she said.

"She's resting. A long trip."

"I'm just glad she's arrived. All that way from California. I don't know what you people could have been thinking."

"She's traveled a great deal, Mother. I'm sure you'll find she's able to handle the toughest situation."

"Still," his mother said.

She saw the box on the table, obviously a jewelry box; her eyes settled on it, but she didn't ask. Tim felt as though he'd swallowed a lit match. His mother had always been a hoarder of details, an amateur detective. Everything was suspect until proven otherwise.

"Mother." Tim stubbed out his cigarette and took her hand, pressing it between his cheek and shoulder. "Would you like to go for a walk, or is it too cold? A carriage? Tea?"

Mrs. Parrish patted his shoulder. "I'm fine," she said. "I thought I might write a few letters before we sail."

And she began ticking off the things and people she needed to write, the process of a letter decidedly unsilent for Mrs. Parrish, rather a one-sided conversation that had to meet the air before she could commit it to a piece of paper. Tim stood to give his mother the secretary, slipping the box back into the breast pocket of his jacket before she got up the words to ask about it.

He'd wanted to give her something.

In the time it took to loose himself from Gigi, he'd remembered all kinds of things he used to like about pursuing women: elaborate dates, veiled letters, the slow unpinning of a twist of hair, endless buttons, whatever clasped at the back of the

224

neck. So much depended on preparation and rate of speed. He could fill an afternoon with a search for a pair of silk stockings. He'd followed a woman two blocks through the theater district the other day, watching the spindle of darker fabric extending from the heel of her shoe to the seam that arched her calf. Cuban-heeled stockings; not the sort of thing you could buy for another man's wife. He'd chosen a bracelet instead, a wide swath of gaspipe chain with a pavé clasp, but Mary Frances had seemed at such loose ends, he hadn't given it to her. Maybe this wasn't going to be so easy.

"Would you write a letter for me?" he asked. "For Alfred Fisher."

The sound of his mother's pen started across the page.

" 'Dear Al. Can't say how glad we are that Mary Frances is here. I have missed her and you both, and know Mother will be all the more comfortable for her presence abroad. Bought her a gift today, your wife, walking to meet her train. Couldn't help myself, a little bauble to mark our time together here. Very excited, and grateful to you, old man.' And that's all. I'll sign it."

His mother passed the stationery over her shoulder, and Tim beat it dry in the air. She looked up at him, her face soft with years.

There was no cause to worry her if he could help it. There was no cause to worry anyone.

In the lobby, Mary Frances telephoned Al.

"You've arrived."

"In body, I guess. Such a trip! What time is it at home? I feel made of taffy."

"It's two." He cleared his throat. "I'm having a sandwich."

"You'll be living like a bachelor by Sunday, won't you."

There was a long silence, static, maybe something else.

"Al?"

"I'm here."

"I posted letters from the train, five already. I hate to spoil them by telling you everything now. I just wanted to say hello. I wish you were coming with us. It won't be near the same without you."

"I'm sure you'll have a good time."

"I've been thinking about what you said, though, about how it's time to put away our distractions and live our lives. I think we would make good parents, Al. I always have."

"Do you mean that?"

She did, for how it squared them up for this time apart, and the enthusiasm in his voice was some kind of permission, re-

226

assurance, absolution all in one. She thought of the boy and his nurse on the train, the way he patted her cheek when she dipped the fork in his direction, the soothe of her whisper through the compartment walls.

"What kind should we ask for, Al, a boy or a girl?"

"I don't know," he said. "I guess I haven't thought about it."

"Well, do. Please do. I think we should."

He told her he loved her, and *bon voyage,* and he hung up the phone before she did, the dead line buzzing in her ear. If she'd promised him the moon, it would seem more possible, and yet she'd have promised him anything. She looked down at her lap, the swath of russet silk, the dress Edith had bought her the previous Christmas. It somehow had become part of all this, her costume.

Across the lobby, Mrs. Parrish stepped out of the elevator on Tim's arm, hunched and delicate in a ruffled velvet cape, a bee working at a flower. Mary Frances stepped out of the telephone booth and into their oncoming path.

"So lovely you could come, dear." Mrs. Parrish brushed her cheeks with her own.

"I was just calling Al. He is sorry he can't be here too. I've promised him an absolute account of everything we do and see, a letter every day."

"Oh, goodness!" Mrs. Parrish beamed at Tim. "When Dillwyn was a boy, I used to take the children all summer to the seashore with my sister. If my husband never got a word from me, he was a happy man."

But Mary Frances could tell she'd pleased her, perhaps even put her at ease. It was important that her feelings toward Al always be clear. She repeated that to herself as they walked to the bar, three abreast, and repeated it again as Tim ordered the drinks, vermouth for his mother, a Gibson for her, and again in the taxi, on the way to Claire's apartment uptown.

Mrs. Parrish could not have cared less about the evening amongst Claire's friends.

"Honestly, we sail tomorrow! There will be so many polite conversations to make at the pensions, the dinner tables. Those friends of Claire's will draw all the clever thoughts right out of me, like blood from a stone. And then what will I have left to talk about over the crossing?"

"I've never known you to flag, Mother."

"I am so much older than I've ever been. Mary Frances, how will you manage?"

"Manage? Oh, I try never to speak until

people have finished with the weather re-
ports."

Mrs. Parrish laughed. "She's such a lovely
girl, Timmy. Where are you always finding
such lovely girls?"

Mary Frances was aware of how carefully
they folded into the car, and the passing,
flashing lights outside the taxi making a blur
of Tim's face. Mrs. Parrish was still talking
and seemed as if she would never quit.
Claire's husband Charles was in the hospital, and yet here they were anyway for dinner, and Mrs. Parrish outlined the other
possible guests: writers like Claire, bankers
like Charles, and behind it all was a kind of
aristocratic code Mary Frances could not
track. This was New York, far more chan-
neled and ornate than California, no matter
what Rex did for a living. She watched
Tim's cool silhouette. How had she ever
found the nerve to touch him?

Inside Claire's building, the elevator was a
birdcage, the foyer a chessboard with walls
of a sour bottomless blue. A man took their
coats, and there was Claire behind him.
Mary Frances recognized her from the
portraits in the house in Laurel Canyon.

Time shimmered uncomfortably, and
Mary Frances thought of the bungalow now
empty, she and Al gone, Gigi gone, and

everything that had started there still rolling forward.

"Are you all right, dear?" Claire asked, her hand at Mary Frances's back. "You haven't got a chill, have you? Timmy, you will never learn how to care for women travelers."

She bussed his cheek roughly, beaming, and thumbed the smear of lipstick she left behind. She was as willowy and beaked as Tim, with wild hair she wore bobbed to her chin and a long silk caftan that parted in dramatic grooves of unexpected skin.

"They always turn up here nearly shattered with all the walking and riding and talking and talking. And then he's gone and fed her something wild, like oriental radishes and sea scallops. Gigi used to *spin* with it."

Her long fingers, still alight on Mary Frances's shoulder, flexed and softened.

"Well," she said, collecting herself around her glass of champagne. "You are probably far more used to that sort of thing, aren't you? Mother is so excited about the trip."

And they were off in that direction, as fast as possible away from the mention of Gigi's name. Mary Frances was unsure if it was Tim's feelings Claire was trying to protect, or her own. So many lovely girls, his mother said, and Gigi was the loveliest. She wondered suddenly what these Parrish women thought she was doing here, if Gigi was the only one Tim had told.

Claire turned to greet another guest, and Mary Frances dropped her voice to speak to Tim.

"What did you explain to Claire?" She couldn't look at him. "About my coming with you."

"She knows I could never handle Mother by myself."

"She seems to know a great deal."

"She's my sister. She thinks she knows everything." He took her by the elbow and steered them toward privacy. "What difference does it make?"

"It doesn't."

"Why are you upset?"

"I'm not."

Tim took two glasses from a passing tray and handed one to Mary Frances, martinis clearly meant for someone else, but the waiter turned and headed back into the bar. Tim drank deeply and looked off over the party.

"My dear," he said. "I have hedged and suggested and connived. I have lied when asked directly of my intentions. I have followed my best instinct to get us this far with fairly spotless reputations. In other words, I have done my part. What's your plan?"

"My plan? I don't know —"

"You knew in Hollywood."

She laughed. Claire was ringing the bell for dinner. "I was terrified, Tim. And that was months ago."

"You came to me," he said. "What are you going to do next?"

For the first time, she got the idea the answer could be anything she wanted.

The dining room was wallpapered with giant melon-colored camellias, almost as tall as Mary Frances herself, their brassy stamens furred and reaching. The service glistened in the candlelight. She trailed her fingers along the backs of chairs, scanning the place cards. In the scripted, careful names, she found herself as MFK FISHER.

She felt a flush of gratitude toward Claire, now arriving in the dining room on the arm of one of her guests. It was a small gesture, but she must have known what this would mean, must have remembered such a feeling herself. Perhaps she was not like Gigi to these people, not small and delicate and pretty, not Tim's wife. But she was understood.

"Claire says you are headed across the pond."

She turned to the man seated to her right, swarthy and round, a plug of a man with a beautiful battered face. He was pouring the inch left in his highball down his throat.

"Yes," she said. "Paris, and Switzerland."

Claire leaned across the table. "Davis, be nice."

"I've hardly said a word."

"I knew this was a mistake, Mary Frances. You have my dispensation to ignore him altogether." Claire offered Davis a glittering smile. "E. Pearson Davis, correspondent for the *Herald* and insufferably right about everything."

"And I love you," Davis said.

"Rounder."

"Tease."

Davis turned his attention to Mary Frances. "Just got back from Spain myself."

She felt Tim watching her from down the table. There had not been a second since she stepped off the train that morning that she hadn't known where he was, felt his attention or lack. What would she do next? She closed her eyes, took a sip from her water glass.

"It's all going to hell," Davis said.

"Spain?" she said.

"Davis." Claire touched Mary Frances's hand, but the warning was in her voice.

233

"You promised."

"A bedtime story then, darling. I'll tell my bedtime stories."

"Mother and Tim and Mary Frances are touring. Mother is elderly. They will not bring aid to the insurgency, nor will they have to fight them off. They're going to Switzerland, for god's sake."

"The Swiss," Davis said, "are in hell."

Claire ignored him. "Timmy wants you to see Le Paquis, the land we've bought above Lac Léman. He thinks we should start a retreat there for artists. The countryside is beautiful. Inspiring. Writers, painters. Mary Frances is a writer."

Davis smiled at her as if he'd just discovered a flask in her handbag. "What do you write about?" he said. "Novels, like Pretty Princess here?"

"No. I —"

"You're such a pig, Davis."

Davis sucked his teeth and looked away.

What difference did it make? Here was a man predisposed to think she was silly. Over his shoulder, Tim's carved cheek, his snowy head, turning again. He had not told her about Le Paquis, and she was sure he had his reasons, one of which was the idea that someday he would go to Switzerland and not come back. She felt the edges of what they knew about each other acutely; what rights she had seemed slim. What would she do next?

"Hunger," she said. "I write about hunger for all kinds of things."

Davis laughed and raised his glass.

Dinner was laid in front of them, tiny shrimps in cream over Holland rusk, and then thin slices of roast beef, potatoes, beets that bled across the plate. The wine was older than she was, and French.

Davis hadn't touched his plate but was well into his fourth highball when he leaned close again. "Was this what you were hungry for?"

She looked at him squarely. He seemed to read her disdain but not care to acknowledge it.

"Claire's not listening anymore," he said. "It's a known tactic — be quiet, and she'll find someone else who isn't. She's talking opera with the gentleman across from you. She knows a little bit about everything."

Mary Frances blotted her mouth with her napkin, a neat red print of her lips left behind. "You say you work for the *Herald*?"

"The *Herald Tribune*. I have a key to their offices. Would you like to, I don't know, see how they run the big press?"

"Mr. Davis. My father has run the news-

paper in our little town of Whittier, California, since I was six years old. I doubt you
could show me something that I haven't
seen before."

"I dunno, doll."

"Doll?"

He leaned close. "I look at you, I look at
this." His gesture indicated the fine room,
the fine people in it. "And I doubt you've
ever been hungry in your life."

It seemed a ridiculous thing to have to
prove.

She leaned closer, reached across his
untouched plate, and plucked the small
white carnation from his boutonniere. She
bit the petals from the stem and chewed.

Tim found her on the balcony, a February
Manhattan lit below. She had wanted him
to come for her; she was so pleased.

"I was thinking," she said, "The first time
I ever ate an oyster, I was in love with a
girl."

"I imagine most of us would say the
same."

"I was in boarding school. Her name was
Eda Lord. We used to have these dances at
Christmas, and the school would serve
special things — one year, oysters."

Tim offered his navy jacket around her

shoulders. "Are you all right?" he said.

"That Davis is a boor."

"He is. I'll go back inside and challenge him to a fistfight."

"What should I have told him? That I'm married?"

"He can see that. And he outweighs me by double, I'd guess."

"Tim."

"And there's all that nasty business he's been into with boxing or bullfighting, parachuting behind enemy lines. I think he shot a tiger once, and he's so drunk he probably does think he's Hemingway, but if it would make you feel better, my dear, I am your man."

"For now."

He inclined his head, turning back to the city, the two of them shoulder to shoulder now, the party a distant background. "Tell me something," Tim said.

"What?"

"Something I don't know about you, like the oysters. Like how you were in love. It's been weeks since I've had a letter from you, and I have come to depend on them."

From far below, the sounds of the city quickened in the cold. Mary Frances buried her face in the shoulder of Tim's coat.

"I won't push you," he said. "This can be

237

all your idea, exactly how much or how little you want."

She lifted her eyes to his. "As much as I want?"

Tim didn't look away, and they didn't talk anymore. She gave him back his coat, and they went back into the party, Davis gone and Tim taking his seat beside her. Claire reached across the table for his hand and squeezed it, turning from her conversation about how to bridle a difficult horse and beaming again at her brother.

"All right?" she said.

"All right."

That night Mrs. Parrish insisted they escort Mary Frances to her room. "It's just appropriate, dear. This is New York."

"I'm sure I'm perfectly safe," Mary Frances said, tracing the carved mahogany of the elevator wall. There was a term for this paneling she could not remember, a French term. *Boiserie.* Her thoughts felt as if they were dripping out a faucet.

"And now we're sure, too," Mrs. Parrish said. She kissed Mary Frances's cheeks at her door and took Tim's arm.

"Good night, my dear," Tim said, and she watched him and his mother down the hall.

The gates of the elevator closed, and Tim

said, "You're not chaperoning me, are you, Mother?"

"I hadn't thought about it. Should I?"

"I am a grown man. I assume you expect me to act like one, whether you're watching or not."

"Whatever that means."

Tim laughed. "Whatever that means, yes."

If he could have explained his true feelings for Mary Frances in that moment, he believed he would have, regardless of the embarrassment it would cause. He did not want to sneak around. He wanted to take her clothes off, to put her body underneath his, he wanted to help her with her work, and it made him want to take her clothes off all again, more slowly, more. When she said something, when she laughed, watching her in the low light of the dining room tonight, he half-thought to tip a porter for her key after his mother went to bed and appear in her room this time.

But he'd left it in her hands. Even more than he wanted her now, he wanted to see what she'd do with that permission, their time at sea. What he would do, with the wait.

"I feel like a twelve-year-old boy," he said.

His mother laughed. "That's none of my doing."

"No, it's not."

The fire had been laid in their rooms, and Tim put a match to it. His mother opened a book in her lap. Tim asked her if she'd care for a brandy, but she said she'd had quite enough already.

"Claire seems well, considering," she said.

Tim settled himself across from her, a brandy not enough to ease the high vibrating ache in his fingertips, between his hipbones. "Did she mention Charles to you?"

"I didn't know Charles was in the hospital until this morning."

"It's like he was out of town."

"Charles has been ill for quite some time, Timmy. And there's his age. I'm sure she's made certain arrangements in her mind, perhaps from the start."

He was constantly impressed with the pragmatic ease of women. He wondered what arrangements Mary Frances had made in her mind for these months away, if that was what she was doing now.

"Are you certain you won't have that brandy, Mother? It might help you sleep."

"No, no. I'm practically asleep already."

She stood unsteadily, offering her good nights, and Tim waited by the fire. He heard his mother in the toilet, watched the light snap off beneath her closed door. He counted the minutes on the clock since they'd left Mary Frances, wondering if it was too late to wake her, if the point was to wake her, and what he would find if he did. God, he hadn't felt this good in years; he could not remember when.

The next morning, Tim collected mail from the front desk, and there was a letter for Mary Frances. He took it with him to breakfast and found her already waiting at a table, a blush-colored silk blouse tucked primly into her belted skirt. He set the letter next to her plate.

"Thank you."

"I would love to hear some news from Al," he said.

She slit the envelope, folding her hand across her mouth as she read. Al's script was small and tight; her eyes scanned it quickly for something she could share. She sighed.

"It's okay," Tim said.

"He just sounds so dissatisfied. A mountain of papers to grade, the students and their inane questions." She folded the letter and slipped it back into its envelope. "He's not writing."

"I didn't know that."

"Not since his father, maybe before. We

241

don't talk about it." She looked at her plate.

He remembered that she used to grade his papers. Was Al intending to make her feel guilty for not grading papers now? It sounded so petty, Tim felt ashamed of himself for thinking it. "Perhaps the time alone will help," he said. "Perhaps we can think of something else."

She laughed. "I can't."

"A secretary."

"That he would pay with gratitude? He needs the job, he doesn't want it. He wants to write, he can't. And meanwhile —" She gestured toward herself, dropping Tim's gaze. "Where is your mother?"

"She doesn't have the stomach for anything but toast in the morning. Mary Frances, if you are to worry about Al, then I will worry about him too."

She brought her eyes back to his face, her gorgeous brow drawn up. "I've got my same gratitude, Dr. Parrish. Are you sure that will be enough?"

That was the girl he remembered.

They had one thing to accomplish before sailing — a visit to Claire's publisher. She sent a car in the afternoon, and a note that she was sorry she wouldn't be able to accompany them, but with the party, and

Charles.

Mary Frances watched the city seem to form itself like crystal out the window, tried to remember to breathe. "Explain to me how this works," she said.

"It's nothing, my dear. It's a roomful of old men. You'll know exactly what to do with them when you see them."

"But have they read it? Are they going to tell me things . . . I don't know. Are they going to tell me what they think?"

"It's an economy like any other, Mary Frances. They wouldn't spend their time if they didn't want something for it."

Her casual remark at breakfast came back to her, a little more true than she had intended. She could she never repay Tim for his time spent like this. What more would she throw at him? The question seemed to be what more did she have at hand.

The car pulled to the curb, and Tim offered his arm, into the slate gray offices of Harper & Bros. The last book Mary Frances had read published by Harper & Bros. had been written by Edna St. Vincent Millay.

Tim whispered something to the secretary, they sat, they rose. Doors opened on a study like Rex's, two old men looking up from pages spread across a blotter behind a walnut desk.

"My goodness, Hamish. Look at her."

"MFK Fisher. You might have mentioned your youth and beauty. Our hearts are not what they used to be."

"Mr. Saxton," Mary Frances shook his hand. "What kind of writer would I be, if I gave everything away?"

The men laughed. Tim let his hand fall from her waist. "Gentlemen," he said, and he was gone.

They loved her. They loved how she traveled and read and pulled from all corners. They loved how she was not a homemaker, not Mrs. Something Something, and her manuscript not like anything else they'd ever seen, written by a woman or a man. A personal history of food, of eating; they wanted 45,000 words as soon as she could possibly write them. They would publish the book here and in London, through Hamish Hamilton. They would draw up the contract as soon as she said yes.

"And?" Tim was laughing. "So you said?"

"Oh, yes. Yes!"

He toasted her with champagne in the dark downstairs bar at the Warwick Hotel. He said how happy he was, and proud, and how he'd known it all along.

"I must write Claire and thank her," she said. "I must write Al."

"Call him. You can go upstairs."

She didn't though. "I want to share this with him, of course I do."

"And yet?"

"Mr. Hamilton said they sent a letter. It must have arrived after I left, but Al didn't mention it when I called, or when he wrote. He would have seen the return address. Everybody knows Harper."

"Your success is not his failure, my dear."

"No. Of course not." And she knew it wasn't. But would these men have looked at her work if Tim had not asked? And would Tim have asked if she were still back in Laguna, inviting him and Gigi to share a pot of stew and some California red?

"Well." Tim pushed back from the bar. "Perhaps it can wait."

"Perhaps." Mary Frances drank down the last of her coupe. "Perhaps."

If she watched carefully, as you would a bird perched on your finger, it was almost a dream. The *Hansa* was white against the midnight pier, the air frigid, too cold to snow, too cold to think. Mrs. Parrish prattled on, only the shrill chime of her voice in the darkness, and Tim, who seemed every-where.

Of all the boarding passengers, their little group appeared to be the soberest, with only dinner's drinks under their belts, and the bottle they had shared of Chambertin in honor of the crossing. They were also the only ones who did not know any beer garden songs.

"You never know with whom we'll be lunching," Mrs. Parrish said.

"That sounds so ominous," Mary Frances said.

"I often find it is."

The steward led them first to Mrs. Parrish's rooms, red and blistered as a poached shrimp. There was a drawing room, with a games table and a writing desk that looked out to the blackness, the sea beyond. There was none of the clever compartmentaliza-tion Mary Frances had so admired on the cross-country trains. Her cabin would be smaller, she was sure, and below decks; she had hoped for privacy. Imagining this trip in California, privacy had seemed filled with much more ease than it did now; she had not been able to think past being alone. Now there was Tim, and the idea of being alone with him or without him, and then what? Her thoughts seemed bound by this mincing, obvious pace.

She could hear the singing and laughter above decks, the jangle of women letting go of themselves. The whole effect was like a very apposite, and clean, bordello.

"Al and I took a German ship home from Dijon," she said. "But it was full of Americans."

"Another time," Mrs. Parrish said.

"But still, I remember there was a woman at our lunch table, a young wife who had run away with an Italian, returning with her mother who had fetched her back. There was such a peculiar light in her eyes when she told the story, she and her mother grasping at each other, as though they were at the opera."

"Precisely what I've been talking about," Mrs. Parrish said. "You can learn the strangest things about people at sea if you're not careful."

Tim was sitting on the edge of his mother's puffy red coverlet, one knee crossed over the other. His mother directed the steward, and he watched Mary Frances.

"Fetched her back," he said. "For her husband?"

Mary Frances nodded. She felt suddenly like crying. She had put herself in a difficult position and locked all the doors on it; for god's sake, she was setting out to sea. Tim was right. What would she do next? What choice had she left for herself?

She pressed the heels of her hands into her eyes, and then stood quickly. She would not be melodramatic, no matter what. And she would not be stupid.

"You're tired," Tim said. "Mother, let her go."

Mary Frances followed the steward down the corridor to her own cabin. She looked back, and Tim stood in the hall.

"You know," he said casually, "it's not like there's a switch anyone can flip."

"I know," she said.

"We'll be at sea a week," he said.

"Yes."

"Ah, Mary Frances. Good night."

She sent the steward away and locked the door behind him. She was an idiot, a schoolgirl, a prude, a coward. She sank down onto her own rose-colored carpeting. She thought if she could get on with it, get over, go on, she would come out the other side of this, but she felt no bottom or end to her appetites. She might just always want this way — after Tim, something else. She might just always be this hungry.

Later that night, staring at the ceiling, she heard a light rapping on her door. Perhaps her door, perhaps the one next to hers, or across the hall. She wanted it to be Tim. She wanted it to be Tim so much, Tim coming for her, that she couldn't bear to get up and check. The rapping stopped, and the ship left the pier without her waving, without her cheering face amongst the crowd, the ribbons and streamers flying, the drinks on high.

The next morning she stood on deck in the icy February wind to punish herself. The ocean was endless in all directions, nearly the same color and texture as the sky, mirrors set against each other toward infinity. Her coat was buttoned to her neck, her scarf around her ears, her arms clamped tight. She was in the middle of nothing, nowhere, countryless, familyless, husbandless, homeless. These two lives she had been living, the one inside and the one out, how much longer could she pretend they mattered when nothing out here held its borders?

She turned from the deck rail to find a young man watching her from inside the lounge, sipping his coffee. She felt her guts shift delicately against her spine with the movement of the ship, an action both effortless and sick at once. He raised his cup in her direction. She needed, first, a drink.

■ ■ ■ ■

Tim answered her knock, and she passed through the door, already opening her clothes. His smile was gentlemanly, and she shut her eyes to it, the buttons of her blouse beneath her hands, the next and then the next and then the next. He cupped her face, his kiss the one she'd gotten after every dance in boarding school, soft and warm and pleasant and over all too quickly.

"I'm very glad you're here," he said.

"Oh, for chrissake. You should be. Turn out the lights."

She sounded brassy, and she could feel the work of the whiskey she'd taken in the bar at the back of her throat. She stepped out of her skirt, yanked her slip over her head. None of it seemed delicate now, and none of it seemed right, but only pushing through to the next thing, and then the next. She felt frayed to tears, and then Tim clicked out the lamp beside the bed, and they went down.

It was not pretty until much later, until they'd made excuses for lunch and his mother's invitation, until they'd pulled the damasked sheets from the mattress, strewn the pillows across the carpeting, until she'd

250

bruised her wrist against the headboard, broken a glass, burned the skin off her tailbone, the room ripe with what they'd extracted from each other, then something turned another way than desperate.

They lay side by side, crosswise on the bare ticking, Mary Frances's face tucked into the bend of her elbow like a bird asleep. Her dark hair spilled over the edge of the mattress. On the floor, a scatter of hairpins amongst the shards of water glass, a few flecks of down, as though a brittle animal had given up. Tim wished he had his sketch-book. He could not think of what to say, and he did not have it in him to go another time, he was exhausted and starving and empty of absolutely everything.

He opened his mouth to tell her how beautiful she was again. She rolled her face from where she tucked it and looked at him from underneath those eyebrows, at first sly and teasing, then seeming to realize what he was about to say.

Her hand shot out to cover his mouth. "Don't you dare, Dillwyn Parrish. I didn't come all this way to be patronized."

He took her wrist and kissed it. The muscles in her chest bowed and arched to hold her shoulders up, to hold him quiet, so many lovely hollows. He reached beneath her armpit; she had not bathed before she came to him, a fine bristle of hair and her travel there. She had not stopped for much of anything, and his hand fit against her perfectly, his fingers cupping against her shoulder blade, and the completeness of it nearly made him sigh.

He pulled her onto her back. He wiped his hand between her legs and across her thighs, slick as paint. He took his mouth across her hipbones and down. She told him to wait, and he told her to be quiet, that she had not come all this way to be patronized.

All the delicate things undone with the mouth every day, and she had never thought of this, never asked for it before, and the sense it made was like threading a needle, pulling the end of thread to a point with her lips and then carefully, with concentration, looping it through. They were lovers now, flesh and beating blood, lovers, and there was nothing to do but dive in, headlong.

At sea, the sunrise was like a bloodletting, and to see it, Mary Frances had been up all night. She was sore. Tim, asleep beside her, her hip now pressed against the length of his back; his nakedness was strange and her alertness to it strange, and outside the small ship's window, the sky pulsed.

She let her hand fall into his white hair, and he stirred, turning to her.

"How do you think I'll get out of here?"

"You're better at breaking in, aren't you."

"It's morning. The stewards."

"The well-tipped stewards?"

"They'll be here soon, regardless. I have to go."

Tim's hand pushed against the sole of her foot, pushing her back against the headboard. "I don't have to open the door." His mouth found the inside of her knee. "You don't have to do anything."

But she would, of course.

She wrote to Al in the mornings from her desk in her stateroom. It took time to settle there, the far horizon outside and nothing but the ocean to watch. She felt herself dividing, everything happening twice, and she filled page after page as though to show him she was busy.

The flowers, she wrote, *are everywhere, little gardens and terrariums, so much that I seem always to be broaching a wall of perfume, lilies big as fists, chrysanthemums, orchids. They never seem to wilt; secretly there has to be a team of stewards whose sole job it is to garden.*

One night, Tim at her door, the bouquet he'd stolen crushed between them in a cloud of sharp green scent. Stargazers, he said. Casablanca, the largest lily in the world. Later he painted her hip with yellow pollen, the flowers never meant for the vase.

The eating goes on at all hours, she said. *You would love the strange little smorgasbords in the afternoons, the pickled vegetables and corned meats, the hard sausages that smell like the floors of the barns they hung in. The chef's consommé is clear as a bell.* And one day it had been sunny, almost warm on deck, and she and Tim took their mugs to the deck chairs, wrapped in blankets side by side, her body still tender from the night before, the morning, already lit in anticipation of the night to come, and the warm consommé in the mug in her hands, in her chest, headed to her belly, Tim's voice, half lost to the water and the breeze, calculating his own pleasure and exhaustion, the tenderness with which he planned to handle her neglected parts: What about your ankles, Mary Frances? What about your little toes?

They were alone, except when they were with Mrs. Parrish, and so at all other times free to say and be what they thought to each other. It was glorious, frightening, to care so little. Passengers stared at Tim's head in her lap in the lounge, his hand inside the low back of her dinner dress at the bar, late at night, all the Germans drunk around them.

Mrs. Parrish thinks it's funny, how I am always setting things aside for you, but I can tell she's truly pleased. I think all the time of our crossings, the little Dutch ships and freighters, how odd and magical it all felt and how it still does, and will again. I wonder what you are doing now, morning here, but still night for you, and I think of what we were doing then, mid-morning, mid-ocean, on our way to France for the first time. I feel all these parallels acutely, Al. At sea, I remember other times at sea, and they overlay these times.

Tim seems better. He looks very well, strong and straight in a way that I remember, and he seems glad to be on this trip with his mother. He rarely mentions Gigi, except in the way that someone speaks about a pet that ran away when they were a child, a passing kind of wistfulness, but maybe the truest kind. I know he will always love her.

In fact, Tim never mentioned her. It was Mary Frances who brought her up, and only the once, asking if he'd gotten news from her. Saying Gigi's name aloud was different from writing it in a letter. She watched it skitter across Tim's expression, a rock on a still pond.

"No," he said. "No, I have not. I'm sure she's married now. She was planning to marry him as soon as she could."

She wanted to ask if it still upset him, but she didn't want to hear him say it. *Have you heard from her, Al? Have you seen her around town? Perhaps she and John have already gone to Laguna.*

You should use the house when it gets warmer. Or drive out now and lay a fire, look out the window, and watch the sea. It is so peaceful there, and it reminds me of the days when we were first married.

I am still thinking of our plans. Perhaps I was never meant to carry a child, and that will be our lot. There are plenty of children in the world already. Surely there is one who would want us.

Against the flat of Tim's inner thigh, she traced the curl of him with the tip of her finger. Something was unbalanced.

"I had tuberculosis."

"Here?"

"Well. Here is where it left me. They had to cut it out."

She cupped her hand around him, and he breathed out languidly. His body seemed to move against his breath: what was slow becoming fast, what was soft, hard.

"Everything seems to work all right," she said.

"Not quite everything."

It seemed somehow another sign. Still, like athletes, winded, they would roll away from each other and eat from the trays the stewards left them, rare roast beef sandwiches and champagne in her room, stout in his, sometimes bracing themselves against the walls, draping themselves like rags. She would tell him not to touch her for a minute, stretching her long white back over a chair, and he would watch the lift in her hips and take it as a dare. They would start again, acrobatically, dynamically, never so much for the coming as for the act itself. There were times she was not sure if Tim came at all, his shoulders curving off the bed to meet hers, the small hot sphere they made together, kept making, kept working at, the thing between them, their own.

It's all right, Al, she wrote. *And I know we have the spring and summer before us to figure it out when I return, and that there is no rush. We are young still, even when we do not feel it, and this life is longer, larger than we think. I feel we are on the cusp of something. Who knows what lies ahead?* Who knows.

She did not mention the meeting at Harper. She was waiting for him to do it first.

When she was finished with her letter, she would stand from the desk and run a bath, the bottle of violet-scented oil from the Warwick rationed out, and she would scrub to her toes with the thick white washcloth. She would dress, and Tim would come to the door and ask her if she'd finished her correspondence, and she would point to the letter on the desk and feel a kind of allowance about it all. She'd follow him down for a beer before lunch, the bar already packed with Germans, Tim with his sketch pad, she with her notebook, and they would sit quietly and wait for Mrs. Parrish.

She loved to write with Tim beside her, to write smart things they would pass back and forth more than they talked, a line, a thought drawn out. He sketched her, sometimes as she sat, and sometimes from memory, from the night, the afternoon before, the arc of her spine over the chair back, only her mouth, her lips open.

They ate with Mrs. Parrish in the little restaurant with the caged birds — Italian, Swedish, Mexican-German food, always heavy and rich, good and strange. Afterward they found conversations and card games and concerts for her, swapped novels with other passengers for her, and invented excuses to be alone. Mary Frances often forgot her wrap. Tim was often curious about the weather. If the elevator was empty, he kissed her. If the stairwell was empty, he ran his hand beneath her dress. Two, three steps away; there was no one here who knew them. He offered his arm, and she fit her side against him, her head sinking back on its stem, how delicious, how well they fit together, what a satisfying lock.

They didn't talk; it was as though they had nothing to talk about, or that the talking would come later, but the current between them was live and thrumming.

The ship felt like their own, something private now, where no real scale applied. They would go to lunch, and then to stroll the deck in the blistering sea wind, and then to play cribbage in Mrs. Parrish's stateroom. Mary Frances had no patience for cribbage and would bring her notebook and write. She marveled at how hard it was for people to find something pleasant to talk about, and how hard they tried even after it seemed unlikely they would find it. It seemed a lesson to her, that we try, even when we ought to know better, to connect with where we are, whom we are with. But whom was she with? She felt Tim's presence in an empty room, she sparked and lifted to it, and when he touched her, her mind went everywhere and nowhere at once. But here, to be here, to feel like she could be here, she rose every morning to write a letter to Al.

The night before they landed in Cherbourg, the little dining room was transformed into a forest. Pine boughs arched the doorways, waxy with scent, and behind them hid the cabin boys with birdcall whistles, trilling at each other from all corners. It was meant to be a woodland feast, some sort of Bavarian tradition, and from the kitchen came huge platters of roasted boar and pheasant and trout, sheets of potatoes, sausages, schnitzels.

Mrs. Parrish clapped her hands like a girl at a play. "Isn't this amazing," she said. "Look at all the evergreens! Where have they been keeping them all this time?"

Mary Frances had no idea.

Tim had fallen quiet, watching. From the bar came the drunken Germans with their champagne flutes full of cherries, their tall buxom women on their arms, and their songs. The cabin boys peeped and twittered, the German women squealed with laughter, and platter after platter poured out of the kitchen on the upturned palms of white-jacketed stewards. There were people in

California lining up for bread; a forest of game in the middle of the Atlantic seemed no more impossible than that.

There were songs, of course, salutes and toasts, all in German. The noise rose around them, and Mary Frances found herself intent upon her food, as if she hadn't eaten in a week. The buxom women pointed and laughed. Some of them wore little felt hats with plumage. Some of them wore dirndl skirts and pinafores. A steward came around with a tray of wooden popguns and a basket of cotton balls.

"For the birds," he said. "For shooting."

Mary Frances leaned forward. "The cabin boys or each other?"

Tim shook his head. He didn't know. The stewards went around, and the first cotton ball took flight, another and then another. Soon the air seemed filled with cotton balls.

Tim fiddled with the hammer on the popgun, trying to figure out the load. The room was getting louder now, the laughter turning coarse, and Tim was frustrated with the gun, prying open the mechanism with a butter knife and muttering something under his breath when all of a sudden, Mrs. Parrish let out a chirp of her own.

"Oh dear, oh dear, I shot him!"

Mary Frances looked up to see one of the

Germans stiffly bending in his tuxedo to look behind him, hand at the back of his neck. He pulled from the floor, not a cotton ball, but a round red grape, the same kind spilling from the centerpiece in front of Mrs. Parrish.

"Mother," Tim said, "if you'd given me a second, I was trying to figure it out."

"Here he comes, here he comes." Mrs. Parrish picked up her fork and took a large bite of roast boar.

Tim set down the popgun.

"Guten Abend." The man's face was pasty and taut; he wore a sort of smile that seemed stretched into place. He bent slightly from the waist, and Tim stood. The man extended a hand, the red grape rolling in his palm.

"Gehört das Ihnen?"

"I'm sorry," Tim said. He lifted his chin, his eyes scanning the room for a steward. Everyone was hiding; everyone was busy, Mrs. Parrish chewing furiously. "I don't understand."

"Ihre Waffe zu haben scheint Befeuert. Ihre Gun. Diese Gun. Ja?"

"I'm sorry." Tim looked at Mary Frances, whose hand covered her mouth. "It was an accident."

"Ein Unfall. Ein Spiel. A game, yes?" The

262

German smiled again, letting the grape roll onto the table next to Tim's plate. *"Kraft durch Freude."*

He bowed again, and Tim repeated the German back to him, *Kraft durch Freude,* as it seemed to solve the problem. He repeated it to himself, then repeated it again to a passing steward whose sleeve he caught.

" 'Strength through joy,' sir. It is a common feeling in Germany now, that we will find strength through joy."

"Of course," Tim said.

"I am really terribly embarrassed," Mrs. Parrish said. "I don't know what came over me."

"It's all right, Mother. Your Nazi was very understanding. And they did hand out the guns."

But neither Tim nor Mrs. Parrish went back to their meals. Mary Frances realized they'd been surrounded by these Germans for the entire crossing and yet she hadn't spoken to any of them, no more than a nod in the passageway, an acknowledgement on deck. It was, in fact, their ship.

Slowly, the twittering cabin boys became less of a spectacle. The whistles and catcalls died away, the Germans pushing back from their tables with their goblets of cherries, making their way back to the lounge, to the bar, to other rooms on other decks. Mary Frances and the Parrishes stayed put, and slowly the cabin boys came out of hiding, shaking the needles from their hair.

Tim ordered another bottle of wine. The cabin boys began dismantling the forest. The stewards cleared the platters of food to the kitchen, snapped clean white linens over the empty tables for the morning's service. There seemed to be a pall settled over them now. None of them were willing to be the first to stand and break it, and they sat there long after their wine was just sips in their glasses. The stewards had finished with their work, a line of white-jacketed young men at attention by the kitchen door, ready for the Americans to take their leave.

They lay in her cabin long after saying good night, the pitch of the ship beneath them. Mary Frances wanted to ask him if he was scared, but it seemed such a silly question now, after all they'd done. All she seemed to have were silly questions.

"Tim?"

His breaths were deep and even.

"What happens tomorrow?"

"Well." He rolled onto his side, his lips next to her ear. "We strike land. We make land travel to Paris. A train, I think. They have beds there too, but I'm not sure we will have the time to make use of them."

"It will be different."

"So serious."

She didn't say anything, and he didn't try to see her face.

"Yes," he said finally. "It will be different, for us. Than this."

"Everything feels a bit more possible at sea."

When the ship docked, they took the train from Cherbourg to Paris, through the wet, gray countryside. Mrs. Parrish seemed unsettled; she spoke to Tim with a surprising intimacy, as though Mary Frances were not there.

"I have real doubts, Timmy. I may well be too old for a journey like this one."

"That's ridiculous, Mother."

Mrs. Parrish made a sound.

"You just got off the ship and have now hurtled yourself off again. You're still catching up. You need a nap, a meal, and then we'll see who can stop you."

Tim crossed his legs, nonchalantly snapping open the paper his French was nowhere near good enough to read. It was interesting to see him bolstering his mother; she wondered where he had learned to do what he did to people. Everybody took his encouragement.

"I could go to the club car," Mary Frances said.

"No, dear, it's fine. The porter will be around shortly. Surely there are porters."

"It's no trouble. Those days on the ship have caught up with my appetite. I'm always hungry now."

"You do look it, dear, healthier. Still, Timmy, fetch the porter."

Tim folded the paper. "Of course."

He slid back the pocket door, brushing against her knees only the barest bit as he passed through. Mrs. Parrish had such firm ideas about what was for her to do, what was for Tim, what she could do alone, and what she needed his escort for. Mary Frances was still learning her place and the expectations therein. She found herself wanting to lean over the rails to test them.

"If I may ask," she said, "what's the matter?"

Mrs. Parrish cut her eyes at Mary Frances, suddenly a much younger woman, capable of far more than prattle and worry.

"Years ago," she said. Then she gave a sigh, the rest of what she was remembering trailing off. "I'm old, dear. Who wants to be old?"

"But you've looked forward to this trip for so long."

"And now I won't have it to look forward to any longer."

Mrs. Parrish turned to the window, the countryside whipping past. Mary Frances followed her gaze, dizzy with the speed at which they traveled. She remembered taking this exact route with Al on their honeymoon, on their way to Dijon by way of Paris. They'd gone to the club car, and she ordered her first French meal, good bread, good ham and butter, a bottle of champagne, and they'd eaten, so happy across from each other, she felt as if she would burst.

When Tim returned, both women sat with their chins in their hands, unreachable in their own places. He opened the French newspaper again and stared at the words until they ran together, blottish, swelling blackness, the opposite of clouds. He could tell fortunes by this newspaper, but he could not read it, and he had no idea what had happened in this compartment while he had been gone.

At the hotel desk, they were holding mail for Mary Frances, a letter from Al and two from Edith. It was cold in Whittier, and with

Anne and the children away, with Mary Frances away, and Rex completely flummoxed by his new editor, Edith had nothing to do. *I miss you, Dote,* she said. *There is nothing so fine as our talks when I start to feel the blurries waiting in the wings.*

Mary Frances took the other letters to the bar. She ordered a whiskey, then another after that, smoked a cigarette and then another after that. In all her travels, even when she and Al had lived in France, this was the first time she'd ever felt so distant from her family. By the time she reached Al's letter, all she was good for was skimming it.

Tim pulled out the chair beside her, ordered a beer. "This hotel is quite modern," he said. "Perhaps all of Paris is modern now."

"Your mother will be disappointed."

"My mother is indefatigable. She knows no French disappointments."

Mary Frances tucked her letters into her purse, to read another time when she did not feel stretched so thin.

"Are you all right?" he asked. "Of course not. I mean, it's hard to be in two places at once."

"For you?" And maybe she didn't want the answer to that, to hear his feelings were

268

divided when he was with her, and who else he might be thinking of, but they had a long habit of being honest with each other, and it was out of her mouth before she could think twice.

Tim fiddled with the cocktail napkin. Finally he looked at her, and all his high fervent promises were in that look: how she was like no one else, how they were like no one else together.

"We could run away," he said.

"You don't really think so."

"I've found it to be a perfectly acceptable response to life's difficulties. Don't I seem comfortable on the run? Dashing, even."

"You're trying to make me laugh."

"So laugh," he said. "Will you?"

It became her job to perform a certain part of every day as though she knew a great deal more about France than she did. She rose to the occasion, offering translation, checking maps, and making itineraries with Mrs. Parrish over lunch, because now that she and Tim stayed up half the night, nobody ate breakfast anymore, and their days unfolded from the table according to the various attractions of Paris.

Cathedral after cathedral, she stared hard at the guide and the French that rolled out of him. She had to concentrate to understand, Dijon two years gone, but worse and harder, Tim at her elbow in his beautiful blue suit, his overcoat open. He stood so close, she could feel the difference in the air inside his coat and out.

He leaned to her. "The church is what?"

"Old," she said. "Old and . . . important."

He told his mother this was a church built during the Dark Ages, with marble quarried from the Hebrides, that every king of France had been interred there, and that the monks now made beautiful cheese. There were no monks or marble in the Hebrides, but he was right about the kings. The guide kept speaking and Tim leaning close to her; everything kept happening.

The guide spoke of an abbey made famous for the marriage of Louis XIV and something to do with lace. There was Tim's hand, and she let her hand fall beside it, this part of France the province of apples, of honey, of sheep, of iron, and like it was an accident of proximity, the back of his knuckles brushed hers and her body leaped and rushed to remember the night before.

Mrs. Parrish asked, "What are they talking about sheep for?"

Mary Frances couldn't say. Her blood thrummed in her ears.

"My dear, are you sure you're listening?"

Tim stood in the gallery at the Musée de l'Orangerie and realized how long it had been since he'd painted. Gauguin's Tahiti before him now, violently affixed to canvas, green and gold and red and cerulean blue in the light that seemed to come from everywhere, an explosion, ecstasy; he loved it. It had been too long since he'd spent time in museums, too long between shows; he'd forgotten what this test felt like, to measure your fire against another.

Of course, he thought of Al. Tim had never been unable to do what he wanted, whether it be to write or paint; he'd opened restaurants and tea shops, torn houses to the ground to rebuild them. He felt a stab of sympathy, another unexpected feeling in this situation. But he could not understand where Al's congratulations for his wife had gone. How could you not be happy for the woman you loved?

Mary Frances stopped behind his shoulder, and Tim turned to look at her.

Her eyes worked fast across the canvas. She would say something, soon, she would say something he'd never thought about, and that made him want to paint all the more, just to hear whatever it was she said

271

next. God, he loved women: young women, smart women with talent, Mary Frances. He was forty-two. There was still time to be a genius in her eyes.

"What do you think?" he whispered.

"It doesn't seem to care," she said, "does it?"

He laughed out loud; heads turned. They drew such attention wherever they went, a triumvirate of statuesque travelers, insulated by their English, their apparent wealth. Tim saw no point in pretending to hide, but Mary Frances brought a finger to her lips and moved away. She sat beside his mother on a green velvet bench in the next gallery, removed her notebook from her purse, and bent to it.

He followed. "Lunch?"

"Timmy," his mother said. "Who can think about lunch at this hour?"

"Most of the Western world. It's two o'clock."

Mary Frances put a hand on his mother's arm. "We could send Tim ahead, Mrs. Parrish. There's no rush. You and I could take a taxi when we feel ready to leave."

His mother looked pleased. "Would you be able to get yourself a drink?"

"I'm capable of the hand signals."

"Here, then." Mrs. Parrish reached into

her purse for a fistful of francs.

"I've got money, Mother. I'm fine."

They agreed on the bar at the Ritz, and Tim set out through Monet's water lilies to the sparkling cold Tuileries. He'd been to Paris last winter, after Gigi left him, and winters before they were married, winters during the war. It was a city he was quite familiar with. But today with Mary Frances, with the stir of work and watching her, the attenuated hours of want ahead, this Paris seemed like the culmination of all those others, the whole point.

Perhaps he would just get drunk at lunch, tell his mother everything she well suspected already, and persuade Mary Frances to really run away with him. Perhaps he would just get drunk.

Sometime over the weekend, when it seemed nothing could be done about it, Hitler marched into the Rhineland, knocking on the door of France.

We go everywhere, Al, and we see everything, eat everything, and the Parrish pocketbook never seems to flag. Soufflé! Omelets with burnt sugar, like we used to get at Aux Trois Faisons, with our initials burned into the crust. The Tuileries! the wind biting at our coats. We walk and walk and walk (so as to wear out

273

Mrs. Parrish so that when they did return, she was exhausted. She begged off dinner. She began to lose weight, they all did, even though they ate the lunches of duck, creamed Brussels sprouts with lardons, terrine, confit, *fromage blanc,* steak tartare with shimmering soft-set eggs, brioche. And they passed cathedral and train station and park and square. They passed women with their prams, old women, tired women — they all made Mary Frances want Tim more, as though he could keep her from the ages to come).

I was so cold this afternoon, I thought about that February in Strasbourg, how the wind was so bitter and we moved into the rooms at the Elisa, where the heat came blaring off the radiators. I would sit at the window and watch you leave for the university in the mornings — how cold you looked, your collar turned up, while I basked like a lizard inside. I welcomed you home warmly, as I recall. I wish for that same welcome now.

Your last letter sounded so melancholy. And I know it's wrong of me to be oceans away and having a high time in all our old haunts, telling you to keep your chin up. But I do worry. His grief seemed like a thick blanket that wrapped him away from her now, as if he too were carrying on a separate life back in

California, as if they both had somehow moved on. She knew this wasn't true, but every thought she had of them together seemed sepia-toned and distant, their youth in Dijon, the ghosts of who they had become.

France reminds me of you every day, and everywhere we go there is a fourth seat for you, my dear, as though you might meet us any moment.

They took a carriage through the Bois de Boulogne, the women bundled in lap robes and furs, Tim on the buckboard with the driver, the wide allée stretching ahead. The wind whipped across the lake, ice still clinging to its edges, but Mrs. Parrish spoke of a sunny lunch fifty years before on the topmost balcony of the Chalet des Iles. Her companion had rowed them across in a tiny wooden boat, her father one boat behind.

"I'm sure Paris was a father's nightmare," said Mary Frances. "My father was a fan of boarding schools when I was young."

Mrs. Parrish nodded. "I wanted desperately to see Paris before taking my place at home. Paris at the end of the century! Of course, now I understand that was something special. Then, Paris was enough."

Mary Frances took out her notebook.

"Are you writing that down, my dear? So unnerving, these habits of writers."

"I'm sorry," Mary Frances said. "It's just that your story reminded me of something else."

She could feel Mrs. Parrish looking over her shoulder as she wrote. She marked her place in the book with her thumb.

"I look forward to reading your book, Mary Frances. Tim speaks so highly of your talent."

"His help has been a godsend."

"He has no doubt you will be published to wide acclaim. I think, when you find yourself in the public eye, careful comportment makes all the difference."

Mary Frances laughed. "It's a very little book. I don't imagine we need to worry about the public eye."

"You must always be careful how you present yourself. For instance, I know you to be the devoted wife of Tim's best friend. I like knowing that about you, and I imagine I would find that reflected in the things you've chosen to write about. There might be other things about you I wouldn't like to know, and they would change my feelings about your book."

She spoke evenly, with the same instructive ease she'd spoken about chaperones and escorts, dinner table conversation and correspondence. "I don't want to read about what I don't want to know. I don't want to know what I don't want to know, for that matter."

"I appreciate that," Mary Frances said, matching her tone. "I will remember that."

Tim turned on the buckboard. "Are you warm enough, my dears? Another fur? A little nip of brandy? Mother?"

But Mrs. Parrish was looking out over the lake and didn't seem to hear him. She reached forward and placed a gloved hand on the back of the driver.

"Once around again, please." She said it in English, but the driver understood.

That night Mrs. Parrish suggested Mary Frances would go ahead to Dijon, and she and Tim follow a few days later.

"You and Al must have friends there, people you'd like to see," Mrs. Parrish said. "And I'm sure Timmy can manage our train."

"I have done it before," Tim said. "No one's gotten hurt."

"It's not necessary, Mrs. Parrish. I'm happy to stay with you."

"I insist."

"Well." She looked at Tim. "Thank you."

"Yes, Mother." Tim sighed. "That's very kind."

Mary Frances bent to her coffee. Her conversation with Mrs. Parrish in the carriage suddenly seemed far more consequential than she'd thought, yet the woman remained personable, chatty, herself. She was a mother, after all. She was capable of many different tacks at once.

"I'm hoping you and Al will come to visit when we return," she said. "I think I should meet him at last."

"You should. He's very curious about you. And grateful."

Mrs. Parrish touched her hand, and that seemed to settle it. "It has been my pleasure."

After his mother said good night and Tim walked Mary Frances to her rooms, unlocked her door, and pushed her up against the papered wall, his hand drawing up beneath her corselette, the thick resistant fabric and belts, her legs opening for him, after they'd made love on the carpet, finally reaching the bed, she told him what his mother had said in the park.

He laughed. "It's nothing compared to what she said to me."

"Oh god, Tim. Really?"

"Something about what happens on a ship

is one thing, everybody packed in like sardines together, but she expects a return to my senses, post haste."

Tim rolled away from her, found his pants on the floor, and extracted his cigarette case from the pocket. Their time together would be over soon, and she could not imagine what would come next, how anything could come next. They would certainly never get another chance like this.

"Shouldn't you be getting back to your own room?" she said, looking at Tim, the smoke from his cigarette rising lazily.

He traced a slow line along her collarbone. "Post haste."

She checked into the Hôtel de la Cloche and left her bags, the day bright and cold, the rooftops sending their wood smoke into the blue sky. She went first and stood in the street at Crespin's, the oysterman still there with his craggy fingers, the gnarled shells. She tipped back a half-dozen oysters with a short cold beer for lunch, the rattle of Dijonnaise around her like the beat of wings in a coop. This was not Paris or Provence but dark gray France, musty and cobbled and muddy and rich. Behind her, she could hear the clock chiming at the Nôtre-Dame.

This was the place she'd first learned to

pay attention to the particular way she noticed things, her perspective, to pay attention as a writer. If these were their last days together, she wanted Tim to know this city as she did, so that something between them might be complete.

She took the narrow stairs to the second floor at Aux Trois Faisons, the narrow hallway to Ribaudot's office, still the short balding man, brusque and pacing, a lit cigarette between his teeth as he yelled into the telephone.

He pretended to remember her. "Yes, of course. Madame Fisher. You look well."

"Thank you. I would like a table for Thursday night. A special table, please, a very special meal. Shall I order it now?"

"Of course, Madame."

Perhaps he did remember. But the lingering feeling of unease followed her to the street, in and out of shops, through the empty rooms in the house on Petit Potet, where she and Al had first lived, and Madame, now poor and alone. Everything was changed. She'd pressed money into Madame's hand as she left, then wandered the quarter, embarrassed, sad, the scent of gingerbread adrift.

When Tim and his mother arrived in Dijon, Mrs. Parrish seemed to need him constantly. She had letters to write and gifts to buy, she was too cold, too hot, too tired — would Tim read to her in their rooms? Mary Frances had other things to do, she was sure.

The one night she shared with Tim was their dinner at Aux Trois Faisons.

There was her table, the menu she'd ordered typewritten on a nice white card. There was the old man who ate with his dog, the four widows in their weeds, the young tourists much like herself and Al. There was her waiter, Charles, with his delicate waxed mustache. Old now, shrunken, his hands fumbled and shook, chasing his tools across the buffet. The Dubonnet ran a purple stain on the white cloth. He was obviously drunk. Mary Frances glanced at Tim, feeling somehow responsible, but he was looking at the swirl in his glass, the lovely deep color there, then at her.

"I'm sorry," she said. "And somehow ashamed."

Tim laughed. "Ashamed?"

"I've talked and talked about this restaurant." She gestured at the purple stain, the pool of soup in his saucer.

"My dear," he said. "What does it matter, where we are?"

And with that, the evening took up its slack. Course by course, the meal became the thing she'd hoped it would be: intricate and subtle and lovely and long, and none of that had to do with the place, which was ancient, or the food, which was perfectly prepared to her specifications, or the service, which somehow improved the more they asked of Charles, his skill finally rising to the surface. It was Tim. He made her laugh, he made her think, they lingered in the restaurant long past hours; the boy with the mop on the edge of their light, sweeping the long hall to the stairs.

A last sip of marc, they settled the bill, and Charles was gone.

They ducked past the boy sweeping up. Mary Frances knew where the coats were hung, but passing Ribaudot's office, he called out to them, "Madame, how was your meal?"

"It was wonderful, wonderful. Thank you."

"I am so happy you remembered us."

"But everyone remembers Ribaudot's. And Charles. Charles was wonderful."

He shook his head. "These days it is hard to say who remembers what. And Charles, I am glad he was able to be here. Yours was his last service."

"Last?"

"He is probably already headed south by now."

"But why?"

It was a horrible question, none of her business, but she couldn't help herself.

Ribaudot drew a small polite smile. "Why, Madame, his family is from the south. And the weather there . . ." He stopped. "Charles is old, intemperate, and now he is gone."

"I'm sorry."

Ribaudot shrugged. "So am I."

Tim took her hand and led her down the narrow stairs, and once they were in the courtyard, the full starlight above, Ribaudot threw the switch, and Aux Trois Faisons went dark. Mary Frances was crying.

Tim gathered her in his arms, pressing her cheek to his. "My dear. It's okay."

"It's not."

"It was a lovely dinner, a perfect dinner. I am so happy to be with you here."

"But, Tim. I wanted this so much. And now there's nothing."

"Everything passes," he said. "Everything changes."

She put her forehead to his shoulder, but she turned her face up, out, away.

"Look," he said. "All those beautiful tiled roofs. The moonlight, Dijon . . ."

But all that was what she was crying for

now, big hopeless tears that come effortlessly, that she did not try to wipe away.

This dinner would become the centerpiece of her book, the story the reviews all focused on, Tim as Chexbres, as he would always be called in her books to come. In her telling, they spark and flirt, they indulge themselves at the table, and at the end of "The Standing and the Waiting," they weep for what they will never have. But most important, Chexbres is not Al, who appears in stories before and stories after, Al who is clearly her husband. Dijon had belonged to them. That she would have this dinner, write about this dinner, and then show it to the world is the most complete betrayal of her marriage she could make.

"I don't think people realize how significant a meal can be," says the librarian, and she has to laugh.

This is one of the things she likes to talk about these days, how people eat in their cars and don't enjoy actual plates or food or company as they much as they should. He's been a good librarian, read her latest interviews. Or maybe he shares her thinking too: she can tell by the way he uses his thumbs against the breastplate, the way he plucks only a few quills at a time, that he knows his way around a game bird. She looks hard at him: a hunter or a cook? She wishes she could blame her glasses.

"God no," she says. "Which is why there's much to be said for dining alone."

He pauses and looks out at the vineyard, the coming darkness. "I guess there is," but he looks unconvinced.

She's not certain she believes it herself anymore. But she's written about the pleasures of traveling alone, dining alone, cooking for one, and she feels beholden to the time he's taken and the distance he's come to hear her say what she always says. She has been alone for quite some time now, and the solitary meals, the big bed, the day that insists on being filled lend an intensity to her smallest conversations. Of course, Norah is here, but that is not the type of companion she means.

She offers the librarian a bag for the feathers and takes the still downy necks of the quail he's finished back to her kitchen. She fills their cavities with lemons, the bay and sage from the pots on the balcony. She trusses the birds, butters their skins. All of it makes for a familiar ceremony, the hundreds of times she's trussed birds, pleased guests, held forth on the significance of daily things.

Then suddenly, he's there behind her with two more birds, his hand to her shoulder, a man accustomed to communicating silently. Suddenly, she wonders about his life back east in Boston, the last woman he touched, the last time he could not keep silent.

"Thank you," she says, and the evening seems new again.

By the time they got to Switzerland, Mrs. Parrish had caught a cold. She wanted Mary Frances to stay with her in Vevey while Tim went to check his property above Lac Léman.

"I'm sure you'll be fine, Mother. We'll only be gone for the day."

Mrs. Parrish blew her nose into her handkerchief and looked at Mary Frances.

"I can stay," she said. "I can go to the pharmacy. It's not a problem."

"I hate for you to change your plans, dear. It's just that I feel rather out of sorts here, and it's not like Paris. I can't understand a word they're saying."

"Of course. It's not a problem."

Tim turned from the window. He pushed his white cuff up his forearm to check his watch, and Mary Frances realized she had not worn her own in weeks. She rubbed the empty spot on her wrist, wondering if she'd even brought it.

"The weather is just too spectacular, Mother. I'll be back in a half hour with the car. You can come with us, or you can stay here and we'll return this evening."

"Oh, Timmy," she said. "I just can't."

"That's fine, then. And you'll be fine. But Mary Frances and I will be going."

Mrs. Parrish redistributed the blankets over her legs. She studied her son, his face even and calm. This was not a standoff, but merely Tim's patience in waiting for her to understand. Finally, she put her head back to the stack of pillows and coughed.

"Perhaps if I can just have a bit of tea sent up," she said, but Tim was already out the door.

Mary Frances picked up the phone to order the tea, lemon, and honey, a plate of sandwiches. She asked if there was anything else, and Mrs. Parrish pretended not to hear her.

"Some brandy, perhaps?"

Mrs. Parrish only shook her head. She looked fragile, her eyes mouse-pink and wet, and Mary Frances felt a stab of guilt. What would Edith do to see her behave this way, Rex, any of them? She sank into the bedside chair.

"You truly are sick, aren't you," she said.

"Well, yes."

She reached a hand to feel her forehead, and Mrs. Parrish pulled away, startled.

"This is beyond my understanding," Mrs. Parrish said. "Really."

Mary Frances let her hand fall to her lap. She was embarrassed to be so obvious, but not so embarrassed that she could stop herself. And what would it matter, to stop herself now? Suddenly the room felt hot, her own face feverish, but Mary Frances kept her seat until the bellman's knock at the door with the tea tray, and then she slipped away.

They drove along the lake, the winding Haute Corniche between Lausanne and Vevey, the Alps still capped with snow. Tim was talking even faster than he drove, his white hair downy in the wind.

"I've wanted you to see this place from the moment we found it. Really. I thought of you immediately."

"You did?"

"I think this place saved my life. Buying this place with Claire, thinking of you, here, this moment we are about to arrive at —" He began laughing. "I think that was it."

They had not really talked about the winter before last, how bad he seemed when he left Los Angeles and what had taken place since then, not in any kind of solid terms. What would be the point in tracing back, what he had done, what she had done to get here? The vineyards terraced up from the lakeshore, and in the meadows between she could see small stone houses built into the hillsides, wending paths, sheep and their herder, a boy and a dog. Tim was talking about the cheeses, the brandy and eau de vie, the summers, the meadows filled with flowers, and Mary Frances rolled the window down to feel the breeze on her face and hear the bells from the sheep as they tripped along. And to be alone with Tim, moving. This was as solid a thing as she could ever ask for.

"We're here," he said. "This is it."

A stone house like the others they had passed, but this one in an open meadow, a fountain bubbling in front, spring-fed, ice cold on her fingertips. He motioned her forward, inside. It was dark and cold and smelled of old hay. The house would need more rooms, a kitchen, but the chimney was sound, and the hearth magnificent. Could they cook on the hearth? Could they chill things in the spring?

She stared at him.

"I have this idea," he said, and he began

to laugh again. "What if we all lived here together?"

And then they boarded the ship home, and it was over. Mrs. Parrish, still under the weather, hardly left her stateroom. The salon, exactly like the salon they'd enjoyed on the trip over, was full of German brewers headed to Milwaukee, the first drink of every evening in toast to the portrait of Adolf Hitler hanging at the end of the bar. They had found a woman, lean and giggling, the silvery drape of her dress like a wing. They were loudly pressing her with glass after glass of champagne.

Mary Frances held her chin in her hand, drawing a small map in the condensation on the tabletop. Tim watched the Germans with a kind of simmering concern; she could feel what he was feeling, as if they had exchanged skins.

"Tim," she said, "what are we going to do?"

"We're going to help that woman get out of here, for chrissake."

"Tim."

He looked at her then, and she saw how tired he was, the dark circles beneath his eyes. He couldn't tell her what they were going to do. He didn't know how they would do it.

He stood and extended his hand for hers, tucking it against his heart, and they left the salon, the pink piano, the girl in the silver dress still laughing with panic, her wrist in the grip of a monocled man. In the dining room, the cabin boys were decking the walls with pine boughs, preparing for the woodland feast. It was as if they were living it all in reverse.

In her room, Tim pulled the red satin coverlet from the bed, and they lay down on the white sheets in their evening clothes. She had begun to cry, and he turned to her so he could see her face, reaching out and lifting her chin.

"You don't need to hide from me," he said. "And you don't need to stop."

She covered her face, and he took her hands in his, pressed them to his own hot cheeks, his neck and ears. She tried to apologize, and he told her to stop. This is what they were doing now.

"And then we will think of something else."

"I can't," she said.

"You will."

"I can't leave Al. He is so very sad. We can't."

"No."

"And you can't come back to California."

"So we have no choice, darling. Imagine that. We have no other choice."

His own eyes were filling now, and she felt something in her head snap and heave forth blackly. The sound she made seemed to come from somewhere else in the room and he put his mouth down on hers to take it from her and that's all they suddenly seemed capable of, throwing their bodies over each other like shields. He pushed the top of her dress down her shoulders to get to her skin.

In the middle of the night, he told her he would write to Al of Vevey, of the orchard and the lake below, the stone fountain and the little house they could make bigger, how they could all go there together and make it something new, for the three of them. Al was her husband, and Al was his friend, and this was a human thing they'd made together, all three of them. She listened to his voice in the darkened room, the spotlight moon shining from the porthole, the ship's rolling beneath her, his breath on the back of her neck, and she knew she'd do anything he asked of her, anything he could think of.

"But this," she said, and she reached over, closing her hand around him, his body already rising to the same thought. She turned and pushed him onto his back, her feet flat beside his hips, her sex settling down. "But this."

He reached between them, and his touch shot through her.

"We can't have this anymore."

Vevey, Switzerland

FALL 1936

Al sat in the café overlooking Lac Léman and knew the decision to come here had been the right one. There were no pages in front of him, no whores chattering past, this was not Dijon or Paris, this was a Swiss town, and the Swiss did not go in for whores the way the French did. And there was no cassis. He drank a strong black coffee and felt the autumn afternoon on his face, the sinking, chilly light off the water, and he knew this would be the place where everything changed.

Upstairs, in the pension, his wife unpacked their trunks, making their home the way she had when they'd first married, and there was comfort in that. They had money; he'd sold the car, whatever furniture Mary Frances had not wanted to store at the Ranch, they had stripped their lives down to the wires — typewriters, wool overcoats, sturdy shoes, a small collection of records and books. Each other, perhaps — it was hard to say.

He had not written in over a year. He had come to blame California.

When Mary Frances returned in the spring, it had already been in his mind to move away from there — to leave the Kennedys, the college, his own mother, still lost in the uncharted territory of her widowhood; it made him guilty to read her letters, made him feel as though he should take the train north immediately, but when he got there, he felt like he should shoot himself. And the Ranch was worse, the Kennedy press and need of each other, all of it suffocating. He had been looking for a way to begin again, and then Tim's letter arrived with this idea that they all return to Vevey. They could make a place to work, and live a life free from the past, and Al knew he was talking about Hollywood and Gigi and the little white bungalow in Laurel Canyon, but also that Tim saw his predicament. Tim had always understood him.

Now he was anxious for Tim to arrive — they had expected him to meet their train at the station, and they had waited with their trunks on the platform, Mary Frances blanching with nerves or travel. She had been so quiet since they left California. Al knew part of her was reluctant to make this leap, and as he watched her knot and unknot the handkerchief in her lap at the station, he realized it hadn't mattered to him. She never talked about her book, and he would have given his eyeteeth for such a contract. She had been reluctant to have children, and he felt as if they'd lost their chance now. They were doing this instead. Sometimes when he looked at Mary Frances, she seemed like a stranger to him; he watched her bring a cigarette to her red mouth and thought how this was not the girl he'd married.

Tim had sent the caretaker Otto to meet them, a barrel of a man, barely topping Al's shoulder with the crown of his hat, which he immediately wadded in his big square hands. Mary Frances kissed both his cheeks. He appeared to be weeping, perhaps with joy at seeing her, perhaps with allergies. The accent here was frighteningly thick; it seemed as if he said Tim would be in on the six-fifteen, that they should all have dinner together and begin their grand plans.

Mary Frances had laughed and closed her eyes. "Grand plans," she said.

Al didn't understand. "What other kind should we make?"

And so what had been quiet between them

turned cold, and Mary Frances did not want to leave the rooms at the pension for a café. She needed a nap, she said, but she seemed skittish. She needed, he suspected, to be away from him.

Al sighed, sipped the last gritty dregs from his cup. It was understandable, of course. They had been married seven years this month, spent the last several weeks crammed against each other in various forward-moving, earth-chewing hunks of metal, and he could not remember their last deliberate contact, their last touch or whispered conversation. It had been weeks of shucking their old lives for this new one, and the fit was still awkward.

Al paid the check and shoved his hands in his pockets. He took the walk along the lake, the Alps hoving up, closing in, already and perhaps always white with snow — he had never been here. He rolled the thought in his head; he had never been here before.

When Tim stepped onto the platform, her pulse thrummed as if she were lined with brass. She called his name, and she felt his eyes catch hers, everything inside her surging forward. Then Al called him, and she turned to see everything she felt in Al's face too, the nerves and joy, the thrill to see the man they'd come to see. Al did want to be here. Maybe this would not be so confusing after all.

"Old man," Tim said.

He and Al made a long handshake, and then he took her by the elbows, their cheeks brushing, and she laughed something tittery, and they all stumbled their words over each other like teenagers.

"A momentous occasion," Al said.

"I can't tell you. I can't tell you how glad I am."

"You look well, Tim. Mary Frances had said, but I'm relieved to see it for myself."

"Mary Frances is a lifesaver."

She couldn't look at Tim for more than a second. "Don't be silly."

And then everything seemed to run suddenly too long, their smiles clinging to their faces, Mary Frances looking at her shoes. It was all so surreal; she felt like a costumed actor waiting in the wings. If they did not move forward, she was going to lose her nerve.

"Well," Tim said. "Let me direct the porter with the bags, and the thing we need, of course —"

They went to Doellenbach's and ordered plate after plate of frogs' legs crusted with garlic and mustard, bottle after bottle of *vin du Vevey,* the thin dry wine Tim said they would soon make from their own grapes. Al put his elbows on the table, and Tim took a pen from inside his jacket and drew a map for Al on the back of a menu card, and Mary Frances kept laughing for no reason and then going quiet, pouring another glass of wine.

She could not look directly at Tim. She studied Al's face instead, unburdened in a way she remembered from before they were married, when he used to seek her out in the library to rattle on about Stevenson or Yeats. She reached for his hand. She wanted Al to be happy again; it had been so long. Maybe Tim could get him talking and planning and writing as he had done when they first met, and she would just be the weather between them: with both, in her way, but with herself most of all. She tried to relax into that thought: *with herself, most of all.*

They walked back to the pension three abreast, unsteady in the early chill. Al felt like singing, but they couldn't settle on a song. Tim felt like another drink, but it was late, the town already closed. Back at the pension, he bartered a bottle of marc from the madame's oldest, son and they went up to the Fishers' rooms for a nightcap.

"Nightcap, my foot." Al stretched out on

the bed in his suit coat. "I couldn't find a place to put a cap if I grew an extra head for it."

"Al?" Mary Frances perched on the edge of the nightstand and poked him.

"I'm fine. Timmy, tell her I'm fine."

Tim handed Mary Frances a drink. "He's fine. A quick toast, and then I'm off."

"A toast."

"Al?"

"My heart is as full as my glass. My heart is as full as . . ."

"Your heart. Sit up, Al. For goodness sake." Al made a sound like a groan, his eyes already closed.

"Ah, dear," Tim said, and then his hand slipped to the nape of her neck and he pulled her to him, holding her tightly. He smelled of the cold and the brandy, and underneath that, he smelled like always, and she pitched into him as he pulled away, unable to keep her balance.

"Good night, old man," he called to Al, now almost out the door, and Mary Frances swallowed the rest of the marc in her glass, setting it down again on the nightstand with a joggle.

If this was the way it was going to be, she didn't think she'd last the week.

■ ■ ■ ■

There was nothing like an empty city at night, and nothing Tim wanted so much — a black lakeshore, a blank canvas, this. It felt as if he'd left Mary Frances and turned off all the lights on the world. He still felt the soft nape of her neck beneath his fingers, bringing his hand to his face, breathing in. Then suddenly there was the morning she'd come to his cabin on the *Hansa,* the scent of her hair, the hollows and folds of her, her salt. He drank from the bottle of marc and watched the stars and ached.

He had not fucked another woman in six months, had not been with anyone but Mary Frances since that morning, and now all that was over for them, which meant, all that was over. Forever? How could he never have sex again?

He laughed. There were a thousand ways to think about it: they would live like family, like monks, like roommates, like freaks. He loved them both, and this was the only way to do it. He shuffled on the cobblestones; he was drunk. He doubted he could stay drunk forever, but in his slurriness he could see a dumb kind of chance for this to all work out. The three of them would make art, maybe great art. There was a theory about it from the Far East, he was certain, about saving your energy for creation. Maybe Claire had mentioned it. She spent a lot of time not having sex. Claire would know.

He put the lake to his back and cut into the city, the narrow streets and slate-roofed houses in their tight, twisting rows.

In the war, he'd admired the men from the east, the Sikhs and Hindus, a Gurkha soldier in the Bearer Corps who'd learned his English from an idiot who'd wanted to climb the highest mountain in the world. The Gurkha lost two fingers pulling an unexploded shell out of a man's chest. He had been a palm healer, or so everyone said, until the incident with the unexploded shell.

The streets Tim wandered were pitch black, not a streetlamp or a candle in the windows. He could still feel the vast flatness of the lake behind him, its unmeasured depth, the on and on of it. The dark streets were safer, but he had no idea where to go.

The Gurkha had died under strange circumstances. Or rather, the Gurkha had gone on to distinguish himself as wildly fearless and skilled with the eight fingers he had left, and when he died, the whole lot of them kind of fell apart strangely. It was

1918, the third or fourth or fifth Somme. They were moving daily. Tim was supposed to be shipped back home (he had not been able to eat in almost two weeks, something rotted inside him, pulling his bones through his skin), but the orders didn't come or couldn't find him, and he'd left the field hospital where he had collapsed and went back to ferrying the bodies from the front lines. No one seemed to notice, until the Gurkha.

Tim needed to go home, go to bed, stop this thinking. But every house suddenly looked like the one beside it, and his way back to the pension seemed to have closed over itself with stone. He drank again from the marc, and kept walking.

The Sikh instructed them on how to make a funeral pyre. According to the custom of his faith, the Gurkha's body had to be burned next to a river, and owning no nearby river, Tim and five other men dug a trench, hauled buckets from a spring-fed pond behind a nearby farmhouse. On the Sikh's count, they poured the water down the trench so he could bathe what was left of the Gurkha's body in what stood in for the Ganges, and the Indian soldier next to Tim began to howl.

The others lunged at him, covering his

mouth with their dirty hands, but the howls drew the attention of the nearest officers. But before they could sort the problem from the scuffle, Tim had lit the fire.

It was stupid, of course, to send a flare like that so close to the enemy line. But it was the end of the war, and even the Gurkha had not been able to heal himself, and this was the best that could be done given the circumstances. It was a magnificent failure, and in that, almost more magnificent. Almost right.

The officers returned to their papers; Tim's orders for home would materialize within days. The Sikh passed a cup beside the pyre (the smell, terrifyingly, made Tim hungry), and in the bottom of the cup, there was a gold coin. Drinking the water released them from the Gurkha's soul, and he from theirs.

He drained the last of the marc and dropped the bottle in the street.

Where was he going? He turned the corner to see a wash of light ahead, and after the next corner, a building still at work at this hour, looming above the houses around it, a man spraddle-legged on the steps in the cold, his white apron spattered with blood. An abattoir? A hospital. The smoke from the man's cigarette mimicked the smoke rising from the chimney behind him.

He spoke in French, and Tim shook his head. He did not want a cigarette, or have one, or need to understand whatever the man was asking him. He walked up the steps beside the man and pushed inside the hospital doors. He was not sick, but he needed to lie down, and it really didn't make any difference to him what it looked like he was doing anymore.

He laughed. It didn't make any difference at all.

The next morning Tim and Otto appeared back at the pension with a hired car, and the four of them drove up to Le Paquis.

It had never seemed more beautiful to her, the golden rush on the ash trees, the meadow rolling endlessly gold alongside the minty brook, speckled here and there with a last snapdragon, the fresh hope she felt now watching Tim stretch his hand toward the clouds, drawing some thought on the air for Al.

She collected a skirtful of small green pears, knobby and hard, dumping them into the trunk of the car, where they rolled like stones. She would make preserves for winter: a knife in her hands, a pot on the stove, something to occupy her senses for long enough to settle here, this meadow that would be their home, these men, gesticulating, energized, who would be with her always.

She followed them into the house, the thick walls that held the cold, the two rooms that would become the many. The strong bones of a granite staircase led to an imagined second story; a terrace off the back would overlook the gardens, the vineyards, the lake beyond. She ducked into the bathroom, still a privy, with one commode for grown people and a small, squat one for children.

She studied the miniature toilet; in a house that seemed to offer such plain charms, near-monastic simplicity, to make such a concession seemed to hint at priorities she had not imagined. She felt a sharp bright pang of something regretful and ashamed, Tim and Al talking just outside the door, their voices echoing and blending. There would be no children here, no chance. Not with either of them, not anymore.

Al stood in the meadow and thought of his father, dead almost a year. He could hear the questions now: *But what will you do, Alfred? How will you support yourself and your*

family? How might you ever find work? His
father, who believed in callings, who had
read his poems once and spoken of the
poetry in King James, a capable man, an
intelligent man, now even more so to Al
since his thoughts had become so fixed and
weighted by his death. His father would
have thought he was as crazy as Herbert in
China, doing God knows what with whom.

Then Tim was at his elbow, sampling the
warming air in deep breaths through his
magnificent nose. Al had the clear sensation
of leaping or falling, and he threw his arm
around Tim's shoulders; he could not help
himself.

"You're like a whole new man," he said.
"It's wonderful, Tim, to see you so happy."

Tim tipped his face back for a moment,
the autumn sun on his cheeks. "This has
been the thing I've looked forward to — Le
Paquis, your company, to have a place to
work again and people I love to share it
with."

Al felt equal pride and discomfort. He'd
never even told his father that he loved him,
certainly not Herbert, and not Tim.

"And the vineyards?" he said. "Whose are
those?"

Tim shrugged. "Ours."

The rows of vines laced the terraces all

the way to the main road, their fruit gone, their leaves already gold and falling. But Al could see the job they would become, next spring, summer. He said, "We'll need to speak to the *vigneron* across the Corniche, see what he says. I don't know balls about growing grapes."

Otto arranged it all. The *vigneron*'s name was Jules; his shoulders filled the doorjamb. He made wine all over the valley and kept his cellar in the catacombs of an old convent behind his home; he would be happy to show them. His face was ruddy and serious, the face of reliable people everywhere, but there was something in his girth, the quick way he moved his weight, that made Mary Frances feel that he would be quick to anger and difficult to stop once he got there.

Jules said they had to drink, that was the only way to learn anything: the thin whites made from these hillsides, a heavier, headier Côte de Beaune, champagne after champagne, too many cigarettes, and more champagne. Before long a young woman descended the cellar stairs, a tray full of sandwiches, pâté and ham, balanced on her shoulder. She was tall and pink like Jules, but slender, beautiful. Her name was Anna; she was sixteen, his only child.

It was a study to watch these men enjoy

themselves; Mary Frances could see how happy Jules was to share his wines, the cases Al and Tim were buying stacking up against the far cellar walls were tabulations in his head, and Al bent on his every word, how the canton of Vaud was the lake and the mountains, how Le Paquis was caught between and so would catch the weather, for better and worse. The lovely Anna, in her long skirts and pink cheeks, reaching to collect a glass. And Tim.

He appeared to be listening to Jules as well, slouched languidly against the cellar wall, tilting his glass to the candlelight when conversation turned to color or body. But Mary Frances could feel the charge of his attention in her skin even from the shadows. When Jules struck a match, she was not prepared for the full blow of their eyes meeting, the sounding that took place in her. Jules blew a mouthful of his uncut rum across the match flame, flaring high then out, and leaving them in darkness.

They were all balanced here at the tip of time's arrow, speeding fast: Al's hand on her shoulder, Tim's gaze across the cellar, the lights out in her bedroom back at the pension in her narrow little bed where she slept alone. She thought of birds that could fly continents without resting, she thought of fish that must swim to survive. They'd keep moving forward, they had to, because there was no going back to any other way it had ever been.

Late that night she and Tim sat in the parlor on the pert fan-back sofa, Al already upstairs sleeping, exhausted by all the shift and change, the possibilities. He had left them to their nightcaps.

Mary Frances smoothed the velveteen. She felt keyed too high, on the verge of tears or laughter, she could not tell which one.

Tim dropped his head back against the sofa and turned to her.

Finally, "I am happy to be near you again. I am trying to let that be enough."

"Oh, Tim."

"Let's not talk about it," he said. "If we talk about it, if it becomes a conversation, then it's fixed somehow. Let's not talk about it. Let's just think our thoughts."

"You think of me?"

He made a low sound in his throat, the skin of his neck and cheeks flushing hot. Mary Frances watched; he was doing this for her and whatever was inside him was for her and she thrilled to it, felt her own skin heat with it, and this was what they had now, instead of what they'd had last winter on the ship, in Paris. This thrill was all they had.

"Tell me how," she whispered.

They found an apartment the three of them could rent in Vevey while they waited for the work to be done on Le Paquis. On All Saints' Day, she watched the old women bundle past her kitchen window, their arms laden with rusty chrysanthemums for the cemeteries, the first snows whitening the deeper folds of the Alps beyond the lake. On the stove, she turned thick brown slabs of wild mushrooms in butter, a salad already tossed of bitter chicory and wine vinegar, roasted walnuts Tim had brought back from Le Paquis, where he'd met with the architects, where he'd hired the workmen, where things were beginning to begin.

He'd never asked her to leave Al, never acknowledged that they were married, only that her relationship with Al was her own, the three of them another thing altogether. He never hid his affection for her: he squeezed her hand, stood close, whether Al was in the room or not. He took walks alone. He stayed out many nights after they had gone to bed. He made space and closed it, every day.

"Al," she called. They were by the fire,

playing cards. "Would you open the wine?"

Music and candles and another bottle of wine. Pastries bought from the shop on the corner, filled with quince or fig, some kind of sweet conserve, and then tiny glasses of marc, *La Vie en Rose.* Tim's hand, still clutching his napkin, extended to her, a dance.

And she didn't think about it, rising into his arms, fitting herself to him, the ease immediate. And perhaps she'd had a glass of wine too many, because she looked into his face, the thing that leaped to her from there.

"Your wife is a better dancer than I am," Tim said.

"Or me. She's had more practice."

"Ah. Finishing school."

"I did not go to finishing school."

"Miss Porter's blah-blah-blah?" Tim raised an eyebrow.

"I think, actually, it was Miss Something-or-other, not Porter's," Al said.

"And you?" She pushed at Tim's shoulder. "You?" She looked at Al.

His face was shadowed in the last glow from the street-side windows, laughing. Of course Al had worked his way through college, while she had been a student at Miss Harker's. And Tim, when he had been that age, was away in France at war, which he never spoke about. But both of them were laughing now, and she was so grateful for that lightness. The song ended; Tim's hands left her. Her heart raced; how lucky she was, for however long it could last.

They bought a car to get to and from Le Paquis. They hired a charwoman, so Mary Frances could focus herself at the table and the desk, without worry for the laundry and the floor-washing, the rhythms of cleaning in this country that were so different from their own. Tim seemed to come by these arrangements with a minimum of fuss and consult, and finally Al just put what money they had into a kitty in the pantry and told Tim to take what he thought was fair.

The charwoman came to clean the apartment on Tuesdays and Thursdays, a slight and dark-browed girl whose father was a tailor. She changed sheets and scrubbed floors, she made bleachy potions and sang in French. She'd grown up around men and men's things, pinstripes and flannel, sweeping scraps of cloth from the floor of her father's shop in the haze of cigar smoke and talk. She seemed to think that was how it was done, by talking.

"Madame," she said, "you would like fresh sheets? For you and the gentlemen, or only for yourself?"

"For whomever needs them, Chantal."

"But you must tell me that, Madame. What do your gentlemen require?"

Mary Frances lifted her head from her notebook and looked at Chantal, her back humped over a laundry basket. The woman looked prickly and teasing, not at all the way the maids in Whittier might have looked at Edith in her day.

"Change the sheets," she said, and Chantal dipped her knees in a little curtsy and left the kitchen for the bedrooms. Mary Frances could hear her talking to Al.

"I'm off, then," Tim said, pulling his overcoat from the hook by the kitchen door.

"Oh, you can't."

"I can, and I am, and there's no need for you to stay here either, you know."

"But, Tim."

"We're paying her to clean."

Al reached around Tim to take his coat as well.

"Not you, too."

Al looked annoyed. "My head hurts. I need a brandy and a café."

"It's noisy enough here, isn't it?"

"She just asked me the size of my shoe and conjectured as to the rise in my pants, based on her father's theories. Her own observation."

"You know, the study of proportion is more exact than you would think —"

"At the café, Timmy. Tell me all about it."

Mary Frances knew how one brandy would turn to two, a stroll along the esplanade to another café, or if it was windy, a tavern with a fireplace, perhaps some fondue. She wondered what they talked about when they were alone; the thought sent a ripple of panic through her, gone as quickly as it had come. She should have gone with them, but god, she couldn't be with them always.

"Madame." Chantal was standing in the doorway again. "Madame."

"What is it?"

"I have been waiting to speak to you," she said. "Alone."

"And so we are alone."

"I am seeking a divorce from my husband."

Mary Frances stared at her.

"He is unfaithful. He keeps a house with another woman, right here in Vevey. He has given me a catarrh —"

"Chantal."

"I must go to the hospital in Montreaux three times next week to be cauterized. I have decided. I will get a divorce, even if God hates me for it. But if you hate me for it, if you will not have me in your home —"

"Chantal, really."

"Please, Madame —"

"Chantal, it's nobody's business, you and your husband, least of all mine."

She put a hand to her forehead; she felt clammy and nauseous. She had drunk too much coffee. Chantal stood before her, still waiting for something.

"Please," she said. "The laundry. The day."

"Of course, Madame."

It was the last they spoke, but Mary Frances pressed at the gape it opened in her thoughts all afternoon. Another divorce. It seemed anyone could do it, even maids, even dark Catholic Swiss women could do it and felt right to do it. What had she agreed to instead? And if you went to hell for your divorce, what would her penance be for what she was doing now?

Al loved the old quarter of Vevey. He loved the purr and bustle of an old city, the cafés on every corner, the winding tempo of it all. And you took up that tempo when you walked these streets, you couldn't help yourself. He knew that was his problem with work. *The Ghost* had ambitions of its own, and he needed to give himself over to them as freely as he gave himself over to his walks.

It had been so long since Al had talked like this to someone, and it felt good, even as what they were saying was how hard it all was, how overwhelming. He ordered them another round.

"So you feel naked and confused, you feel intimidated — goddamnit, you should." Tim pulled on his cigarette. "Or what's the point."

The point was, Al couldn't stand nakedness and confusion, messiness, mistakes. But he could never admit as much to Tim. He nodded, staring over the bar to the mirror beyond. With his white hair, Tim looked old enough to be his father.

"You've read Mary Frances's work," Tim said. "What do you think?"

"Well," he said. "It's lovely. Clearly."

"Lovely?"

Tim went on talking, but Al stopped understanding him, like a radio that had slipped out of frequency. All this time, all the size and strength and passion Tim was urging, Al thought they had been talking about *The Ghost*. About him. But really it had been Mary Frances all along.

When they returned to the apartment, she was still pacing the kitchen, still trapped, though there was no sign of Chantal anywhere.

"What is it?" Al said. "What's wrong?"

"Nothing."

"Mary Frances?"

"Nothing. Did you boys have fun?" she said, banging a pot down to start supper.

Tim and Al sat by the fireplace, the last of the evening's wine in their glasses. Mary Frances was in the bath. The walls of these rooms were old, the carpets thick, but Tim was in the chair closest to the bathroom door and he could hear the water moving against her body, the lift of her limbs from it and the clinging rush back into itself, a kind of suck and kiss of something slick drawn away, the sound of mouths. He wanted to be in the room with her; he didn't have to touch her, he remembered fully. He wanted to see her face, to hear her talk. He closed his eyes: they never stopped fucking, somewhere in his brain, they never stopped. They were inexhaustible in this regard.

"That bad?" Al said.

Tim opened his eyes, his book fallen flat across his chest.

"This? No." He looked toward the bathroom door. "Just listening. Like swans on a lake."

"Ah," Al said. He studied Tim, not saying anything more.

"It's a beautiful sound. How many paintings of a woman at her toilette? I'm thinking of Degas here, the series."

"I don't know them."

Tim rose to the occasion. "I'm so grateful you are here, that we will live and work together. I'm so long out of practice at companionship, and so eager. Forgive me."

Al smiled. "Nothing to forgive."

Tim stood and smoothed his shirt into his trousers. It was time for him to take a walk.

When Mary Frances returned from the bath, Al sat reading by the fireplace, his lanky form folded on itself, and the glasses he had taken to wearing perched on the end of his nose. He looked older with them, brittle. A draft whistled in the bedroom window.

"What are you reading?" she said.

"Oh. This."

"Al."

He looked at her. "Just reading."

She draped her forearms over the back of his chair and looked over his shoulder, the newspaper, the names of generals and cities not in French. She wanted to tell him something suddenly, something it would make him happy to hear.

"I could sit with you," she said. "You could read to me."

"I don't think so."

"Come on, Al."

He looked at her long over the tops of his glasses, then snapped the paper out roughly. "They bombed the Plaza de Colón last week, six or seven different bombs in a single square. Sixty people dead, most of them women, most of them waiting in line for milk. And so I keep thinking about milk. Milk, mother's milk, my mother, you. Madrid is the exact center of Spain, and it's Spaniards in the airplanes, dropping the bombs. On their own honest-to-god mothers, see."

She backed away from him. His head lolled against the chair, his eyes closed now.

"Where's Tim?" he asked. "We were just talking about this, I think." He looked at her now, lazily. His voice was even and calm. "Go find Tim for me, would you?"

She felt like such a coward, unwilling or unable to meet what Al was saying with the truth, her own truth, their truth. What was wrong with her? She went into their room, closed the door, and went to sleep.

Sleep came often and easily for Mary Frances now, a nap after lunch and perhaps another before supper, but also five or ten minutes drifting off before the fireplace, her book open in her lap and her eyes floating closed, a measure of escape. Al and Tim played cards in the kitchen, long hands of rummy and pinochle. She canned beets and ground mustards, made late apples into sauce. Al and Tim pored over the plans for the house. She knit endless cabled scarves, watch caps with brims that could be doubled, tripled around the ears. She walked the esplanade along the lake when the sun was high, basking in the thin winter light that seemed to shatter on the water.

She had slipped this life for another, where time and event and memory all blended together into some other kind of sense altogether, traveling from one fantasy to the next. Sometimes words were the conduit, and sometimes food was the conduit — cooking, eating, talking about food — but always at the other end was this imaginary life, and she realized suddenly how much time she spent there. How much time she spent there alone.

She wakes in the fan-back chair to the squeal of the front door hinges, and it takes her a few moments to place herself correctly: Switzerland, San Francisco, Sonoma. The kitchen smells of roasting birds.

The librarian returns from the carport, where he's loaded the van full with her boxes of papers. There is a wide plunge of dark fabric between the shoulder blades of his shirt where he's been sweating. She gives him a bottle of wine, a corkscrew, her hands too weak.

"There was much more than I realized," he says. "Or else I'm older than I realized."

This pleases her in some way she can't completely account for; she has worn him out. "It's my whole life," she says.

"With all due respect, I'm sure you kept back a thing or two."

This too, a pleasure. She thinks of the letters she burned, the journals after Tim died, the journals since that she and Norah sorted out and put away. She'll burn those as well. But something in her almost tells him about them anyway, a sudden urge of trust. She stands, feeling fluid and graceful on her feet for the first time in weeks. She hardly needs her cane. She pours the straw yellow wine and offers him a glass.

"Would you like a bath?" she says. "The bathroom is the most wonderful room I have."

He seems startled at her question, but she doesn't let that stop her.

"We have all the time in the world," she says.

"I wouldn't want to trouble you."

"It's no trouble."

He plucks his shirt away from his chest. She can see him weigh what he thinks he should do against what he wants; she has watched so many faces. She's always been easy to flatter, quick to flirt. It feels like a limb that needs stretching now.

She flips the switch, and the red bathroom comes to light, the drawing by Picasso, the small Miró. The portrait Tim painted of her turning away, the long white swath of her back, a thin strap across her shoulder. She pulls two clean towels from the cabinet and sets them on the chair next to the tub.

"Is there anything else you need?" she asks.

"I don't think so." He raises his glass and touches the rim of hers.

"Oh. What are we toasting?"

He takes off his hat finally, his thick white forelock long enough to graze his eyebrows. Her breath catches, and she tries to hide it.

"Just right now," he says. "Just, I don't know. A toast."

In January the stonemasons broke ground on one of the three cellars planned for Le Paquis. They took the roof and the back wall from the kitchen, the body of the house open to the cold, as it hadn't been for a hundred years. Mary Frances and Tim and Al drank their good champagne and watched the men in their matching black hats and woolen pants, their breath smoky in the winter air.

"How do they know what to do?" Mary Frances said. "To just rip into a building like that and expect it to stay standing."

"For the parts you want to stay standing," Tim said.

"Exactly."

"Practice," Al said. "And of course, one of them is in charge."

Mary Frances studied the tangle of men, all dressed alike, moving easily together. "I can't tell them apart."

"Well, it's like war, I guess," Al said. "If you knew whom to blame, it'd be too easy to shoot him."

Mary Frances lifted her face to his. "A lot of things have come to seem like war to you."

"Nature of the age, I suppose."

He drained his glass and rested it on the rock wall, stuffing his hands into his pockets. Al could still look quite casual when he wanted to, quite at ease when she knew he was not. There was a kind of dare in his posture, and she took it. She threaded her arm through his and pulled him down the wall to the work site, telling him to show her what he knew, tell her how he knew it.

Tim watched them: the beautiful dark knot of her hair, her cheeks pink against the cold, and lanky professorial Al, a professor anyplace you put him, in farm clothes, in a bathrobe, eminently wise and awkward at once. He felt love for Al, and pity, and brotherliness. He had never had a brother; he assumed this was the same kind of love and envy, pride and fear.

Tim had a sense for growing things, and he'd read a great deal about the French way of gardening, about cover crops and planting pairs, making your own fertilizer from kitchen scraps and saving seeds from one harvest to the next. He made sketches, watched the weather, watched the things they threw away.

Mary Frances, cracking eggs over the sink. "Wait," he said.

He bent and picked the eggshell from the trash, holding it by its jagged white lip under the tap. She lifted her eyes to his face; he was watching her, not what he was doing. He was always watching her. He shook the water from the shell, rinsed another, reaching across her to stack them neatly on the windowsill.

"For the garden," he said.

She beat the eggs into a glass of port and downed it at the sink, the winter day beyond.

"The middle sags." She turned from the window. She could pick up their conversation, from days or minutes ago with equal ease. "I need to write another piece for it, and all I can think about is now. I was thinking about our dinner in Dijon."

She went to the table and opened her notebook. She pushed the page before him, just an opening, a few lines of dialogue, a sketch of little Charles as he had been, and what he had become, but it felt as if she were peeling open her skull for him to look inside. Her wispy thoughts — undigested, undisguised.

Tim's eyes moved fast across the page.

"I toasted our pasts," he said. "You laughed."

"I'm not afraid of time," she said.

"Well, that's fine, dear. That's all we've got."

She sat at the typewriter and made the moment again, the two of them people not quite themselves having dinner in Aux Trois Faisons, concerned mostly with the passing of time. The layers of the truth in it stacked upon themselves.

"Oh, Tim," she said.

Al came from the bedroom, his boots in his hand. He had heard them talking and turned toward the kitchen to say something about soup or lunch or fireplace construction, and in the yellow light of the kitchen bulb, still on in spite of the brightness of the day, he saw Tim bent over Mary Frances, leaned into her shoulder; she put a finger to the page and said something. Tim looked into her face, and Al felt a catch in his own chest. They both went back to the typewriter.

Al couldn't remember the last time Mary Frances showed him what she was doing; certainly it had been before her book was sold, the book that he had yet to read, that would be published in the summer. Maybe he would never read it. He couldn't remember the last time she had looked at him as she was looking at Tim now.

It was a small space to share. That was the bulk of the problem, the bath on the hall, the tiny stove and three cups. The madame kept the radiator high, which never would have happened in Dijon, and the air was always close and dry. Too, at the table, Tim's charcoals sometimes, his sketches sometimes, sometimes of Mary Frances or himself, the both of them working. Al felt idle by comparison, and uncomfortable thinking much further than that. He put on his boots; he wondered if they'd hear the door close behind him.

Mary Frances had gotten pages from her publisher to proof, a great stack of them, and a red pencil, the markings in the margins some kind of shorthand not easily decipherable at a passing glimpse. And she talked in a way she'd never talked before, a new bold language vaguely directed at whichever man seemed to be standing nearby, and Al had nothing to say. He'd never published a book. That belonged to her and Tim.

But out at Le Paquis, the walls were still going up. This place might still become whatever he wanted it to be. The sun had cracked the treeline now, and he looked down the pasture, the run of rock wall to the lake below. The men would arrive soon and begin, slowly, to ruin it all.

He unlocked the trunk of the car and folded his overcoat neatly inside. He would stand in the sun; he would work to stay warm. The blade of the ax was still sharp against his thumb, and he set off down the hillside to the banks of the brook in search of the hardwood they would want next winter, when all of this was done.

He worked for hours. He felt efficient and clean. He sweated, he tore through winter-stripped brush and drank from the cold brook. Tim had just been saying how they needed to plan ahead, prepare for winter, not this waning winter but the next. It seemed a long way off today. How much wood could Al chop?

At the base of the property, he caught a glimpse of a pink flap of cloth from the *vigneron*'s house across the road, Jules's lovely daughter hanging out the wash.

Perhaps it was time to begin his education in wine.

He knocked at the heavy door of the convent, knowing he should have sent Otto, that he should have made sure he was expected, but Jules had offered. They were to be neighbors, and Al would have to make his own arrangements in the months to come. Otto was not his man, after all.

He turned his back to the door, the vineyards bare around him.

"Monsieur." It was Anna, her fine blond hair caught back against her head with a ribbon, a pail of soapy water she set behind the doorframe, shyly.

"I'm sorry to disturb you," Al said. "I was looking for your father."

"He is in the Fribourg, Monsieur. He will

not be back until late in the day."

"Of course."

"He is checking on the vineyards there."

"Of course."

She had been working too, her hands red and cold looking, the dark underarms of her dress, woolen, he guessed. There was the slight animal scent to her, and a mask of soap. She was so young.

"Where's your mother?" he asked. "Are you here alone?"

The girl nodded. She stood there, waiting for whatever he wanted next.

He stepped away from the door, into the strong sun. He wished he had a card to leave, something to leave with her, a message, but he just kept stepping backward. He thought of the picture he carried of Mary Frances as a girl, of Gigi, and he wanted to warn Anna now, to keep her somehow just as she was, and in an unspeakably dark instant, he realized that was how men came to do horrible things, how horrible mistakes were made.

It was late when he returned to the apartment. Who knows what they had done with themselves all day, but Mary Frances was already in bed, and Tim in the kitchen, making a late supper for himself. He offered and Al accepted, the thick plate draped, three eggs sunny side up, the edges gilded and crisp. There was bread run beneath the broiler, a dish of salt. The men put their elbows on the table and ate.

"I'm not writing anymore," Al said.

Tim looked at him, still chewing. "What?"

"Go look in my room. There are pages everywhere. I've stuck them to the walls, and I stare at them for hours, but I haven't worked on *The Ghost* since last winter. Since my father, and the weeks Mary Frances traveled with you. I had another story since then, but *The Ghost,* I fear, is dead."

Tim wiped his chin with the back of his hand, glanced through the parlor to the bedroom door where Mary Frances slept. She might stay in bed through the next morning, pulling what she needed to her, her pens and paper, her notebooks and tomes.

"Al —" he said.

"And I'm trying to figure it out. I go to the house. I work all day there. I chopped wood today and stacked it higher than the roof beams. It felt good to do it."

"Give yourself time, Al."

"There's been only time. I thought coming here would change things. I mean, Dijon was the last best place for me in this regard, and here we are, in the middle of . . . it's the same kind of place, Tim. It feels the same, but I've lost something."

His voice was quiet. His eggs ran on his plate. He prodded them with his fork, not raising his eyes to meet Tim's.

"And I haven't told her. I'm trying to figure out why I haven't told her that."

"Mary Frances is very understanding. Resourceful. She could help you. I could help you, too."

"Because," Al said, "if I'm not working, what am I doing here?"

Tim leaned back and lit a cigarette. And as though he had been released, Al picked up his fork and ate.

But with that, whatever means Tim had used to rise above these days of tension evaporated. He wasn't sure what he'd thought might happen, but they'd all entered this arrangement far too passively, with basic understandings they did not hold in common, and though he'd kept away from Mary Frances, he didn't want her any less for it. And she had withdrawn into whatever private world she tended in her head, and Al was suffering. He had been suffering long before he came to Le Paquis, Tim knew that, but still. He was hurting his friend and could bring himself to do nothing but continue to carefully hurt him further.

He began to have horrible dreams, to stay awake to avoid them. He smoked more, smoked all the time, and Mary Frances watched him with worry in her face, but she didn't ask any questions. First he tried leaving the apartment more often, giving the two of them space and time to be together — he didn't care what they did, he wanted them to be happy — but he would return to find Mary Frances napping in her room and Al gone, gone all day to watch the work at Le Paquis. She would flutter awake to see him, her eyes round with something desperate, and then she'd go down again, sometimes for hours, for the rest of the night.

He started making plans for the three of them together. A trip to the casino at Chillon, where Byron had written; Al loved Byron. A blustery night walking the old quarter for fondue, dinner, drinks, tickets to a play. He kept pushing, thinking they could push past this to something else, but each outing was less successful than the last, and finally he broke.

They were sitting in the mezzanine of the Théâtre de Vevey, the lights just coming up for intermission, and Tim went to stand and found he couldn't, went to speak and couldn't, only a last spasm, then blackness.

"Tim."

Al turned, and Mary Frances was crouched over him as he sprawled, collapsed, his limbs flung out and stiff.

"Is he all right? Is he breathing?"

"I don't know, yes." She gathered his head into her lap, her voice low and even. "Tim," she said again, "Tim."

Al reached a hand to his cool cheek.

Panic filled him, Mary Frances's calm voice, repeating and repeating. He wanted to shake Tim awake, alive, and then that's what it became in his head, Tim dying in the red aisle of the Théâtre de Vevey after a half-baked performance of Cocteau, a hundred people milling past them and not stopping, not even looking long at the man collapsed and Mary Frances. This couldn't be how it ended for the three of them. What would he do with her now?

And in that moment, Al realized how that would never be his problem. He was watching Tim and Mary Frances drift out of reach, sink beneath the surface, a slow but inexorable slipping away. They grew smaller there in the aisle, Mary Frances clinging, her voice a plea; she wanted Tim back, yes, but too, she would follow him anywhere,

anywhere he went.

And then Tim rolled away from her, pushing himself back and away, very pale now and beads of sweat bursting across his forehead, his mouth slack, his whole body. Al stepped to put his hands beneath his arm. He folded over himself in the theater seat, clutching now at Al's hand, clammy with whatever had overcome him.

The panic still roared in Al's ears, uncontained.

Back at the apartment, Mary Frances bustled at the stove, heating broth, toasting yesterday's end of bread, her silk dress creased and rumpled, her hair loosed from its pins. Al poured everyone a brandy, shot his back, and poured another.

"I feel so embarrassed about all this," Tim said. He propped his hand against the side of his head as if to hold himself up, studying nothing on the far edge of the table.

"I'm sure you're fine," Al said. "A bit of bad potato."

"We're past the season for that." But he smiled. He was grateful and confused, very much alive.

Al left the kitchen for the fire, and he could hear Mary Frances still bustling with the pots and pans, the low sound of their talk together, but he didn't need to weigh and measure it anymore. He understood now that whatever they were saying was so much more private than he might have imagined.

He threw his empty glass into the corner, the way you'd toss a coat or a newspaper. It splintered into a hundred shards.

"Would you look at that," he said. "It slipped."

He got no answer back, and he doubted they had even heard him. He left the pieces where they fell and went to bed.

In the kitchen, Mary Frances turned from the sink. She was crying.

"Oh, darling," Tim whispered.

She shook her head. "I have to go," she said. "I have to go to sleep now."

"Please." But he couldn't finish that thought. What more could he ask of her than he already had?

But she could not sleep. The sheets were musky and suddenly too long unwashed; the radiator heat so dry it seemed difficult to breathe. Again and again she thought of Tim lying on that carpet at the theater, all the blood drained from his face and the white of his hair, the whiteness of him monstrous now, her mind unable to shake loose of it. Tim, at her feet, and only this tenuous arrangement they'd forged left for her to navigate without him.

Escape was not peace, she realized, not ever.

Al left the apartment before dawn.

Tim watched the knob on their bedroom door for long minutes. He needed to go for his walk through town in the cold, to do whatever it was that made him not think about her so constantly, but he lit another cigarette instead, and watched the bedroom door, and remembered the pale skin of her hip beneath his hand their last night aboard the ship back to New York, the last night he'd truly touched her, and he felt something bleakly rocket through him, the last thin restraints breaking free.

And then it all seemed so easy.

He crossed the room, knocked. She opened the door for him, still in her white cotton nightgown, the strong winter light from the windows behind her outlining the arcs of her body in the fabric. He didn't say anything, and didn't touch her, but crossed the room to the bed and lay down. She lay beside him, but it wasn't like the times before, where he wanted to eat her alive, where he could not bear his need for her any longer. It was deeper and darker; he loved her, he was certain of it. Why else would he do this thing to be near her?

When he told her so, she wept.

He took her hand, and they whispered, staring at the stamped tin ceiling of the apartment. This was their life, their second life, their shadow life, and they were living it inside their heads and on the promise that things would someday be different. That someday needed to be now.

"How?" she said, and she was still crying, her mouth swollen and red.

He did not know. In fact, it was a question he could barely understand, and he felt dumb and childlike looking at her, filled with a child's sense of relief, as though someone had only turned on the lights and everything was better.

"Stop crying," he said. "We'll think of something."

"What?"

"We thought of this."

"This is horrible."

"Then the next thing will be better, no? Mary."

He took the hand that held hers and brushed her hair from her eyes, again and then again, he couldn't stop his hand now, tracing her cheek and jawline, the fine bow of her clavicle where her pulse hammered, he could see it against her skin, another thing that seemed impossible, and yet here it was, her blood, throbbing. He brought his mouth down, wanting to feel it, his lips opening, he could not stop himself, his hands beneath her nightgown now and pushing up, her blood against his mouth and pushing, Mary Frances.

"He knows."
 "Are you sure?"
 "He knows something."
 "Maybe that's a good thing, a better thing. Maybe that's just the next step."
 They were quiet a long time.
 "I don't think so."

On the funicular to Mont Pèlerin, they were the only people in the car. The calliope played, and the cables tightened and drew overhead, the winter-dead meadows giving way to alpine shale and pines, sharp and true against the ever-blue sky. They stood at either end of the car, their backs to the rails, Mary Frances looking down at Tim. She seemed, to him, to be flying, only the sky behind her as they went up. Her grip on the rail to her back was tight, her body moving with the groan and shift, the music like something plucked on a saw.

"I love this thing," he said.

"Let's buy it. Let's live here."

"You say that of everyplace we go, dear."

"Well, I mean it." She shrugged prettily, or perhaps it was just the rocking of the car. He loved to watch the way she absorbed motion, the way she landed in the world.

"You are magnificent," he said. "I mean that too."

At the top, they passed the Hotel Mirador, its elaborate balconies and patios, and took the trail along the mountain's ridge at a pace that left them just enough breath. The air was thin and still cold; they walked fast to keep their blood moving, and they did not talk. Tim listened to the solid grind of her boots on the trail, the wick of her pant legs. In her satchel, she carried a thermos of warmed red wine, a bar of chocolate, and a loaf of bread. Her breath heaved white ahead of her, her lips parted. She licked them, and smiled.

There was more money in the kitty than Al had put in it; he emptied the can onto the table and counted it twice, almost three hundred dollars. Tim had been adding to it rather than taking away. The yellow light buttered everything in the kitchen. He was suddenly ashamed to have trusted one man with so much without thinking, ashamed to have trusted anyone at all.

There, on the table, was Mary Frances's notebook.

The thing was, it was nothing to open a book, to read it. It left no marks, no broken seals or waste. He had never thought about it so brutally, but really — all this fuss over who was writing, not writing seemed suddenly ridiculous. There was no way Mary Frances would ever know if he read her notebook or not. It was the thinnest line, requiring the slightest effort. How many of these lines had been crossed in his marriage? What was one more now?

He poured himself a drink, pulled out a chair, and sat. He opened the book, and he was still reading when Tim returned to the apartment.

He pushed the notebook away, pushed back from the table, but it was the quick move at the hot stove; he'd been caught. He grinned stupidly. His reflexes were failing him.

"Any good?" Tim asked. His face was neutral, passive.

Al tried to see him for the first time as the man who had stolen his wife, but it was almost impossible to forget what he already knew and loved.

"Drink?" he said.

Tim looked at his wrist; Al didn't see a watch. "I can't. I've got another meeting with the dealer from Geneva at four."

"Geneva." Al rolled the short glass between his palms. "Are you headed to Geneva soon?"

"Hopefully, some paintings will be."

"But you won't need to go."

"No. I'll stay."

Suddenly Al was standing, his chair pitching back behind him, and he grabbed Tim by the shoulders in a rough embrace. His body felt enervated, terrified, and he clasped Tim closer, unable to form words that might make sense. He could feel Tim's breath push against the bones in his chest, breakable. Al was sweating now. Tim's hands came up to free himself.

"I have to go, Al," he said. "I'll catch up with you at supper. Perhaps a night on the town, say. We haven't done that in a while."

Al shook his head. He could not fathom the kind of arrangements Tim must be managing within himself to suggest such a thing. What, exactly, had they all been doing?

"The other night —"

"It's okay, Al." Tim reached across the table and took the notebook, slipping it back into the cupboard where Mary Frances kept it. "I'm fine, now."

"Fine?" This was insane. "Fine?"

Tim nodded, rapped the tabletop twice with his knuckles, and left the kitchen empty-handed.

This couldn't go on any longer. Al took the bottle to his room, dragged the armchair across the floor to wait for Mary Frances.

She knew what he was going to say as soon as she walked into the bedroom, as soon as she saw Al's face. She sat on the edge of the bed with her skirt smoothed over her knees and stared at her lap like a scolded child. The conversation ahead lay in blackness. If she took a deep breath, it would be over soon, she'd learn her punishment and take it. They just had to get through it.

"Al —"

"I'm leaving."

"What?"

"I'm going to Salzburg for the summer. George will be there, and we've talked of writing a paper together."

"All summer?"

He laughed. "Yes, my dear, all summer. You and Tim will have to find some way to make it without me."

"Well. I'll come visit for a few weeks. We

can —" She met his eyes and the sentence evaporated, the anger and hurt and drink dangerously plain on his face.

"Visit," he said. "Visiting your husband while you live here. That's very bohemian of you, MFK Fisher."

"I only meant —"

"Of course." He reached blindly for the bottle beneath his chair, knocking it over. There was no glass. He must have been drinking for hours. He pushed himself upright and came to stand too close in front of her, all gray flannel and loom.

"You haven't the slightest idea what you're doing," he said.

She didn't answer, but lifted her eyes finally to his and was surprised to feel the measure of sadness there. She had been so insulated for so long, had felt so little; this sharp pain made her flinch.

"Do you?" he said again.

"No."

He made a dismissive sound, bending to where his sport coat had slipped from the back of the chair. He dove his arm into the sleeve once, twice without shooting it; the sleeve was inside out. He wadded the lapel in his fist and seemed, almost, to tremble.

"Here, let me," she said.

"Let you what? What now?"

But she took the jacket anyway and reached into the sleeve, drawing it right. She held it for him while he slipped into the shoulders. He focused on a spot on the wall above her head to hold his balance.

"I'm going to get a job teaching, back in the States," he said. "I don't care if it bores me to tears. I haven't written in months, years, and *The Ghost* is dead now. A great poem, squandered on . . . this."

He was winding up now. The next thing he said would be truly devastating, and she tried to scan the possibilities, to prepare herself: Would he disparage her writing, her parents, her fidelity, her pride? Would he call out children they'd never had? Would he say he'd seen this coming? The room was close and airless. If she could just stand still enough, she could think of what came next.

Instead: "You're not even going to try to convince me to stay, are you."

She looked at him evenly and said nothing.

"Ah, Mary Frances. I would have thought you'd learned some potent new persuasions. To get where you are now."

He took his hat from the rack and slowly, carefully, pushed it forward on his head. The door did not slam behind him, and at the window she watched him cross the street below, ducking into the tavern on the corner.

She opened the armoire and considered her suitcase, her neat stack of shoes and the clothes hanging there. Al had taken the keys to the car in his pocket, but she had money tucked away. She could take blankets, she could wash in the fountain at Le Paquis. She could stay with Jules across the road; she could pay him. She could pay anyone. She did not have to wait for Al to come back and go at her again.

She thought of her parents, somewhere in the midst of the Atlantic, on their way to visit her; she could not go home now.

She folded her face into her hands, and he was there.

"Are you all right?"

"No," she said. "Not really."

"Are you hurt? Did he hurt you?"

"Al?" And then: "Not physically." She was crying.

"I saw him in the kitchen with your notebooks. I knew, then . . ."

There seemed no way to complete that thought. Something bad, messy, ultimately survivable, but they would none of them be without their scars. He knew that, and yet he would do anything to take what she felt now onto his shoulders. How was it Al did not feel the same? If he loved her, if he was honest, they had all done this together. What was there to gain in casting blame?

He sat beside her on the bed, his hands clasped between his knees, and wanted to kill someone for hurting her.

"Can I take you out for dinner?" he said.

She laughed and swiped at her running nose with the back of her hand. "I doubt that would be a good idea."

"You don't have to stay here, Mary Frances."

She shook her head, even as she'd been packing a suitcase a few moments before. "He's leaving," she said.

"I heard."

"I'm going to ask him to stay through my parents' visit."

Tim lay back on the bed and put the palms of his hands to his eyes. "Of course."

"It would be so difficult on Rex and Edith, you and I without Al. There would be so many questions, so much lying."

"As opposed to this measure of lying."

"Tim."

"Look. It doesn't matter to me anymore who knows what and how they feel about it." He wanted to throw his arms around her in this moment, but the moment itself would not allow it. Maybe she would not allow it. "I've done the best I can."

"You've done the best you can."

Her voice was flat and cold, and Tim found himself prickling with it. "So why is he leaving?"

"Really?" She stared at him, her eyes filling with something tender and heartbroken. "Because I'm his wife."

The word seemed like a dropped stone they were waiting to strike bottom.

She said, "I remember when you had one of those."

In the middle of the night, Mary Frances cut on the kitchen light and made a pot of coffee. She had begun to think it possible that Al might have hurt himself, accidentally or otherwise, and the idea set off a string of vague panics: scandal, of one sort or another, was coming. Tim joined her at the table. He'd fallen asleep in his clothes, his shirttails long and rumpled, the back of his hair on end. She poured him a cup of coffee, and they sat without anything to say.

He got up and returned with a sheet of writing paper and an envelope, copying a long address from his notebook, a formal letter. Mary Frances listened to the scrape of his pen across the page. She thought she could put her chin down in her hands and close her eyes, that then she might be able to sleep here, upright, with Tim nearby, even with all she was waiting for to happen. How was that possible?

"I could almost fall asleep," she said, "knowing you are here."

He slid the envelope across the table, a letter to a friend of his in Paris who was in charge of the exposition for the world's fair.

"Is it open yet?"

"He's a good friend. And there's a painting they're going to show, a huge Picasso. They've exiled him over it. Take Rex and Edith to see it."

"What about you?"

"You can tell me about it. I'll see it that way." He looked at her then, just as helpless as she was to chart their course forward. He pressed the envelope into her hand. "Just please," he said. "Go."

Al stood in the street and pissed like a Frenchman, remembering only at the last moment that this was not France. For some reason, that was funny. It was dark, but he had no idea what time it was, what day it was about to be. They'd closed the tavern on him, he'd been playing the piano for hours, but there was no way in hell he was going home. He turned to the girl who'd taken him on.

"And where do you live, my sweet?"

"Ah, captain. I can make anyplace feel like home."

Or that's what he thought she said. There was a lag in his language skills this evening, possibly due to the vast amounts of gin he seemed to have bathed in, and she seemed to be slurring as well.

He drew some wadded bills from his pocket. "We might," he said, "get a room."

She took the bills in her fist and smiled at him, shaking her head. It was too late to wake anyone in town.

He noticed she was missing an incisor, and her mouth looked swollen. He drew his thumb across her upper lip and it came away bloodied. "What happened, dear? What happened here?"

She laughed. "It's all right now."

He stroked her lip, the red paint there. He had a faint recollection, not much more than a flash — earlier today, yesterday? He looked at the back of his hand, the livid marks on his knuckles. She'd told him it was time to go home to his wife.

He took the woman's face in his hands now; he could not even remember her name. She was dark-skinned and sturdy, her face plump. He could see other scars there now, a cut beneath her eye that had healed badly, a rash. He was so sorry. It must have been an accident. He must have been confused. He was rattling now, maybe crying. He hardly remembered, he hardly remembered anything.

"Désolé, désolé," she said. *"Vous êtes désolé."*

So beautiful, desolate. "Just take me home with you," he said. "I am so sorry. Just take me home."

When Al came back to the apartment, it was already Thursday morning. He stank of cheap alcohol and cheaper perfume, his eyes shot, his shirtfront bloodied. Tim and Mary Frances still waited at the kitchen table with their empty coffee cups and their worry, he could see it as soon as he walked in the door, and he felt a sharp stab of guilt on top of everything else.

He pulled out a chair and sat between them. "I fear I might have tarried at the bar."

Mary Frances stood and ran more water in the pot packed with fresh grounds.

Al wheeled himself around to follow her. "I fear I might have made a scene, Mary Frances. I might have had too much to drink and been an ass."

She did not turn from the stove, and Al shifted his attentions to Tim.

"Did you hear what happened in New Jersey? A zeppelin burst into flames as it was trying to moor, to moor in the air, of all things, and filled with air. Just impossible. Anyone could tell it was impossible. Thirty-two seconds, and all was lost."

"We were listening on the radio," Tim said.

"How old are you, Tim?"

"I'm forty-two."

"And you have no children," Al said. "I'm thirty-two and I have no children. Time just flies, doesn't it? You turn around, and you're . . . I don't know. Tetherless, and far from home."

"You should lie down, Al," Tim said. "Let me help you to your room."

"I don't need your help."

"But I'm offering nonetheless."

Later that night, in the shaft of light from the open door to the living room, Al snored and Mary Frances packed her bags.

In the morning, he took her to the train station in the car. They could have walked, but it was not clear he would have made it; his eyes were black in his head, his hands shook. She had not ridden in the car in weeks. The floorboards were caked with

352

mud and crumpled lunch wrappings, a wool blanket across the backseat and what appeared to be a change of clothes. Al had been using the car for more than driving.

"When will you be back?" he said.

"My parents arrive next Tuesday. I don't know. A week?"

"What will you say?"

Mary Frances sighed. "They'll stay at the Trois Couronnes. We'll show them the house, Chillon, frogs' legs. I hope you will stay to see them."

Al pulled the car to the station curb and kept his hands at the wheel, clutching. The people of Vevey bustled past, pushing their carriages, their market carts, everyone carrying something, the efficient flood of Swiss. The car was unbearably hot. She put her hand to the door latch.

"I'm sorry." Al heaved himself out and came around for her door, bending to kiss her cheek, an unnecessary gesture. Of course he would stay until the Kennedys returned to the States. Really, there was no rush.

"Thank you," she said. And she was gone.

Al did not return to the apartment. He took the Haute Corniche back along the lake and into the hills to Le Paquis, this place that would never now be his, the

353

beautiful orchard bursting into bud, the pale green break in the vines, the garden Tim had planted, the house, the three rooms there meant for the three of them, solid rooms with thick stone walls, the roof still open to the pale alpine sky.

It was how he felt now, lidless, open. He killed the engine, took the blanket from the backseat. The foreman approached, and Al nodded to whatever he said, whatever he wanted to do. He walked down the terrace to the crest of the vineyards, the foreman following after, and spread the blanket in the grass to lie down. He closed his eyes. The sun was bright in its glint off the lake; all he felt was its warmth. The foreman stood at his shoulder now, no longer asking. Soon he would go away. Al pulled the corner of the blanket tight around him and waited.

When he awoke, the sun was very high, and Tim was there beside him, looking out across the vineyards to the lake below. Al sat up, scrubbed at the back of his head with an open palm. Tim handed him a paper sack, greasy and warm with a roasted chicken. Al tore open the sack and ate. He wondered if he would ever be surprised by anything again.

"How'd you get here?" he asked.

"Chantal." He rolled his eyes. "She saw Patrice in town. I don't think silence is her virtue. She understood you might have collapsed."

Al took the beer Tim offered, smiled into the neck of the bottle.

"I'm tired, Tim."

"I understand."

"I'd kill you if I wasn't so tired."

Al finished his chicken, wiped his mouth on the brown paper; Tim finished the bottle of beer. Tim had always been a generous man. But no matter what he offered, Al knew everything belonged to him; they could call it whatever they wanted, a commune, a threesome, but all of this was Tim's.

They rested back on their elbows and took the spring sun on their faces, not talking, not thinking, should either prove too dangerous, but Al realized they would have to leave this meadow, that the next things would have to happen.

Finally he said, "I'm sure you know. I'm going to Salzburg for the summer. You'll have to finish it without me."

"You mean to stay longer than the summer?"

Al shook his head. "I need your help. I need to find a job."

Back at the apartment, they typed up Al's

credentials, sent letters to people Tim knew on the East Coast; at Harvard, he'd been friends with Cummings and Aiken and Dos Passos, had gone to Paris with them during the war to drive ambulances, and now told a funny story about Aiken falling asleep with a whore and waking up to no boots, no wallet, and no cigarettes save one and the match to light it with. Al had read *The Enormous Room,* Aiken's *Nocturnes:* he had marked their pages, returned to them again. To hear of these men as if they were men, to be writing them for favors, it felt surreal, ridiculous, even in the context of what all else was going on.

Aiken was in London and married to his third wife, Dos Passos in New York or Baltimore, possibly Spain, everyone in flux and travel these days, but Tim would track them down. He spoke confidently, intimately about these men; they had shared a war and a decade of time Al was too young to remember; but instead of fatherly, Tim seemed supernatural, his penumbra of hair, the voluminous sleeves of his jacket, the way he seemed to always know what to do.

"I had no idea," Al said, "the people you called friends."

"You're my friend, Al. I'd do anything you needed."

"Right."

He stood to get the coffee from the stove; he didn't want to look at Tim but could feel the heavy blanket of his words regardless, the suggestion there, the opening, if he wanted to take it. His head pounded. On the back of the stove, there was a mustard crock from Dijon filled with the first violets of spring. Mary Frances must have saved the crock, picked the violets, all this time. He set the coffeepot down on the eye and would not have been surprised to watch it pass right through.

"I'm going to need some cash," he said.

"How much?"

He turned from the stove. "How much is she worth to you?"

In Paris, Mary Frances was alone for the first time she could remember. There were hotels to arrange, and flowers; she bought novels for her parents and champagne. She made reservations all across the city, more meals than they could eat in a month of Paris, in a lifetime. But mostly she walked the springtime boulevards and felt alone.

It was the season for tourists. People from other places filled the hotels and museums and cafés, crowded the benches in the Tuileries; it was Mary Frances's least favorite time, yet now she felt anonymous here, relieved to be unrecognized. For months in Vevey, the introductions and conversations, the raised eyebrows, had always been about the three of them, and why three? Here she was just another woman from out of town.

Paris was full of Germans, and talk of Germans, the sound of their voices in the sunshine. When she had been in Dijon, there were plenty of Germans at the university, squat, thick-legged women, dough-faced and sour. But in Paris this spring, they were girls. Lithe and beautiful, their golden hair loose around their necks, suntanned, sculptural girls calling to each other across the cafés, their accents softly German, musically German, German with smiles and light, their lean arms lifted in greeting. They wore smart suits, delicately cut shoes, a kind of easy uniform that drew your eye, as though at any moment they might all come together in a chorus, they would all break out in song.

She delivered Tim's letter to a gallery on the Right Bank, to a secretary who would not grant her an appointment but took down her hotel information and said the monsieur would contact her, that he was very busy, and that afternoon three tickets arrived to a special preview of the exhibition, a private showing.

She tried to write to Al several times to apologize, but she could never say what she was apologizing for. She could not admit to him what she had done; she hadn't done it to him, it wasn't his to know about. Finally just a note, on the hotel's stationery, that she had arrived and was waiting, would see him in a week.

She met Rex and Edith at the Gare du Nord on the platform like a heartsick puppy.

"Dote, darling, look at you," Edith kept saying, though Mary Frances was unsure whether she meant this in a good or a bad way, and Rex never let go of her arm.

They sent the trunks by porter to the hotel, and Mary Frances led them upstairs to the restaurant at the top of the gallery. The grand ceiling arched above, muraled with scenes from any place you might think to travel on a train, and the brass lamps shone, and the floor sparkled. Lifetimes ago, her last trip to Paris, she and Tim and Mrs. Parrish had marked that first solid day together at these tables with champagne. She remembered hoping she would never return to that restaurant and compare that day to another, that there would only ever be the one morning at the Gare du Nord with Tim.

She ordered sweet ham and bread and butter and the cold Pommery as before. She had been so foolish; it was a train station for going to and from everywhere in Europe. Her mother would not stop staring at her.

Finally Edith said, "Dote, what's wrong?"

She found she could not open her mouth to speak and so only shook her head and raised her glass.

"To us," Rex said. "May we all be safe and warm."

Mary Frances burst into tears.

Back at the hotel, Edith put her to bed. She was overworked, overtired, she had been alone in Paris too long; Edith both offered and accepted her own excuses. Across the room, Rex stretched out on the tiny sofa, his big feet hanging from the edge, a small hole in the toe of his black sock Mary Frances would have given anything to mend.

"I have missed you both so much," she said.

Edith laughed. "You can always come home, darling."

Mary Frances shook her head. She had made such a mess of things, and it would only get worse when they returned to Vevey and the Kennedys saw for themselves. She could not imagine now the kind of blindness with which she'd been living. She felt

360

as if she were bursting from a dark room into one where every lamp was burning. There seemed nothing to do but close her eyes again.

She woke hours later to Rex and Edith sitting on the edge of the sofa, dressed in their evening clothes. They seemed so much older than she remembered, so much more delicate and frail without their big house around them, the spaces they called their own.

"All right, then," Rex said, rubbing his hands together. "Let's get this show on the road. I could eat a horse."

"Daddy."

"Freshen up, Dote. We'll meet you in the bar."

Downstairs the marble lobby of the hotel sparkled with people. It was well past the hour when everything in Vevey would be closed, but Mary Frances found Rex and Edith finishing their cocktails, and they loaded themselves into a cab. Across the arrondissement to Maison Prunier, because this was Paris for Edith and Rex, as grand as anyone could make it. Inside the brasserie felt like an aquarium, the black marble walls inlaid with bubbles of gilt, the low candles and lush carpets and cut glass. Sweeping her hand along their banquette,

Edith found a woman's earring, skinned over with rubies. Their waiter tucked it into his pocket as though he were embarrassed for them both.

They ordered all the things they'd never eaten before, things from the sea: Venus clams and whelks, potatoes pressed with caviar, champagne and Chambertin, Rex finally pulling the waiter aside and asking for more caviar, making a bowl with his giant hands, the best caviar he'd ever eaten, and by god, he wanted his fill.

They would eat caviar all across the city that week, in fine restaurants and cafés and bistros, mounded in ice bowls, from tiny ivory spoons, spread on toast, on blinis, on eggs and potatoes, but Rex would always return to that first night, his first bite, and how he would never have another as good. He would smile at Mary Frances, and she would feel ridiculously proud and wistful, and they would pay their check, stroll through the park or the Louvre or the gardens by the Palais Royale until they were hungry again.

She felt as if she were bearing something, that her job was to do it quietly. She listened to Edith exclaim over the flowers, to her worry about David, his graduation around the corner, about Norah, her boyfriend of

362

the moment. She listened to Rex's deep sighs of pleasure, his first vacation from the paper in as long as he could remember. They did not ask about her writing; she had never shown it to them, so it was not a part of how they thought of her. She imagined inscribing a copy of her book to Rex and Edith when it was published, packing it off to California in the mail. What could she say to her parents that might prepare them for the version of herself she'd put in those pages? The version she would be next year, when they read them?

There was never any news for her at the hotel.

The Spanish Pavilion was still under construction, the painting temporarily kept in a gallery nearby. Mary Frances led her parents down the Champs de Mars, the lattice of the Eiffel Tower at their backs, the snaps of flags and mist from the fountains in the breeze. Everything about the World's Fair was still going up, except for the eagle-topped fortress of the German Pavilion, which seemed taller than the Russian hammer and sickle across the mall.

They found the gallery off the Trocadéro and presented their tickets, but the curator

acted as if they'd forged the things themselves.

"I am sorry, Madame. It is not possible to
see the *Guernica* today. You will come back
in July for the gala opening?"

"We will not be here in July. We will not
be in Paris."

"Regardless, Madame, that is when the
painting will be ready. You should be our
guest, then, in July."

Mary Frances looked at the doors to the
gallery. Two large men stood ready, North
Africans in uniforms she could not place,
their hands on the butts of guns, their eyes
fixed forward.

"There have been many threats, Madame.
I am sure you can understand."

She felt a kind of panic rising, and she
thought of Tim sliding the address across
the kitchen table, his face drawn with last
resort. She did not like to become upset in
French, but here she was, and all she had at
her disposal was the declarative command.
"We have special permission," she said. "Do
you have a telephone? Call the gallery."

The little man sighed. He folded her
tickets into the pocket of his shirt, made a
clicking sound of disdain or concession, she
could no longer tell the difference. He
stepped between the guards and opened the

doors to the space with a kind of flourish. Mary Frances and her parents stepped inside.

The painting was enormous, stretching along the entire wall, and there was no way to step back far enough to take it in at once. She walked alongside its black and white clutter and mass, gaping mouths and trampled figures, beasts and people, the high looming outline of a bull, bleeding newsprint colors into the tangle at his feet.

The first thing she thought of was Al. She looked into the slantwise flattened face of a figure in the painting, arms lifted, supplicant and abject, and she understood what Al was getting at, with all his talk of Spain and war and what was coming. This was the kind of pain we could only bring ourselves.

She turned to find Edith and Rex standing behind her, chins lifted to the painting, now small and shyly holding on to each other, as if they were watching something about to fall atop them. On her mother's face, a sickened expression was dawning, and Mary Frances knew she would not be able to tell her about what had really happened with Tim and Al. She would not be able to come clean.

They collected themselves in a café around the corner. There was no conversation; not even Edith tried. When the waiter came, Rex did not look up, and she ordered champagne and rillettes for the table in French, though the waiters here served thousands of tourists. They would have understood Rex, and the way he silently handed the job to her made her somehow mournful.

Across the street, he watched tall blond German girls stirring in and out of an open doorway, a clutter of Nazi officers drinking beer and playing cards.

"Austria," he said, "is very close to here."

Mary Frances made a sound in her throat, but he didn't say anything more, his high, clear brow drawn tight. It was her brow, too; she got it from him. She wanted to think about that, not Austria or Germany, not any of the things that seemed to be looming so clearly in the future now.

"Let's take the train tomorrow," Rex said. "I'm anxious to see your home."

In spite of herself, Mary Frances said she was as well. Back in Vevey, she was surrounded — by the news, the Alps, by what was on the other side.

Mary Frances's suitcase arrived with a porter from the train station sometime late in the afternoon. It was very heavy, probably filled with books and things her parents had bought for her that could only be bought in Paris. Al tipped the porter and put the suitcase in her bedroom at the foot of her bed. He looked at it for a long moment, then closed the door.

The porter had given him a note: the Kennedys would be arriving for a drink at five, Mary Frances had made reservations for dinner later at Doellenbach's. She asked that Al be in the apartment to greet everyone and signed her initials, nothing more.

He wondered what kind of notes she had been sending Tim.

It was an honest wondering; the fury he'd felt, the hurt and stupidity, the shame had all burned out, to leave a shell of removed curiosity. He wondered about chronology and timelines, which one of them had lied to him first — his guess was Mary Frances; he'd come to feel she was always lying to him, while Tim had been honest in all but one respect. He wondered why it was so much easier to hate Mary Frances than Tim. Perhaps it was simply that she had been gone, and once Al was gone, they would both seem equally, monstrously, to blame.

All of Le Paquis had been a lie; that he could chart for certain.

It was a matter of days now, a matter of

survival. There was an envelope in his packed suitcase with five hundred dollars, a ticket for a ship that would depart England in August for New York. Just this last act of his marriage to get through, and then blackness, nothing, not even grief. He just saw nothing.

When he heard the Kennedys coming up the stairs, they sounded loud and happy, Mary Frances's laughter loudest and brightest of all. Al suddenly remembered, lifetimes ago, arriving at Tim and Gigi's house for that cocktail party right before Tim went back to Delaware. Tim had been broken. He certainly seemed fine now, and Mary Frances coming in the door of the apartment with her parents in tow, she was fine too. Al stood and extended his hand to greet Rex, bent to kiss Edith's cheek; he could feel the muscles in his face grinding to work, and with a kind of grim kinetic force, the evening slid into place.

He offered martinis, the Kennedys accepted. He asked Rex about Paris, and he heard about their walks in the Tuileries, the Champs-Élysées, the dogs, the bread, the art. He asked Edith about the children, and he heard about Norah's French tutor whom Norah had to correct half the time, and David's company exercises, his handsome uniform, his skill, it seemed, with a gun.

Then Mary Frances laughed, low and private like a curse slipped out by accident, and Al wanted to slap her. He couldn't look at her. He focused on what Edith was telling him about the children.

God, if they'd had children.

Edith was blinking, making a small open gesture with her hand toward the silent room. For a moment, Al worried he might have said his thoughts out loud, but there were a thousand possible reasons for discomfort: Rex and Edith had traveled all day, did not know this place, or what their daughter was doing here. And Tim was nowhere to be found.

"Tim will be meeting us at the restaurant," he said, because it felt like the thing everyone had been waiting for. Maybe Tim would be meeting them; the man had an uncanny ability to know what he needed to know and to be in the right place at the right time. Mary Frances laughed again, and Al stood up to mix himself another drink.

Out the window on the street below, Tim sat at one of the café tables on the sidewalk that had appeared with the spring weather. His white hair blew forward across his face, an open sketchbook, a short glass of wine at his elbow. Al felt a nauseous flipping in his

369

gut: this had all happened, and would keep happening. The window was open. He leaned out.

"Al?" Mary Frances said.

"We're ready to go, then?" Al said. He sloshed some of his martini, streaking his shirtfront as he took it down. He pointed to the window. "Tim's waiting."

Tim raised his hand for the check. Mary Frances would be gathering herself for dinner now, coming down the stairs. He had marked this day in his head when she left for Paris, and he'd thought about it constantly since she'd been gone. He'd known when her train made the station, the route she would take home; he had known she was in the apartment when he took his seat at the café. It was all a tremendous scale of increments and numbers: how close, how soon. With enough patience, he decided, anything was possible.

His head felt too large on his shoulders. The night at the theater had begun to dog him, the way the ground had dropped away. He could still feel it, maybe because of her, how she filled his thoughts. She was coming down the stairs. He closed his eyes, opened them. *Here she comes.*

She stepped onto the sidewalk across the

street, and it was as though someone had dialed in a radio, the frequency tight and every register clear. She touched her throat with the flat of her thumb, and he could feel the pulse there, the thin skin, her nail.

She looked for him. He stood to meet her gaze.

Mary Frances.

He crossed the street and greeted her parents, Al. He took her hand too, pressed her fingers to his cheek; she wore a new perfume. He had not heard a word from her since she'd left for Paris, and it didn't matter what they said now. He wanted to crush her in his arms.

He was not sure how they made it to the restaurant.

Her parents filled the silence; they could not stop asking questions about the future. They asked what Al was working on, and wouldn't her book be published soon? Edith even started to tell stories of Sean and how wonderful he'd been as a baby, the sort of baby you might have taken anywhere, perhaps overseas. Mary Frances and Al sat blanched and paralyzed at opposite ends of the table. Even what they were going to do tomorrow proved a question to fumble between them.

The waiter stepped away, and Mary Frances turned as if to follow him, straining toward something unreachable.

Tim felt responsible. This had all been his idea, the three of them together at Le Paquis. As much as it had once seemed the way into this life, it would have to be the way out now.

"Tomorrow we should see the house," he said. "We could pack up the car and take a picnic."

"Oh, lovely," said Edith.

He thought of that early spring a year ago, taking Mary Frances to see Le Paquis for the first time, and now he told the Kennedys about it, none of it a lie but rather a last, late abstraction. Everything was lush and green, the meadow blooming, the house rising up from the foundations. The peas were almost ready in the garden, and there was nothing as good as fresh spring peas. They could make a picnic, push the carpenter's tables together, and spread a cloth beneath the sun, the stars. They could cool their wine in the spring-fed fountain. They could see Mary Frances's new home.

"That sounds fine," Rex said. He turned to Al. "So different from last time around."

"Sir?"

"I remember when you and Mary Frances were in Dijon, it seemed like you were off somewhere new every weekend. This apartment, then another. I must have wired once a week for a while."

"Daddy," Mary Frances said.

"You were so young." Rex reached to touch the back of her hand, almost shyly.

Al cleared his throat. "It's different this time, sir. Tim has provided us with everything, the house, the garden." He met Tim's gaze evenly across the table. "I'm afraid he's gotten very little in return."

Tim inclined his head and smiled, opening his fist against his thigh.

"The experience, though," Rex said. "Invaluable."

"Yes, sir."

The waiter delivered their nut-brown roast chickens, more cold bottles of Dezaley. Across the low-lit table, Mary Frances excused herself. Minutes later, Tim realized he'd left his cigarettes back at the café. He would be right back.

He found her leaning against the wall outside the restaurant, rolling her head back and forth against the brick. He did not say anything, what was left to say, but went to her and put his hand to the nape of her neck, drawing her mouth to his, her cheek, her earlobe, his thumb on the pulse at her throat he had begun to feel hours before.

373

She had not yet allowed herself to imagine what this life would be like when they were gone, but she could see it now. It was almost here.

The quail, when she pulls them from the oven, are golden and crisp, and she wishes for some fresh spring peas to go with them, for a long table on a stone terrace and a warm season coming on, her family gathered around. And always Tim.

She remembers now their afternoon in the trellises, Tim and Al snapping off the new pea pods, each one a bell in the bowls they were filling for Edith, who slit them open with a sharp thumbnail, Rex draped against a chair, looking out over the lake, still and silver in the lengthening light. Then everyone gathered at the table with steamy platefuls, the color of brand-new anything, perfectly green and bathed in butter and salt, bursting with themselves — the first spring peas. All around, only the sound of knife and spoon and china, the bent heads of the people she had loved most in the world, the place she had loved most, the time. For better or worse, the last time they were all together.

She feels dizzy and rocks back in her joints to rest her head on her forearms. She has spent too long on her feet. Perhaps she is tired. Perhaps what she needs is to lie down.

A fire stammers warmly in the grate, and the marmalade cat is curled in front of it: down the hall, her own personal librarian taking his bath. She thinks she can hear him humming some old show tune, but her hearing has become a creative sense these days, filling the gaps as they occur. Maybe that's what time is doing to her now, filling in.

She finds herself drawn down the hallway toward the line of light at the bottom of the bathroom door, the song becoming the sluice of water from his limbs as she imagines them, her imagination still sharp. She decides he must be strong to have loaded that van, dexterous to have plucked those quail. A flush seeps through her: this too, still strong enough to follow.

Her fingertips trail the shelves of books that line the hall, their slick jackets and spines. This is her last house; she knows every inch of it by heart. She slips her shoes from her feet, letting them fall, one by one, to the floor. At last she reaches for the knob. And turns.

IDYLL
1937

They were deeply in love. There were other things in their lives that were not so effortless, but those things were far away from Le Paquis and their garden and their books; those things were in other countries, across oceans. News arrived by mail and could be opened at their leisure, on the radio they could turn on or off. There were whole weeks they did not drive to town, they did not see another soul. What pressed them were their appetites and what they grew themselves.

The house was finished as they had planned, space that opened one room into the next, where they sat to where they ate to where they cooked, the large stone staircase winding to the second floor and Tim's room, filled with summer light. Mary Frances had the only quarters left over from the old house, a tight warren beneath the stairs, and her refuge near the stove.

She cracked blue-shelled eggs from the *vigneron*'s chickens across the road, beating them for omelets, a nub of butter skating the pan. Out the window, boys were reaping in the pasture, the tall purple thistle and chamomile coming down with the hay, but this was the second reaping of the summer; she knew the flowers would return and be more for it.

She called to Tim, breakfast.

He kissed her; his mouth tasted of cigarettes and honey. She could see his relief after all those months on tenterhooks. It was hard to understand now what had taken so long, what they had thought they were doing, what they had been trying to protect. She promised herself she would not waste another moment not sure of what she wanted, not with him.

They sat next to each other at the long Valaisanne table, a streak of cadmium in Tim's white hair, the fletching on an arrow. They talked of the novel they would write together, a woman's story, maybe a woman trapped in a desperate life. They were still imagining it. The omelets were lacy and fine, a few crisp lettuces from their garden dressed with mustard, a bottle of cold ale from the fountain. Mary Frances stood to get her notebook, and Tim to the kitchen, returning with a bowl of strawberries, a pitcher of thick cream. The woman would be a widow perhaps. What would a widow long for? They had a pseudonym: Victoria Berne.

Her book *Serve It Forth* arrived from New York, as well as a clutch of the first reviews. Some of them were very good, and there was also a small check. But when she read the clippings, she could hardly remember the motion of the essays referenced there, as though she'd written them in a trance, in another life. She was flattered, of course, but after the first few, they stopped making her feel flattered, stopped making her feel any way at all. That had been so long ago.

Shards of hay spun in the shaft of light from the open window. It was already late in the morning; they had work to do outside. Tim looked at her wistfully. He reached out and ran one square finger down her collarbone, her chin tipping back to receive the length of his touch.

"Happiness becomes you," he said. "You are happy, yes? You're not coming down with a fever."

She laughed. "I knew there was something."

"Yes, something." He pressed his hand flat against her chest, what beat there, and time passed the way it seemed to now that they were together: right by them.

The garden was a tyrant, and they lived off it. Tomatoes, the reddest she had ever seen, their stalks twined up the cages Tim had built from galvanized wire. The peas were gone now, but Tim had planted radishes beneath the lettuces so that they might be shaded longer into the summer; each plant provided something for the other. Eggplants and peppers and squash, tents of beans, they were good for the soil. Basil and chives, a few melons, potatoes for the fall and keeping. And down the terrace, espaliered apples and pears that had fruited for decades, farther down the grapes, all this lushness, and then the wide blue stretch of the lake, a plate of glass.

Mary Frances stepped into the rows with her basket, pulling down what was ripe, Tim behind her, tying stalks back, turning the crumbs of their eggshells into the soil. The sun was hot on their necks, their shoulders brown, fingernails ragged and stained.

Tim said, "A child. A widow would long for a child."

And Mary Frances's hand stilled in the vines for just a moment, her head already nodding but a kind of alchemy taking place inside her. A child.

"She could marry again," she said. "Someone with children."

"Someone who already had them."

She couldn't see Tim in the mass of green behind her, but she could hear the rasp of his fork in the ground. He was thinking now about how that would work, about the novel, the man their widow might meet and how they would meet and why. And in that silence, her mind flashed across the baby Al had wanted and how even that had gotten smeared between the three of them: Al wanting the baby but not the thing they had to do to get one, Mary Frances wanting Tim. She could examine it now; she could talk about it with him. They talked about everything, sometimes folded inside other things, but still. Light reached all corners, now that it was just the two of them.

Her basket was full of tomatoes and beans; she would need to can some for the winter. Their last trip up the mountain to the orphanage in Fribourg, the car was overflowing with zucchini, leafy bundles of chard, carrots. They could not eat enough to keep up.

"What about the orphanage?" she said. "Perhaps she goes to an orphanage for a child?"

She stood and pressed her hands to the small of her back, arching; she looked around for Tim, but he had gone inside.

The bed in Tim's room was wide and white. From there, she could look out the window toward the lake, and afternoons when he was painting, sometimes she would come to his door and drop her muddy pants, stretching out full on her stomach, her round white behind an invitation. She counted in French the seconds it took for him to cross the room. He pushed the back of her shirt up, over her head, away. He pressed against her. He did anything he liked, his canvases stacked against the walls again: his home, their home, together.

"For the first time in my life," he said, "I regret not being able to father a child."

Her forehead pressed into the sheets. The talk about their widow had brought this on, another thing they'd made together. She felt a vibrant new potential open inside her, not for some tangible baby, but the desire they carried for each other, their constant want taking shape.

"Say it again," she said.

"I would have liked to have a child with you."

Not everything was possible, but they had

learned how want was a powerful thing.

The first hints of fall came in the night, the chill they closed the windows against, the extra blanket they drew across Tim's bed. In the pasture, the asters bloomed, the grapes ripened, the tart apples and pears, the last vegetables pressed for their seed. Then it was time to rake things clean, to turn the soil so that in spring they might start again.

Mary Frances needed a divorce.

"You can send for it," Tim said. "It's a piece of paper and travels quite easily. Much more easily than you, in fact."

She pulled the quilt around their shoulders and studied his face in the firelight. "I want to see the children. I want to arrange for Norah and David to visit us here."

"And Anne?"

"Oh, Anne." Mary Frances felt a stab of something in her guts. "Anne will have plenty to say to me, I'm sure. And Rex, and Edith. I want to get it all over with, face to face and then be done."

Tim pushed her back against the pillows, his hand skating along the flat of her belly. She breathed out.

"And back here to you," she said.

He dropped his mouth to her skin. "Ah,

Mary Frances. What could I do to make you stay?"

And all night long, he tried.

But after Christmas she took a train to Cherbourg, and a ship out. As soon as she lost sight of land, she knew she'd made a mistake. Out in the world, time passed in the usual way; she felt her guilts and regrets, the things she wished had happened differently, as though she'd left the shell of herself back there with Tim and now she was only jelly. She would be gone for the short, dark days of winter at Le Paquis: their rest, the rhythm of their work together, their long nights. What had she been thinking?

In New York, it was a matter of signing her name where the notary indicated.

"Is it still mine?" she asked. "The Fisher. Or does it go back?"

He shrugged; this was just his job. "You bought and paid for it, I guess."

His bright blue necktie lolled against the desk as he leaned over her. He pointed to another line, and she signed "MFK Fisher," again and again.

It took three days to get to California, but still it felt as though the Kennedys were not quite ready when she arrived. Rex was busy at the paper with another change in editorial staff, and Edith was fluttery, dithering, older than their last visit in Paris. The children were not yet home from school. Mary Frances told herself she'd wait to tell everyone at once about the divorce, get it over with and be done.

But whatever she once would have busied herself with seemed lost to her now. She didn't want to bake or can or listen to Edith's gossip about town; she remembered trips from their house in Eagle Rock to the Ranch when she had first been married to Al — it had always been a whirlwind of activity. Perhaps she had made it so, not wanting to sit too long and think about her life away from home. Now her comforts were shifting.

She took long drives in Rex's coupe, into the city, out to the ocean. She'd heard that Gigi and John Weld were living back in Laguna, that they had married and bought the newspaper there. Gigi had changed her name: she was Katy now. Mary Frances asked at the post office where she might find their house.

It was a big, sprawling house covered in weathered cedar shake, the yard filled with juniper and purple sage, maybe other things like bicycles or toys; Mary Frances hadn't even considered the possibility that Gigi might have a family now. When she appeared on the porch, her hand shielding her eyes from the sun, she was still beautiful, still young.

"Mary Frances?" Gigi's face opened. "Hello! What a surprise."

"I'm sorry to just show up." Mary Frances smiled but did not get out of the car. She looked up the lane to where it met the coast highway, as though she were still driving. "I'm not in town for long."

"Come have a drink. John's at the paper. It's just me. Come inside."

"Oh, I can't. Edith is expecting me for dinner."

Gigi leaned to the passenger window, resting her elbows on the frame. "We'll have lunch in Hollywood, then. Next week — you pick the day."

"That would be lovely." Mary Frances put the car into gear. She needed to get away.

"Give my best to Al," Gigi said.

Mary Frances nodded. "I will."

Driving away, she watched Gigi in the rearview mirror watching after her, just as electric in her shape as ever. Mary Frances wondered if she missed her life in Hollywood and the talent she had spent there, or if she'd even know what to do with herself if she went back.

There was no score to settle here, nothing to be lost or won. Their lives had changed hands fluidly, and if there was anyone who would understand how Mary Frances was feeling, it was Gigi. But she had been unable to set her straight when she mentioned Al. She had not told her about Tim. She was not going to have lunch in Hollywood. She had no idea what she'd come out here looking for, or what she was afraid would happen if she told the truth, but she needed to start saying something.

She lost her footing after that. She told Edith that Al had left her, and she wept hysterically as Edith stroked her hair.

"I'm sure it's just a passing phase, Dote."

"He's found a job in Massachusetts."

Edith began again. "You'll move home then," she said. "You will always have your home here with us, darling."

This only made Mary Frances cry harder.

Later, in Rex's office, she explained it another way. "Al and I have separated. Unless something drastic changes —"

"Your mother told me."

"I'm afraid that got rather muddled."

Rex sighed. "Well. We've been through this before."

"Daddy, it's not like that. I thought —

and I guess Al thought — returning to Europe would be good for us, that he might write again, and other things would fall into place. But he only became more distant, and then my book was published . . ."

The more she talked, the clearer this version of events became. She had wanted to be a good wife, to have a baby with Al. He had come to not like her, to even despise her. She had tried. She had failed. Wasn't that confession enough?

"So you are home to stay," Rex said.

"I'm working on another book now," she said. "A novel set in the hotel in the mountains at the end of the funicular — you remember it."

"A novel." Rex said. "How much longer to finish that?"

He sounded as if he were asking for corrections to the sports pages, or maybe how much it was going to cost, her staying on in Vevey.

"I don't know," she said. "I don't think you can know."

He leaned back in his chair, pulling his ankle across his knee. He was her father, and she owed him an explanation; they had always been close, and she wanted to give him one. But there was only so far she was willing to go.

Finally, "You're a smart girl, Dote. You'll figure it out."

It seemed like the only kind of blessing she was going to get.

The next afternoon a letter arrived from Tim. Her mother handed it to her with a heavy sigh, as though Tim had presumed too much welcome to think he could write her here, now. Mary Frances made a point of opening it in front of her, the leaf of paper perfectly transparent. Tim missed her and felt compelled to count the ways.

"He needs some supplies when I return," she said. "Some paints. I'll have to go into the city." She folded the letter and tucked it back into its envelope, her face flushing hot. "Shall we make a day of it?"

Her mother waved her hand vaguely, and Mary Frances walked away.

In her room, she read Tim's words again and again, her fingers finding the parts of her he made rise and swell. Each day there was less of herself she would share with her family, these people she loved and now lied to freely, had even come to dread. Anne would be arriving by the weekend, all her righteous pride in tow.

And Sean, with neatly trimmed hair and short pants and knee socks, saddle shoes, and teeth, a mouth full of them when he grinned. He didn't remember Mary Frances and whimpered when she came too close. She knew she shouldn't be surprised. She'd hardly seen him in the last year and a half, but for some reason, his distance weighed against her heavily.

She and Anne sat underneath the lemon tree while Sean collected fruit, still green and hard as baseballs. He placed one at a time in Anne's lap.

"I guess Mother told you, too," Mary Frances said.

"Mother? Oh, Dote, come on. Your letters have been so dodgy. You hardly mention Al anymore. I just assumed."

Mary Frances sighed.

"I know the signs," Anne said.

"Well. You were right."

"Yes."

"Little comfort in that now."

"You shouldn't count on comfort for a while, Dote."

Mary Frances agreed with everything Anne said but still refused to ask for her advice, to relinquish her position as the eldest. Sean kept with his back and forth. David stepped onto the porch, his hands hanging at his sides as he'd been taught. It was hard to remember him as a boy, like

Sean now, doing anything so pointless. It felt as though they'd all assumed these places long ago.

There were only a handful of days left before her train.

But then Norah, who loved boys, who loved romance and intrigue and secrets, Norah came home! They stretched across her bed on their bellies, Norah still in her slip and stockings. Her date would be here any minute, but he was the sort of date you kept waiting. She and Mary Frances had been talking all afternoon.

"When did you know?" she asked.

"Oh, I was far too young to get married. That's where you've been so smart, darling. You're in college now, you've focused on your writing, your life."

"Not really. Not enough yet, or like you."

Mary Frances ran a palm down Norah's glistening head. "But you will. And you'll see how that changes you. And you'll see which of these boys likes the way that changes you."

"But with you and Tim?"

Mary Frances ducked her chin. "I loved him the moment I met him. I knew it was hopeless — his wife was beautiful, and he adored her. And I was married, and I thought I would stay married forever. But one night when he and Gigi were coming apart, we were there for a party, and I sat next to him on the piano bench where she had been practicing a song for a part in a film, and I was plinking along a bit, and I just said it. I turned to him and confessed I was deeply in love."

Most of all this felt like the truth, voluptuous and flush with the sort of undercurrents that carried a good story. She could almost hear Tim asking what MFK Fisher longed for, that night at the piano. This version was as clear as any of the others she had conjured up the past few weeks: the stubborn sister, the dutiful wife, the abandoned woman. And what if she had confessed she was in love with Tim on that piano bench, all those years ago? Could they have saved themselves the trouble and just run away together then?

Were they running away now?

Norah laughed. "Oh, god, you are so fearless."

"I was terrified! But I did make the direct approach."

"And that was years ago."

"Lifetimes," she said.

Norah stood to slip her dress over her head, and Mary Frances felt a wash of something permanent and sad, something like mourning. She would never be so young and beautiful as Norah again, getting ready for a date. She could imagine suddenly the distance their conversations would acquire as Norah chose her way, and she returned to France.

What really happened, how it happened, that belonged to her and Tim.

At Le Paquis, he was waiting on the patio. She pressed herself against him, kissing the spot where her mouth fell against his neck. A warm wind stirred the meadow, beginning to green at the edge.

"It feels like a Santa Ana," she said.

"The foehn. You brought it with you."

She closed her eyes against it. "At home they said the Santa Anas drove people insane. I remember one winter our cook slit her mother's throat then killed herself." She turned to Tim. "She had the most beautiful long-handled French knife."

Tim burst out laughing. He reached for her, his fingers playing at her neck, and she folded herself once again into the tight wrap of his arms, the rising, licking need to get inside. He pulled her down against him on the chaise, her hands already inside his clothes; the newspaper he had been reading fell away in leaves.

"I'm starving," she said. "I haven't eaten since breakfast."

Something stirred in him to hear this, starving. Why would she neglect to feed herself? He put his hand on her knee and guided her back in the chaise as though she were a lithe craft under his sail.

Spring was coming. They started seeds in the perfect cups of eggshells and lined their sunny windowsills. They drove to the casino at Chillon for a dinner dance, for blackjack, took the funicular and hiked the mountain ridge. They strolled the market in Vevey, these last moments of leisure stretching out on the cusp of the season to come.

They listened to the news when Hitler walked into Vienna, the ringing of church bells, the cheers and singing, to the royal suite at the Hotel Imperial and the throngs in the plaza, their palms raised to greet him. Men climbed trees to see him on the balcony, people raised their children overhead. Mary Frances clicked off the radio. It was all so close. Tim stared out the window, his cigarette burning to his fingers.

Late that night, his arms wrapped around her: "What if we have to go?" he said

"Go where?"

"That's my point. What if we can't stay

here anymore?"

Mary Frances pushed herself up to look him in the face. He loved to see the edges of her suntan; he traced them with his fingertip.

"Poland, Austria. France has left the doors open. What's left but here?"

"But there's nothing here to want."

"There are the banks."

"Are you serious?"

Tim let his hand drop. He looked at her a long time.

"I won't stay here through another war, darling. Not again, and not with you. I couldn't."

They would wait and see. There was time, and outside their window, the garden was coming all to life again. Soon the radishes and peas. Soon the tomatoes, the peppers, the corn, the berries and apples, the plums. The grapes, their skins hollowed out by bees; she stepped close in the vines to hear them rattle in the husks. Soon Norah and David were coming, the chance to show all this again to people she loved, to show herself, finally, for the first time, happy. Herself. There was too much here to leave behind.

They would, of course. It was only a matter of time.

■ ■ ■ ■

But before they left, the children would come to visit from California, one last great Kennedy gathering, and they would tour the Swiss countryside, they would have a grand night in Berne.

When she thought back on the evening, she swore she could tell the moment it happened, the moment their lives changed forever. The table was loud. They were all drunk, the wine light and full in everyone's glass, dinner long ago eaten, and some other kind of hungers rising. There was a band swinging, clarinets and brass. Norah danced a tight little circle on the seat of her chair, and the boys at the next table looked up at her with wonder on their faces; Mary Frances had been thinking about the wonder of boys, about David across the table, laughing for the first time since his horrible girlfriend slunk off to Austria and god knows whatever might happen to her there, and she turned to Tim, his hip pressed against hers in the banquette, and she was about to tell him what all she would do just to see such wonder on his face, but something else beat her to the punch.

She saw everything in him shudder to a

stop, and start again.

The sound he made was awful. The band stopped playing. The solid parts of Tim sheared away, in exchange for pain that seemed to dim the lights in the room. He wouldn't let her touch his leg. Someone called an ambulance; she heard it roaring toward them in the dark.

In the Viktoria Hospital, a surgeon opened a vein in Tim's thigh and removed an embolism the size of her thumb, then went back the next morning and removed another. Somehow, and at tremendous cost, his blood kept making more.

The surgeon's name was Dr. Nigst: he was square and Swiss. He explained what they had found, explained the process of the surgery, and then explained it again another way. Mary Frances was quiet, looking at Tim's leg. A blood clot. A blockage. The wound seeped through its white bandage.

"Why?" Mary Frances said. "What is it?"

"I can't tell you these things, Madame. I can only tell you what I've done."

"But why again? And why his leg?"

"I do not know."

She was grateful somehow, for this small honesty. "Then when will it be over?" she said.

Dr. Nigst lifted his heavy shoulders and

explained the surgery again. They didn't know what was wrong with him, what was making this happen, only that if one of those clots stopped the blood to his leg, he would lose his leg. To his heart, a cardiac arrest. To his brain, he'd have a stroke. It was the worst story Mary Frances had ever heard. In her head, she began to write another.

In the morning, Tim's foot was blue, then white. He thrashed and moaned but never seemed to rise above the morphine; he sweated through his sheets. The children came and went. David brought newspapers. Norah brought her notebook, some chocolates and clean clothes, but Mary Frances's silk party dress was like a wilted corsage; to take it off would be to give up in some way. She left the clothes folded in their bag.

David asked Dr. Nigst if he thought there would be another war.

Again, his shoulders rose and fell. "They say it is a pact in Munich, but yes. Yes, it feels like war again to me."

"Yes," David said, as though he could feel it, too.

"But who knows?" Dr. Nigst said. "Who knows."

Rex and Edith knew. A cable came from California; the children's passage home had been arranged. Norah's German lessons, the accordion she hoped to learn to play, David's last pining thoughts of his horrible girlfriend, they would have to leave it all behind.

"But Dote," Norah said, "we can't leave you alone with this. We can't."

Mary Frances looked at Tim, still and white under the wash of drugs.

"It's already done," she said.

Norah wept. David stood tall between the women, his hands clasped behind him, and Mary Frances could imagine him in the uniform he'd worn in school, perhaps another uniform, if things took the turn they seemed to be taking. Before all this, she would have cried with Norah, she would have begged David not to do anything rash. She would have gathered their thoughts into a neat package to take with them, all sorted and saved for later. Now it was all she could do to get them to their train.

In the morphine, Tim lay perfectly still. He sighed and hummed and slept, he ground his teeth until his jaw clicked against itself, but he did not move. When the morphine wore off, he prayed. He wept. He writhed as though someone had set the sheets on fire. When she touched his hand, he yelped as if she had struck him, and she had to learn not to touch him anymore. It was a whole new kind of horrible conversation they could not stop having.

She hovered near the bed, waiting. They could not tell her why he was still in pain. Sometimes she held his water glass while he slept, waiting until the same thing started up again.

When Tim's foot turned yellow, Dr. Nigst said they would have to take his leg.

"How much?" Mary Frances said. Even just a little was too much, but she would give anything now, anything they asked to have Tim back.

"Please, just a moment, Madame, and I will tell Mr. Parrish about the surgery. If you would step outside —"

"Outside?"

"He is in tremendous pain. I'm sure you do not want to see —"

She didn't even have to think about it; this new sure thing rose in her now and pushed her forward. She leaned over Tim, her lips to his ear. His hands were already twisting at the sheets.

She said, "Darling, that leg is going to kill you. They are going to cut it off."

"Oh Christ please," he said. "Cut it off,

cut it off."

She looked at Dr. Nigst as if she had won something. That would be the last of it: Tim would heal, he would come to walk again, and they would return to Le Paquis. It was just his leg. She had never been the sort of woman who allowed for the worst.

"Cut it off," she said.

But somehow the pain got left behind.

Tim reclined in the hospital bed he had not left in weeks and held a book open in his lap. He turned pages he did not read. He looked at the book without seeing it, looked out the window, looked at her. She thought how hard it was not to hate the thing that pulled your lover into himself, no matter what it was. She wrote that down.

She wrote everything down now, what Dr. Nigst said or the nurses, what Tim said when he was lucid, what he screamed when he was not. She wrote to keep a stitch running through her thoughts, to have something to do with her thoughts, because what was happening was important and someday she would need to remember. Someday she would need to remember everything, even this.

And the words across the page, page after page, meant time moved forward. The light falling across the room, the nurse that came at noon, at four, the meals that came, uneaten now, she wrote to move from one to the next to the next. It was the darkness that was uncountable. In the dark, when all Tim could manage was a whimper, he begged her to drag him to the window, break a mirror, lift a pillow, please — would she help him? Of course she would. In the dark, she would do anything.

But in the morning, the shots would come, he seemed better, and they bore on.

"Do you know," he said, "from where they cut it on down, I can't remember one goddamn thing about my leg."

She lifted her eyes from her notebook. He was looking at the place it should have been, the drape in the sheets, the leg that wasn't there but still somehow throbbed and burned and itched.

"I can't either," she said.

"It might have had an ingrown toenail, but I'm not sure now. I can't remember. It looked like all the others."

She had the sudden thought maybe she would cut her hair, cut it all off in a handful at the base of her scalp. She would like to be shorn. She would like to lose something that didn't matter.

"We'll find something," she said. "Something that works. And once you're better, we'll go back to Vevey and our house and our garden."

"Our garden? It will have to be your garden now."

"Don't be silly, darling. We'll starve."

Tim had started to tremble and blanch. The nurse was on her way.

"Tell me, Mary Frances," he said. "Tell me how we will go back."

And she began.

Vevey, Switzerland
SPRING 1939

It would be the last time they took the train to Milan. They had no reason to take it now, no business in Milan, but they used to love to take the train, and these last times were what was left to them. Le Paquis was sold, their trinkets sorted, boxes packed. At the end of the week they would take the *Normandie* to New York, and on to California, the new home they would buy in the desert, the whole of Europe slouching toward war.

They spent money as if it were paper now: they bought books and left them in cafés, they drank gimlets and good wines and ate whatever they pleased: potato chips and beer for dinner, plates of fried minnows sparkling with salt. They bought gifts for everyone they knew, vellum stationery and broad-nibbed pens, Italian paintbrushes, hats, perfume. They bought fourteen months' worth of Analgeticum, each ampoule wrapped in a cardboard comb and sleeve, nested like honeybees in a steamer trunk she'd pushed beneath the narrow bed at the Hôtel Trois Couronnes. When the Analgeticum ran out, Tim would lose his other leg. If he lived that long.

They bought the drugs from Dr. Nigst, and only the Analgeticum helped Tim's pain, not the cobra venom or bee stings, the careful diet or the mountain air, not morphine or whiskey or beating his head bloody against the hospital wall. And they sold the Analgeticum only in Switzerland, where the end of the world was coming soon.

The full trunk beneath the bed became a kind of liquid calendar. They had fourteen months. They knew how it was going to go; they had it all locked away. What was there to do but take the train once more to Milan? What was there to do but be together?

Tim woke, his midnight shot run out and the electric licking in his guts already chattery and loud. He watched the ivory face of the clock. He could hear Mary Frances breathing like the breath of the clock, slow measured rounds, the minute hand, the seconds, the dial spinning in him now faster and faster until he keened on his springs. He reached for Mary Frances, and Mary Frances reached for the ampoule and sy-

404

ringe. She scored the glass top with her teeth to break it open, drawing up the dose, fast into a muscle, any muscle — his arm, his hip, his thigh. He watched her face now, still sleeping or half sleeping, the thick hum of sleep on her breath and the needle aspirating in her closed hand. She rubbed the spot she'd hit and whispered things he could not focus to hear. Seconds more, seconds more; they waited.

It took longer to do everything now. Once the shot hit, she swung herself across his lap, one foot flat on the bed beside his hip, watching as he pressed himself against her. She smiled at him — oh, the mornings, the slow turns she made, her dark hair loosely braided down her back, her eyes always open, her hands on the sharp new jut of his ribs. It was June; they had been married now three weeks, four days, and they rubbed themselves against each other every morning in one way or another, like flints and sticks, and half the time, miraculously, they caught.

The shot took hold and gave him time.

Later she bathed and dressed. Her head was empty in the morning; the day had yet to wear her down. She was working on a new book, several books, the coupling of sentences harmonic and loud like the coupling of trains. *The love-life of an oyster is a curious one. Spatting and spawning, spawning and spatting.* She relied on rhythms now, the blue ribbon in her hair matching the blue in her sweater, the blue shadow she painted on her eyelids down by the lash. *Spawning and spatting, spatting and spawning.*

She called the line aloud into the other room.

"Tim? What do you think?"

He was probably asleep. But she knew one day she could do something wrong with the needle or the dose, she could leave too much within his reach. She knew he was probably asleep, but her hands gripped the edge of the marble vanity, and for a full five seconds, she couldn't bring herself to go and see.

Then, "Darling," he said. "I didn't hear it. Come tell me again."

The train left the station at ten, Tim navigating the narrow passageways with his crutches; he never stuttered at it, as if the leg had never been necessary in the first place. He loved the swaying motion of the cars along the tracks, loved to watch Mary Frances sway in front of him, would follow her anywhere. To their compartment, and then the restaurant car, the dark scarred tables and wide views, the faded advertisements off-kilter above the windows, as they had always been.

And the same people worked the train as always; in the restaurant car, the old waiter and the young, their black jackets and long Parisian aprons, leaning against the bar of the kitchen with small glasses of vermouth and cigarettes. When the old waiter came for their order, tears leaked from both eyes that he did not wipe away; they might have been for them, for this journey, his country, it didn't matter, really. Mary Frances told him she had missed their trips together. Tim asked about the weather. No one acknowledged the cause or need for crying.

"Your Asti, as always," he said. "And something else?"

Tim tipped his hand to Mary Frances. She didn't look at the menu, and the old waiter didn't write anything down. In all their trips to Milan, all the things she'd eaten on this train, the old waiter had always pretended to listen to her order and then brought her what he wanted to, whatever was fresh and good from the kitchen, what he thought she'd like. She was flattered to be treated so carefully. Still, she said some things, he nodded and left, and she turned back to Tim.

They leaned into each other across the table, threading their hands together; they touched whenever they were near enough now, Tim's foot resting on the seat next to her, his crutches by the wall. The train chuffed and runneled through the Alps, still distantly cragged with snow. Their Asti arrived, popped and poured for them to toast their future or their pasts, but they just drank it down.

Soon the tunnel would appear ahead of the tracks, and always before they had dreaded it: the echo of their own travel, where they had been and where they were going disappearing in the blackness. Their waiters dreaded it, too, and the chef in his high white hat. But today they sat across from each other, and the dread never came. Whatever was happening to them had already been cast, was here, now. As they slipped into the darkness, Tim whispered something to Mary Frances, and she laughed the kind of low, throaty laugh not heard in public places anymore. The young waiter watched them and sighed.

When the train stopped at Domodossola, they made their way back to their compartment to wait for the border guards. In the corridor, they passed two Blackshirts, a man between them, his hands cuffed to each. You saw that sort of thing all the time now, their three faces sharing the same empty look, and Tim met it squarely, stopping to let them pass.

Their compartment was full of German tourists, their backpacks and girth, their ruddy faces and long legs a tangle in the aisle. They stood politely, to make room.

Tim was hurting now, she could see it in how his hands seemed to shimmer in his lap. She looked at her watch; it was too soon for another shot. She went into her bag for the pills to hold him, but she would give him a shot if he needed it, she didn't care anymore. She had come to hate this as much as he did. The border guard appeared at the compartment door, but Mary Frances kept her eyes on Tim, his beautiful birdlike face so taut, his eyes so fragile. She swore she heard something shatter and bent to her purse again. The pills were in here somewhere.

Finally she pressed a tablet into his palm. The compartment door slammed; the guards were running in the corridors. The Germans smelled of hay and sweat, their words chinking low in their throats, but Mary Frances watched Tim. Slowly his face released; he might have been asleep.

■ ■ ■ ■

The train had been stopped for too long by the time the young waiter came to fetch them for lunch. He was anxious, his French rushing from him all at once, how wonderful, wonderful to see them both again. He had thought — but then he couldn't finish that sentence. He hoped — but that one fell short too, finally asking them only to be careful, monsieur, be careful. There was a spot on the passageway that was slick.

The border guards stood by the spreading puddle, and a woman with a broom swept the shards from a broken window into a pile at their feet. Inside, the train had been hosed down. Water still dripped from the glass caught in the frame.

"What happened?" Tim asked the waiter.

"It was nothing, nothing. An accident."

But the waiter's voice hitched as he rushed ahead, leaving them to their table, little dishes of pickles, salami and sweet butter, a basket of warm bread. He brought a bowl of peeled fava beans, Mary Frances's favorite, as though that were answer enough.

The old waiter was yelling in the kitchen; he'd torn the sleeve of his black jacket. He waved his hands; the chef continued to smoke passionlessly.

As the old waiter passed, Tim reached out for his arm. "What happened?" he asked again.

The old waiter jerked away. "The bastards," he said. "It is not my business. I was not there. I didn't do anything, but look what the bastards did to my coat."

He turned his head; he might have spat. His face, always given to coldness and crease, seemed fully hateful now. Mary Frances looked out her window, the small station, the black toe of a guard's boot. Tim leaned back against his seat. He was on the downhill slide of his shot; he'd need another soon, and she'd left the works in the compartment.

Finally, slowly, the train began to move.

The young waiter appeared with a bottle of Chianti. He was sorry; the old man was upset, he was crazy.

"What happened back there?" Tim said.

The young waiter leaned close. "There was a prisoner on the train since Paris, with the Blackshirts. They were bringing him back to Italy. In Domodossola he broke the window, leaned his head out, and pressed his throat —"

The old waiter had seen it happen. It was why the train had stopped so long at the border. Mary Frances looked at Tim, his eyes fluttering closed. She noticed for the first time that the restaurant car was not empty; other passengers seemed poised and listening, the clatter of their plates quiet, their forks in midair. Outside the window, the blue blur of spring rushed past as the train picked up speed. The young waiter touched their arms, and left.

Tim was exhausted now.

"Eat," she said.

"I'm not hungry."

"Tim?"

"But you should," he said. "You've had too much to drink."

She looked away. They never talked about too little or too much anymore; they just ate and drank. The accounting would come later.

Their plates arrived, little nests of pasta, and the first mouthful tasted like ashes; she could barely swallow it. Long ago they had been different people who had seemed as complete and solid as the ones they were now. Mary Frances put a hand to her chest, the knot there. She no longer thought of home and the Ranch and the Kennedys, of Al and his new wife and the baby they would finally have, she never thought of Le Paquis, now full of boxes, their cellar full of stores they would never use, and she didn't think of Tim, standing tall in the rows of their garden, his face tipped back to last summer's sun. What she had was right in front of her, and she thought, only and always, of that.

But now, bite by bite, the train shattered and heading south, their past lives leaked in. What was there left to do but go along?

Pasadena, California
1943

It was basically done. She pushed away from the desk, her hands coming to rest atop the full basket of her pregnant belly. It pressed before her everywhere now, insistent, ponderous, entirely her own.

She had been writing all day in the tiny rooms at the boardinghouse, rooms that reminded her of so many other places she had written in her life. Her emotions seemed so close to the surface now, and the heat, the last throes of July made her melancholy anyway, but this book was finished, and it was good, she knew it. She'd written it in ten weeks flat.

She'd written to Edith and Rex, the rest of them, that she was taking a leave of absence, that she'd been hired to do some government publicity work, secret, for the war effort, that she'd be incommunicado for some time; she threw in as many official words as she could think of. She'd also said she was thinking of adopting a child.

Instead she had come to Pasadena and rented these rooms through August. She'd spoken to no one but Dr. Bieler and the chambermaid, and because she was weighted with consequence, and because she had nothing better to do, she pounded at her typewriter day and night. To begin at the beginning, to take the measure of her powers, to taste the first thing she remembered tasting and wanted to taste again: from there, she'd written the book she was meant to write, about how she came to be herself, *The Gastronomical Me* by MFK Fisher. She had written about her grandmother's boiled dressing and dour face, about Aunt Gwen and the hills above Laguna, about making curried eggs with Anne when they were children, so hot her face flamed for days after. She wrote about crossing the ocean, about Al and Dijon and Tim. Tim was everywhere; she owed this book to him, and in her mind, would owe every book after, would owe everything that happened to her for the rest of her days.

This child, when it was born, would have his name.

And if she said it, by the state of California, it was true. That was the miraculous thing she was learning, that the power to say something with conviction, with grace and beauty, made a story that felt as real as whatever might have been the truth, that these were equal forces in the world, just as powerful as records, maybe even more so. Memory, love, pain: these were the things that people believed. These were the things that made her believe herself. And now if she wanted Tim's child, this was how she was going to get it, and this had always been how she was going to get it, by saying so.

He had been dead for almost two years, the trunk of ampoules beneath her bed long emptied, despite her half doses, her stretch and pull. In the end, there had been no lying about it. Tim watched her with the last needle in her hand.

"So that's it," he said, and she said yes.

She'd turned from him and slipped her dress over her head, a gesture she'd made a thousand times in their life together and yet one that always felt filled with anticipation, his first light touch, the way they always began, and she lay down beside him in the heat and waited.

They looked out over the desert, the blistered sunset. He had a gun; he'd asked her to hide it, but what was a hiding place between them? The night came on, the sounds in the darkness, and she tried to listen only to that, not what she knew would come, but only Tim now, his arms wrapped around her, their lengths pressed together on the bed, and night in the desert beyond.

The sound of the shot, all the way out in the canyon, woke her at dawn.

The tightrope of his pain had required all their time and concentration. They had carved themselves away from everyone to manage it; she wrote to read to him, she cooked to feed him, she lived way out there in the desert to pour herself into him, and now he'd left her. It was a long time before she found a reason to continue on.

Her hand dropped along the dark seam of her belly and disappeared in her lap. She had six more weeks to go. Sometimes it felt as though the parts of her she couldn't see would never return to her, that she would have to learn to live without her feet, the thatch of hair around her sex. She hadn't thought about sex in years, though she'd had plenty of it. She hadn't thought about sex since she stopped having it with Tim.

She was hungry. She ate tiny meals these days, craved lemony things, and spicy things, and beer, which Bieler had said was good for the production of milk. She wouldn't nurse this baby, though, no matter what Dr. Bieler wanted. Because this baby

417

had been adopted; that was what she planned to say. Until the day she died, that was what she planned to say.

She stood slowly from her chair, the full arc of her form pulling her forward. She needed to move. She stacked her pages and flipped the coverlet up over her pillow, drew a smock over her head. She wanted nothing against her skin these days and dressed only to leave the room, her hair pulled back tightly, her sunglasses and a bright slash of lipstick. She would be back in twenty minutes, but leaving felt as if she'd peeled herself from the cocoon.

Heat shimmered on the asphalt. Sweat ran from her scalp, the backs of her legs, places she had not known sweat was made, and she walked slowly so as not to melt away. Back in her rooms, she would fill the basin with tepid water and sponge herself off, she would wash her hair and let it dry across her pillow as she took a nap, and so dreamily she stepped into the grocers' on the corner, the fan pitched down hard from the ceiling, blowing its hot breeze against her skin. She collected a bagful of small yellow tomatoes and a carton of blackberries, a loaf of semolina bread, some soft white cheese. She pulled two bottles of soda from the cooler and a chocolate bar: she'd had a

418

sweet tooth and saw no reason not to satisfy it.

The cashier loaded her brown paper bag, and Mary Frances slipped her sunglasses off the crown of her head, stepped back through the fan and into heat of the day.

She was waiting for the light to change on the corner, of all things innocuous and simple, of all things daily, she was waiting for the light to change when someone touched her shoulder.

Even before she turned around, she felt as if she were falling, her getaway disappearing. This was it. It was all over. She'd been found out.

"Mary Frances."

It was her sister, Anne.

In a single motion, they both reached for her belly, high and firm and real, steadying themselves against it. Anne's face was pale, round-mouthed, and Mary Frances could not help but laugh.

"Dote," Anne said. "Jesus Christ, are you all right?"

She couldn't get a breath, the baby high and tight in her rib cage, and the laughing that was both nervous and true. She thought of little Anne, years ago in her pinafore, her mouth on fire, her sister, the only person who might and might not understand what she was doing, her toughest audience, her first. How could she explain?

Anne had her by the elbow. She was headed for a park bench.

"Shhh," she said. "We'll sit down, Dote. What on earth has happened? What is going on?"

"Oh, Anne," she said, still laughing. "Where do I begin?"

ACKNOWLEDGMENTS

This book was written over the better part of a decade, with the support of so many good people to whom I will always be grateful.

It began with about two dozen pages of Joan Reardon's luminous biography, *Poet of the Appetites: The Lives and Loves of M.F.K. Fisher.* That biography, read and read again, sent me to Fisher's body of work, her letters and published journals, and late in the game, to Anne Zimmerman's *An Extravagant Hunger: The Passionate Years of M.F.K. Fisher,* all of which provided insight, friction, and answers to questions I had not even thought to ask about a charming, enigmatic, and brilliant woman.

I would like to thank the National Endowment of the Arts, Queens University of Charlotte, the South Carolina Governor's School for the Arts and Humanities, *edible*

Upcountry magazine, and M. Judson Booksellers and Storytellers, as well as the
management and staff at Ballcrank Indus-
tries — namely Carla Damron, Stephen J.
Eaonnou, Dartinia Hull, Beth Johnson, and
Holly Pettman — without whom I would
quite literally be lost.

Writers I admire greatly read this book in
manuscript and provided invaluable feed-
back and care. Thank you to Lauren Groff,
Jo Hackl, Fred Leebron, Mamie Morgan
and Jim Walke.

Thank you to Kathryn Court and Lindsey
Schwoeri at Viking for sharp and sensitive
editorial skill, and to the incredible Marly
Rusoff, for putting me in their hands.

Thank you to Ron Friis, who always
thought this would be a good book.

Thank you to my family. And to my
children, who mean everything.

ABOUT THE AUTHOR

Ashley Warlick is the author of four novels. The recipient of an NEA Fellowship and the Houghton Mifflin Literary Fellowship, her work has appeared in *The Oxford American, McSweeney's, Redbook,* and *Garden and Gun,* among others. She teaches fiction in the MFA program at Queens University in Charlotte, South Carolina and is the editor of the South Carolina food magazine *edible Upcountry.* Warlick is also the buyer at M. Judson, Booksellers and Storytellers in Greenville, SC, where she lives with her family.

The employees of Thorndike Press hope you have enjoyed this Large Print book. All our Thorndike, Wheeler, and Kennebec Large Print titles are designed for easy reading, and all our books are made to last. Other Thorndike Press Large Print books are available at your library, through selected bookstores, or directly from us.

For information about titles, please call:
(800) 223-1244

or visit our Web site at:
http://gale.cengage.com/thorndike

To share your comments, please write:
Publisher
Thorndike Press
10 Water St., Suite 310
Waterville, ME 04901